Lemon

A NOVEL BY
CORDELIA STRUBE

Coach House Books, Toronto

first edition

  Canada

Published with the generous assistance of the Canada Council for the Arts and the Ontario Arts Council. Coach House Books also acknowledges the support of the Government of Ontario through the Ontario Book Publishing Tax Credit and the Government of Canada through the Book Publishing Industry Development Program.

The author gratefully acknowledges the support of the Canada Council for the Arts and the Ontario Arts Council.

LIBRARY AND ARCHIVES CANADA CATALOGUING IN PUBLICATION

Strube, Cordelia
    Lemon / Cordelia Strube.

ISBN 978-1-55245-220-2

    I. Title.

PS8587.T72975L44 2009   C813'.54   C2009-904271-1

for Carson

1

'If I hadn't been reading about a Jewish girl in Nazi Germany, I might have let Zippy kill me.' This gets Blecher scribbling in her notepad. I knew it would. She's a psych-major-dropout-turned-guidance-counsellor, the only thing between me and another suspension.

'She tried to kill you, really?'

I nod, sucking on my Tootsie Pop.

'Let's talk about all your mothers.' Blecher always wants to 'talk'; she learned that in Psych 101. I don't want to talk, especially about my mothers. It's not that I have anything against them. I don't go around blaming them for my inability to attend classes regularly, or to find the meaning of life, but mental disturbances seem to be a recurring theme, if my current mother's crack-up is any indication. 'Why would a student want to stab *me*?' she keeps asking. The fact that she was the school principal eludes her. Which is why another suspension must be avoided. Rattling around the house with Drew freaking over her stab wounds is no joyride.

I keep sucking, staring at the mottos taped to the wall behind Blecher's desk. 'HANG IN THERE!' one of them says. 'TOMORROW THIS WILL BE YESTERDAY!' assures another. 'TIME IS THE GREAT HEALER!' Beside the slogans are smiley faces. I endure Blecher because our 'sessions' keep me out of the halls crowded with buttheads, but the woman is seriously damaged. She dyes her hair orange and fries it with a curling iron to make it puff off her head. She wears little pointy shoes and stashes food in Tupperware in her desk. You can be talking about something personal, like how you wish you could develop an eating disorder but you can't stop eating, and she'll reach into a drawer and pull out a cracker and one of those cheese triangles wrapped in foil. You'll have to sit there watching her tear the foil off the cheese in little tiny strips. Soon the cubicle-sized office will stink of Blecher's digestion.

Pen ready, she looks probingly at me. 'Let's talk about how your first mother tried to kill you.'

'Pills. Plus a jump off the balcony, holding hands so we wouldn't be lonely.'

'How did you stop her?'

'I said I was reading.' After *Anne Frank*, I was hooked on persecuted-Jewish-girl stories. Compared to them, living with Zippy wasn't so bad. Or putrid Damian for that matter. Shared custody meant I was in constant motion. Like the Jews, I had no homeland.

Blecher pats her puffed hair. 'Why do you think Zippy wanted to commit suicide?'

'To teach Damian a lesson. He was always bumping uglies with other dames.'

The truth is I considered *pretending* to swallow the pills, faking the jump, then shaking myself free of her, watching her body flail through the air in her fluffy bathrobe. Then I twigged to the awful truth that I'd be left all alone like the Jewish girl. Her father had gone into hiding and her mother was constantly volunteering at the orphanage. Jews had been forbidden to attend German schools so the girl had to hide out in the apartment all day. 'I love you more than anybody, Mother,' I said, which wasn't saying much as I didn't love anybody – except my hamster, Alice, who'd died – but I understood that dramatics were required, that our death warrant was Zippy's cry for help. I dropped to my knees, grabbed her around the waist and wailed into her bathrobe. 'I don't want to die and I don't want *you* to die! Why do we have to *die*!?'

'Because nobody gives a fuck about us, honeybunch. Nobody gives a *fuck*!'

Blecher twirls one of her gold stud earrings, winding up her brain. I spare her the sordid details of Zippy's debacle because Blecher's one of those living-in-a-Disney-movie types who get hysterical when you reveal life's atrocities. 'It must have been terrifying for you,' she says.

'I just wanted to finish my book.' The Jewish girl was walking alone in streets full of Nazis. She bought sausages from an 'Aryans Only' butcher. He even called her *liebling*. I was scared shitless he would discover her true identity and snatch her bratwurst.

'You've always found solace in reading, haven't you?' Blecher's powers of observation continue to amaze. I only have a book on me 24/7. 'I love to read,' she says, which is outrageous because the only thing she reads is *Archie* comics. She hides them in a *New Yorker* or something so you'll think she's intellectual.

'How're you taking Archie tying the knot with Veronica?' I ask, suspecting she's pro-Betty and pretty broken up about the wedding.

'We're here to talk about you, Limone. What did Zippy do when you refused to co-operate?'

'I distracted her by begging for another hamster.' The Jewish girl begged her mother to promise she wouldn't send her away with the orphans to England. 'Promise me, Mutti,' she'd pleaded. But Mutti pushed her away and told her to finish her latkes. Zippy didn't push me away but the fluff on her bathrobe was tickling my nostrils. *Thump thump thump* banged through the wall as the neighbours cranked their stereo for another Friday-night beer swill. If we made it through the night, Damian would be there in the morning, stinking in his Buick. We'd go to the Golden Griddle and I'd stuff my face while he'd sweat over the sports section.

I never told Damian about the botched double suicide. He'd already left Zippy anyway to shack up with Drew who's ashamed of being a neat freak and tries to mess things up once in a while, do something really radical like leave her coat lying around. I'm a chronic slob so there have been tensions between us. At first Damian tried to get me to call Drew 'Mother.' Drew didn't care what I called her. We got along alright, passing the Shredded Wheat and all that. Damian was busy bossing around illegal immigrants on construction sites, so Drew and I spent a lot of time alone, in separate rooms. Mostly I read, got into the dead Russians, especially Dostoyevsky because everybody in his books is so totally damaged. *He* must have been totally damaged what with that secret society business, being sentenced to death and all that, then being carted off to Siberia.

Blecher digs around in a box of Ritz Bits. 'Did Zippy get you another hamster?'

'Negative.'

'How did that make you feel?' She's wearing her concerned-counsellor expression, lips pursed, eyebrows merged. Best to defuse things before she contacts Children's Aid.

'I watched Bob and Bing movies.'

'Who?'

'Hope and Crosby.'

Blecher masticates Ritz Bits, clearly ignorant of the twentieth century's primo comic duo. I've got all the road movies. Bob lived to be a hundred. I think about that when I watch him being blown out of a cannon or something. I like movies made before 1950, when women had soft bodies and something to do in flicks besides strip and fake orgasms. Dorothy Lamour never flashed her headlights. Rossi and Tora, my non-compos associates, can't stand anything that doesn't have sex or special effects. 'How can you watch black and white?' they kvetch. When I tried to get them to sit through *Harvey* Rossi said, 'Is this supposed to be funny? Like, anybody can see there's no rabbit.'

'Maybe the rabbit shows up later,' Tora suggested.

James Stewart's alright, but Cary Grant's my man. I almost read his biography once but decided I didn't want to know what a fuck-up he was, twenty-five wives and all that. I know he was born Archibald Leach then remade himself as Cary Grant. I wouldn't mind doing something like that.

'You have your whole life ahead of you, Limone,' Blecher says, shaking the empty Ritz box. 'You should be full of hope and enthusiasm.'

'It's hard to get enthusiastic when adults keep telling us everything sucks.'

'When have you heard me speak negatively about anything?'

'Not you, the usual noddies who yak about the good old days before kiddie porn and pollution. When people left their doors unlocked and kids walked home alone. When employers paid benefits and didn't downsize every three seconds.'

This stumps her. She scribbles on her pad.

'These days,' I continue, slowly so she can get it all down, 'unless you're a super-brain or gorgeous, you're going to end up in some bottom-feeder job at some corporation that's going to restructure every time you take a crap. If you make it through the first cuts, you might as well chain yourself to your cubicle because they're going to want your soul.'

That's why boys get into guns. It's easy and you can scare people who wouldn't give you a job interview if you offered to blow them. Well, maybe if you offered to blow them.

'There's no room out there,' I say. 'It's way too crowded. We need more war and pestilence.'

'You cannot,' Blecher says, 'you simply cannot expect to function with such a bleak outlook.'

'I don't expect to function.'

'You'll break your mother's heart.'

'Which one?'

2

Drew's hunched over the crosswords again, still in Damian's old PJs.

'Do you want anything from the store?' I ask. 'There must be something you'll eat.' I think she shakes her head. She's stopped picking up after me. The place looks like a tornado hit.

Instead of jail, the knifer's getting medication and treatment for PMS, plus therapy for depression and anger management. She's supposed to keep an hour-by-hour log of her mood and seek counselling if it's negative. She wears a wristwatch that beeps every forty-five minutes to remind her to check her mood. She hasn't returned to school. She told the judge she was sorry and that she wants to meet with Drew to apologize in person. Drew can't face her, couldn't even attend the court proceedings. The letter opener was twenty-three centimetres long. Drew had to have surgery to remove it. I caught her trying to look at the scar in the full-length mirror. She couldn't turn her head enough to see it properly but I saw it, red and ridged, like something out of a horror movie.

I push my cart around the Valu-Mart, sniff and squeeze things, pretend I'm like other people, buy some Black Forest ham thinking Drew might go for it instead of peanut butter. Her first husband's son is coming next week. He's a tree saver, climbs trees and lives in them. He gives the trees names and has a special tree-saver name himself, Thor or something. I stare at the frozen foods trying to figure out what a tree saver might eat that I can nuke because old Drew won't be playing hostess any time soon. Zippy was always buying prepared foods and becoming hysterical when the food didn't look like it did on TV. Me, the seven-year-old wizard, explained that TV wasn't like real life. Zippy had a problem with this concept, was always comparing her daily grind with the smoke and mirrors on the one-eyed monster. 'It's not humanly possible to look that good,' she'd say, regarding some liposuctioned model type. I decided there was no way *I* was going to spend my life sitting in front of a box that told me I was ugly. I quit TV and even movies, the modern ones anyway, because they get inside my head: all those hard bodies jumping in and out of cars and rutting. Plus the violence. Rossi forced me to watch *Gangs of New York* and I couldn't handle all that butchery. What's his name, who was in *Titanic*, was in it and Rossi's got the hots for him. Ever since her breasts sprouted, Rossi's only concern is whether guys think she's sexy. I tell her they'd ram a tree if it had a hole in it. Tora has small breasts and writes poems in lower case about her isolation. She's been working on an ode about the stabbing, depicting Drew as some kind of girl Jesus. The three of us were eating fries at the time of the incident, heard a hollering and saw Drew with the letter opener sticking out of her back, still holding her food tray. She must be the only principal in history who eats in the cafeteria. Anyway, preoccupied with the greater good, she didn't twig to the fact that she'd been seriously wounded. She carefully set down the tray, switching to conflict-resolution mode, but the knifer didn't seem too interested and started swiping at Drew with her paws, calling her a cunt-shitting bitch. This got the mob's attention; even the geeks looked up from their techno-crap. Finally Mr. Coombs, super-jock phys. ed. teacher, tackled the girl from behind and held her arms behind her back. She kept wiggling around, shoving her ass into his crotch, making Coombs' eyebrows pop. When the paramedics arrived, Drew was lying motionless with her legs sticking out at weird angles.

'How's your mother?' Damian asks.
    'Which one?'
    'Has she left the house yet?'
    'Negative.'

Ever since Damian started feeling guilty about leaving me on suicide watch for mother number one, he's been taking me out. We started with doughnuts but have progressed to beer. The waitresses act wenchy around him and don't ask my age. I guess he's good-looking, though his hair's thinning a bit. He's alright. I've never expected much from him. When he isn't chasing pussy, he's stomping around in a hard hat on building sites. He met Drew when he was the site manager for our school reno. Now he's with some other tomato he really wants me to like. They play tennis and drag me out so I can miss every single ball.

'She should be seeing a therapist,' he says.

'To which mother would you be referring?'

'Drew, obviously.'

'Obviously.' I like saying that word, stretching out the *ob* then gliding into the *vious*.

One table over, a couple are shoving tongues down each other's throats. Damian's pretending he hasn't noticed.

'I'd like some nachos,' I say, knowing the cheese will stick to my thighs.

'Whatever you want,' he says, wiping sweat off his forehead with his napkin. He always sweats around me. I figure it's due to his high blood pressure and compulsive lying. 'A little bird told me your biological mother wants to meet you.'

I don't say anything because I know *he* will.

'That's exciting,' he says. He always says, 'That's exciting,' or 'How exciting.' It never is. I ask the waitress for nachos.

He leans over the table, giving me his undivided attention. 'Aren't you just a tad curious about her?'

I don't tell him she's probably trailer trash who hopes my existence will give her life meaning.

'Zippy phoned the other day,' he says. 'She thinks you'll never forgive her.'

That's sweet, the two of them talking behind my back. 'They let her out?'

'She hasn't been institutionalized for some time, Limone. If you paid attention you would know this.'

'Are *you* paying attention? I mean, she was your wife. Maybe if you paid her more than a dollar a month, she wouldn't have to clean toilets.'

'For your information, she is no longer with Molly Maid. She's working at Marty Millionaire.'

'That's exciting.' I try to picture Zippy in her fluffy bathrobe hustling couches.

The nachos arrive and I start shoving them in my mouth. When I was eight I decided to stop reacting to humans. Reacting gives them power, which they can use against you. Registering nothing shields you. The attackers throw jibes and punches but go unrewarded. You're still inside your body feeling the pain, but the ass-faces can't see it. This is particularly useful when boys stalk you. I'm classified as a 'dog,' which means they pass me off to a friend: 'How 'bout some sucky-fucky with my friend here, bitch?' What is it about boys and packs? A bunch of them are currently swarming total strangers. Even if the victims offer up their iPods and cells, the dullards still beat the crap out of them. So I take precautions, dress baggy, cover up. Avoid all techno gizmos.

'Why don't you give her a shout?' he asks.

'Who?'

'Your real mom. It can't hurt and, who knows, you might like her.'

'What's it to you if I call her?'

'Limone, you're a little short on role models right now. She might be just what you need, with Drew in rough shape.'

'Drew's fine.'

'I don't think so.'

'Don't think, okay, do me a favour, *don't think.*'

He does one of his walrus sighs then takes a gander at the couple swapping spit. I ingest more nachos, thinking about that woman who adopted two unbelievably cute Guatemalan babies only to discover that she couldn't 'bond' with them. Nine loveless years later she passed them back to the adoption agency. 'I made a mistake,' she said. 'They deserve so much more than I can give.' Of course the boys weren't cute babies anymore and nobody wanted to adopt them. They're in foster care. I cut out their photo and put it in my mother/daughter scrapbook, even though they're boys.

'You're really growing up,' Damian observes. 'If you wore some decent clothes you might even be pretty. Whoever would have thunk it?' Not only does he say *thunk* but another favourite phrase is *How d'you like dem apples?* It is truly painful being associated with him.

'Do you need clothes? Some summer dresses?'

What's he got in mind? Something short and sheer? A pair of fuck-me pumps?

'You know,' Damian says, breathing beer, 'you're always welcome to come and live with me and Goldie.' He only asks me when he's drunk. I push the plate of carbs and fats at him.

'I gotta go.'

'D'you need a ride?'

'Negative.'

'Don't be a stranger.'

Late shifts at the hospital don't bother me. I like talking to the kids who can't sleep. The lucky ones have parents dozing on sofa beds in their rooms, but there's always some loner whose parents work nights or have to look after other sibs. My job is mostly to make sure the younger ones don't pull out their ivs. Contrary to popular belief, kids don't usually die from cancer these days. Unless it's neural blastoma, which is pretty rare and only happens to the under-fives. Leukemia is usually treatable, although sometimes the chemo and radiation cause infections. The worst is when the brain gets infected, because it can result in brain damage. If the kid makes it, she has to learn how to walk again, hold a crayon, a spoon. By the time she's up to speed on feeding herself, chances are the cancer's back. But mostly the kids pull through. In the short term anyway. In the long term they're more susceptible to adult cancers but nobody talks about that. So I don't sweat the cancer ward.

The parents can be a problem, freaking out where the kids can hear them. The parents check their brains when they step through the hospital doors, morph into emoting blobs in the elevators. I always ask them to fuss and blither in private because their children don't want to hear about dying, they want to party. Sometimes they're too weak to do much so I perform puppet shows by their beds, the more violent the better. The girls always want a wedding at the end. The boys want everyone blown up. I tell them somebody has to live to keep the human race going. 'Why?' they ask, which is a good question.

I really like this six-year-old named Kadylak whose parents are Ukrainian and clock long hours at shit jobs to pay for the cancer drugs their daughter needs when she's not in the hospital. Even though Kadylak knows making extra cash is why they're not around, it's obvious she misses them like crazy. She rocks in her sleep and calls for them. I put my arms around her and hold her steady till she relaxes. You can always tell when a kid's fallen asleep because suddenly they weigh an extra fifty pounds and have no bones in their bodies. Most children with cancer become pretty self-absorbed what with the treatment and pain and the feeling that the world's left them behind. But Kadylak keeps an eye on things, people's moods. If I'm sad, angry, frustrated, Kadylak wants to know about it. 'Why are you so fussterated?' Usually I tell her and she listens. Nobody else does. Blecher's head bobs but she's not hearing what I'm saying; I'm tempted to ask her why she doesn't do something useful, like learn how to masturbate, but I can't risk another suspension. Kadylak's a big believer in 'tomorrow,' which is wild considering she's got cancer. 'It'll be different tomorrow,' she says. She never says, *It'll be better tomorrow*. Just *different*.

3

The truth is I want a biological mother like the Jewish girl's. When the Nazis evicted them, Mutti sent her daughter on the *Kindertransport* to England even though losing Marianne was killing her. Mutti told Marianne that she had to let her go to a better life because there would be no life in Germany. Mutti sacrificed herself for her daughter. She pinned a letter inside her dress that told Marianne how much she loved her, that she couldn't bear the thought of not watching her grow, not fixing her hair, not lengthening her dresses. That's how my real mother is in my heart. In my head she's that girl who gave birth in the can at Walmart and left the baby in the toilet bowl. Gives new meaning to the phrase *shop till you drop*.

I'm digging through the debris in my locker for that French textbook I pretend to read to keep Babineaux off my case, when Tora thrusts one of her poems at me:

> *i'm in my own world*
> *all alone in this*
> *icy blue sky*
> *i see no one*
> *hear no one*
> *i cry tears of pain*
> *but i no longer ask*
> *why am i here*

'Awesome,' I say, avoiding eye contact. I've considered telling her the truth re her verse but suspect this would mean losing an ally, which I can't afford. Personally, I think telling the truth is overrated.

Rossi shows up, smearing on lip gloss. 'So what are you guys doing for lunch?'

'Sitting in the yard and flicking boogers,' I say.

There's a party none of us are invited to, at Nicole's. She's one of Queen Bee Kirsten's followers. Being excluded has Rossi in a funk.

'That's like, the tenth party this year,' she whines.

I can't imagine going to a 'party.' I'd have to look interested.

'She's invited *everybody*,' Rossi says. I'm worried about her. She doesn't see what's happening, that she's been labelled *skank*; that soon they'll be dissing her in the halls and online, pelting her with rocks and toilet paper. Last year Kirsten pushed a broken bottle into a skank's face. Of course there were no witnesses. And yet somehow word got around that the skank's chin had been hanging off her face. I want to protect Rossi from a similar assault. We've known each other since JK, swapped Winnie the Pooh stories, cried at the end when Christopher Robin asks Pooh to remember him always no matter what happens.

'Why should you care?' I ask.

'Unlike you, Lemon, I like to meet guys.'

'Do you actually *want* their dicks up your snatch, Ross?' I ask. 'Do you get some kind of power surge when they grab your tits or do you just want to be loved?'

'You should talk. Everybody says you're a dyke.'

'That'll keep 'em off me.'

We used to talk about other things than sex and guys. We used to have confidence. We spun cartwheels and handstands. We got A's in math.

'Lemon's saving herself for the ghost of Cary Grant,' Tora says.

The skateboard boys arrive in the yard. Dressed in grunge, long-haired with toques pulled low over their foreheads, they slam their boards around. Rossi arranges her body for better viewing.

'Do you think the words *personal hygiene* hold any meaning for them?' I ask.

'I think M. Babineaux wants to have sex with me,' Rossi announces.

'You think everybody wants to have sex with you,' Tora says, penning another poem.

'It's the way he leans over me when he's helping. He's like, all over me.'

'Do you want to have sex with *him*?' I ask.

'It might be different.'

'With him being French and all.'

'He's got halitosis,' Tora points out.

Babineaux is ambidextrous. When he's conjugating verbs on the board you have to copy really fast because as he's writing with his right hand, he's erasing with his left. 'So,' I say, 'you're thinking he can work you with both hands?'

'What would *you* know about it?'

'I know I wouldn't have sex just because it would be different.'

'You wouldn't have sex, period.'

I don't know if this is actually true. I didn't want to have sex with Doyle, even though I let him shove his tongue down my throat a few times – only after he'd taken me out for fancy dinners, of course. Having a boyfriend flush with cash has its upsides. You get to go places other than Tim Hortons, and drive around in his daddy's car. But the whole sweaty, slobbery, groping process is pretty base, particularly if he's been drinking beer and eating oysters.

Sex with Kadylak's father, on the other hand, has some allure. He's attractive in an earthy-but-sensitive-labourer kind of way. He doesn't speak much English which might be part of the attraction. He's been asking fewer questions now that Kadylak's on her third cycle of treatment. Watching orangey-red and bright yellow fluids dripping into her is the new normal for him. They've put a portacath in her chest because her arms are burned out from the first two cycles. What Mr. Paluska hasn't witnessed is the intramuscular needles three times a week. The nurses put numbing cream on her but still Kadylak screams. It's the only time she shows her pain. The nurses wear masks, gowns and gloves when they give needles or handle chemo drugs. They look pretty scary. They even gown up when they're removing bed pans because any bodily fluid coming out of these kids is toxic. The first time Kadylak bloated up from the steroids and her hair was falling out in clumps, she looked terrified. Now she's just resigned. She sees things for what they are: drugs that'll save or kill her.

'I'm like, so totally bored,' Rossi anounces.

Tora hands me the latest.

> *the world is in unrest*
> *innocent people dying*
> *afraid to go out after dark*
> *violence*
> *we must end it*
> *give of ourselves*
> *show that we care*
> *the world needs*
> *a river of peace*

I watch Zippy through Marty Millionaire's window. She's checking herself out in a gaudy full-length mirror. She looks fatter. The medication always puffs her up. Makes me think of those Guantánamo prisoners being mainlined antidepressants until they get so stupid they don't know who they are anymore. They start calling the guards their daddies and do everything they tell them. Zippy doesn't know who she is anymore, if she ever did. She used to heat pins over a flame then stick them into her wrists. She didn't go for the arteries, just wanted to cause pain because she said feeling pain was better than feeling nothing. She'd make a pattern of black dots with the pin. Over a week the dots would turn from black to yellow and she'd start picking at them to make sure they wouldn't heal. The open sores stuck to her clothing. She'd yank her sleeves over her hands. Even after the wounds healed they'd remain swollen for months. When she progressed to razor blades, I told Damian. The way I see it I was partially responsible. She *couldn't* feel love for me so she cut herself. I've quit trying to be loveable. Being adopted makes it easy: I was damaged from the start. Unwanted goods.

Zippy sees me and jumps up and down as though she's just won something. She grabs me and pulls me into the store. 'How *are* you? Sweetness, it's so good to see you, you look ... you look so grown-up.'

'Damian says you think I'll never forgive you. I forgive you. Don't carry that around.' I can't stand being somebody else's baggage.

Already there's nothing to say. She sits on a bloated couch and pats the spot beside her.

'I've got to get to work,' I say.

'Just for a sec, honeybunch. Just give me a minute.'

The truth is I want her to hold me, make it all better the way she could before the pins.

'You were the most beautiful baby,' she says, like she always does. 'I took one look at you and knew I'd love you forever.'

What a careless word *love* is. People toss it around.

'Do you like working here?' I ask.

'Oh, Lloyd's fabulous.' I see an ape man in the back watching us. She's always been a good lay, all those years tranked in a bathrobe.

'I'm still in training,' Zippy whispers. 'Lloyd's been so patient. Let me look at you.'

I stare back at her, see the fear in her eyes. 'I forgive you,' I say again.

'Why won't she buy you some *pretty* clothes?'

'I've got to run.' I quickly kiss her forehead. It feels moist. I've made her sweat.

Sometimes I think I'm going nuts. Usually when I'm scooping ice cream for overfed *Homo sapiens*. I start freaking about being trapped underground with a thousand humans. I watch them clogging the mall, picking their noses, trying to figure out what to consume next. I start visualizing their gastrointestinal tracts, plugged with burgers, fries, wings, pizza, slushies. I start thinking about toilets and all the shit in pipes all around me. I look at the paraplegic who buys frozen yogourt for his parrot. The parrot sits on the handlebars of his motorized wheelchair. The paraplegic feeds the parrot the yogourt with a stir stick. I stare at the old guy in the Speedy Muffler cap who orders vanilla soft-ees and grabs his crotch when I hand them to him. I see parents shouting at their consumer trainees then buying them more stuff. I think about China, all that economic growth blackening the rivers, lungs and faces – killing people. I think about all the wars going on for no good reason, and those Africans fighting over diamond mines, cutting off the arms and legs of children, and I just can't see how it's possible *not* to go nuts. That's if you think about anything for more than five seconds. If you can stop thinking after five seconds and move on to some new topic, you'll probably be alright. Drew knows about every stupid human trick going, and it doesn't get her down because she thinks she can do something about it. She's a member of every human rights and environmental protection organization going. She reads up on all the shit that goes down. She seems to think reading is taking action. She drives a low-emissions car and has solar panels attached to her roof. She thinks she's making a difference whereas I know IT MAKES NO DIFFERENCE. Although, since the stabbing, the mail's been piling up. She doesn't read the 'Save Our Water' pamphlets anymore. Mostly she chases the cats in the backyard. She pitches plastic containers of water at them but always misses. She says the fucking cats shit and piss and dig around in the flower beds. This is not news to me, but Drew used to have a day job and no time to sit around staring at the yard. The cats aren't afraid of her. She's collected gravel from the drive-way and is planning to ambush them. At least it'll get her out.

Doyle's standing over me wearing his Dairy Dream hat at a jaunty angle. The hats are mandatory; we all look demented in them. The main reason I went out with Doyle is he's six foot four. I felt like a little woman beside him, wanted him to pick me up the way Rhett picks up Scarlett.

'Are you washing the scoops regularly?' Doyle demands. Ever since I stopped going out with him, he demands things.

'How regularly?'

'You're not cleaning them at all, are you? You're just *soaking* them.'

Doyle likes to make explosions in chemistry. Mr. Conkwright will stress that certain chemicals should not be mixed because they're combustible and sure enough old Doyle will mix them to make a bang.

'I don't want to have to report you,' he says.

I could say, 'To who?' Mr. Buzny, who shows up to collect the cash, who wouldn't notice a dirty scoop if it was shoved up his ass. I don't say this because that would be reacting. Doyle wants me to react. Doyle has spread word that I'm frigid.

'Have you checked the toppings?' he demands, flipping the lids. 'You're almost out of sprinkles here. What the fuck have you been doing?'

Is it always going to be like this when I tell a boy I don't want him slobbering all over me? I didn't actually say that, of course. I think I said I wasn't ready for 'this,' which I'm sure our hero took to mean sexual intercourse in general as opposed to sexual intercourse with *him*. At our hero's urging, we'd been imbibing banana daiquiris at a bar with a tropical theme and, I have to admit, those drinks were good. Those drinks even made Doyle look good, until his tongue started weaseling around my mouth. He shoved me up against a fake palm tree beside the toilets. Men walked by zipping their flies. Women flicked their hair. Nobody cared that some guy twice my size was squashing me into a plastic palm. They assumed I was enjoying it, which is what I'd always assumed when I saw couples pushed up against immobile objects. Now I know better. You get yourself into these situations and sometimes it's not so easy to get out of them.

Drew's always told me that if you get into a difficult situation with a boy, tell him you're going to puke. It worked with Doyle. He backed off and I dashed to the Ladies' to scrub his spit out of my mouth. Drew knows a thing or two. She's alright. Which is why I'm sad she got knifed. I've never told her that. Maybe I should.

4

Mr. Huff, who's about a hundred, has us studying *A Midsummer Night's Dream*, which has to be Shakespeare's all-time most boring play – all those halfwit lovers and fairies flitting around. Mr. Huff squints at us. 'Who's going to read?' he asks. I know he's about to pick me because I'm the only girl whose name he remembers. He only remembers it because I was in his class last year when he made us read *Love's Labour's Lost*, Shakespeare's second all-time most boring play. I can't stand all this love-at-first-sight bilge, couples obsessing over each other before they've even had a conversation. People are always blaming Hollywood for our screwed-up perceptions of romance, but as far as I'm concerned, it started with Shakespeare. All those guys and gals swooning over each other from a distance. Get them alone in a room to hash it out, don't make us numb our asses for two and a half acts before they get it together. Even then they don't have a serious conversation, just exchange the old wedding vows. Happy happy happy. All those pretty boys in dresses. No wonder Will was a queer.

'Limone?' Huff says. 'Why don't you have a go at the fairy queen?'

Limone is the name Zippy cursed me with. I changed it to Lemon when I was six. This upset Zippy because she thought Limone was French and classy.

'Why,' I inquire, hoping to delay reading until the bell, 'does Titania cave to Oberon?'

'Interesting question.'

Huff always says, 'Interesting question,' because he's so excited anybody even has a question.

'Why,' he repeats loudly, I guess because he's hoping to wake a few dozers, 'does Titania succumb to Oberon?' He peers over his reading glasses. 'Any ideas?'

'It's because she's drugged,' I point out.

'Is that the only reason?' Huff queries, hands clasped behind his back in scholar mode.

Queen Bee Kirsten puts up her hand. 'I think she was attracted to him all along.'

'Based on what?' I say without putting up my hand. I never put up my hand. I figure these duffers are lucky I bother to participate. They're just passing time, counting paycheques till the pension kicks in.

'He's sexy,' Kirsten says. 'That's obvious.'

'How is that obvious?'

'Interesting question,' Huff says. 'How is that obvious?'

Kirsten thinks hard, twirling her hair.

'She talks about him all the time,' Nicole of the party we're not invited to says.

'She doesn't talk about him,' I say. 'She talks about the changeling boy. She doesn't give a rat's fart about Oberon, she wants the boy.'

'She wants the boy because she wants Oberon,' Kirsten says. 'That's obvious.'

Everything is always obvious to Kirsten.

'How is that obvious?' I ask again.

'Interesting question,' Huff says. 'How is it obvious she wants Oberon?'

'She's always talking about him,' Kirsten says.

'She's not *always* talking about him,' I repeat. 'She's talking about the changeling boy.' It could go on like this for hours. Huff starts pacing, excited by the stimulating discussion.

'It's date rape,' I say. 'Dope 'em and do 'em.' Gasps are heard, then snorts. Huff takes off his glasses and rubs the bridge of his nose. The bell goes. I jet out of there.

In need of air I head for the track, hang my head off the bleachers and watch the world upside down. Looks better this way. People have to work at holding on to the planet, they can't just loiter. Feet are put down with purpose, bodies move with conviction.

I don't think Zippy actually meant to hurt me when she attempted to kill me. I think she was trying to save me from suffering. That's all it's been for her, one big trial. She often said, 'This is a trial,' or 'What a trial.' I don't know what she was on trial for – burning the macaroni? Failing to keep up with the laundry? Failing to provide sucky-fucky for old Damian? I think he was happy with her for about five seconds, before her tits fell and her neediness got on his nerves. She was supposed to be a homemaker, which in those days was pretty radical because everybody was enslaving themselves to corporations and shoving their kids into daycare. Classmates used to tell me I was *so lucky* to have my mom at home, which I was before she started self-mutilating. We made popsicle-stick castles and baked cookies. She taught me how to ride a bike. She and Damian were on some list to adopt another kid but it was impossible to find one who wasn't damaged by drugs or alcohol. I wanted a brother or sister, preferably a sister. I imagined we'd be one happy family like on TV. I pretended to talk to my sister at night when I couldn't sleep. She couldn't sleep either and always agreed with me about what jerks people were.

There must be some twisted reason why my biological mother wants to meet me all of a sudden. Maybe she's got cancer and wants to fill me in on my rotten genes. Or maybe her legitimate spawn got killed in a car crash. Or her son got an AK-47 and shot up a cafeteria and she can't cope with the revelation that she raised a monster.

The football-slash-hockey crowd trot onto the track. You'd like to think such cretins are extinct, only to be resurrected in Hollywood movies. Unfortunately, jocks still rule. We girls watch them jog around, warming up for some macho-man activity. According to Doyle, the football-slash-hockey boys can get any girl they want. He said this as though it doesn't get better than being able to shove your noodle up any girl you want. Rossi was given the honour of being nailed by one of the football hulks. She said he 'fucked me hard,' which doesn't sound too charming. She said it was 'athletic sex.' I said, 'Did you like it?'

'He's got a great body.'

'Did you *like* it?'

'It's not that simple.'

'Why isn't it that simple?'

'There are parts you like and parts you don't like.'

'What parts didn't you like?'

'He kept pushing my head down to his crotch. He's like, a total blow-job freak.'

I watch the blow-job freak do some stride jumps. I want to grab his head and shove it into some jock's stinking crotch. I've never been able to compute why girls are expected to suck boys off and yet the ultimate degradation for a straight male is to suck another male's penis. 'Suck my cock, you cocksucker!' they yell at each other. So why is it an honour for girls to get on their knees and gag on some dullard's jewels? No equality of the sexes there. Rossi started out providing fellatio as an alternative to sexual intercourse because she knew her mother would freak if she found out Rossi had lost her virginity. But the boys got bored with that pretty quick.

'What about *you*?' I asked her once. 'Are *you* bored with it?'

She shrugged. *She* doesn't factor into it. I don't know how that happened. She looks in the mirror and frets about what guys will think of her. What *she* thinks of herself doesn't matter anymore.

The twist with the current supremo jock is that he wants to be a rap star even though he's white and is going to end up selling insurance or something. His car stereo always blares gangsta rap about 'what that ho needs.' Meanwhile, Queen Bee Kirsten and her ladies are cheerleaders. The revival of cheerleading is a twenty-first-century tragedy in my opinion. It is truly painful watching them twitch their glutes and spread their legs. Rossi auditioned but they wouldn't have her. Somebody taped a bottle of Rid, the poison you smear on your pubic hair when you get crabs, to her locker this morning. I grabbed it before she saw it. Kirsten's crowd has been staring at her, hoping for signs of humiliation. Rossi, of course, thinks they're paying special attention to her eensy-weensy tank-top-and-capris combo.

In Social Studies Mrs. Freeman told us that we have to rid the world of the notion that young people today don't have ideals and morals. 'Prove them wrong!' she bellowed. Like everybody else, she wants us to get educated so we can score some pod job, licking the assistant VP's loafers. Work sixty-hour weeks so we can earn the benefits we won't get after we burn out and get laid off. I'd rather make soap. I read about some burnt-out human-rights lawyer who transformed himself into an organic farmer and hooked up with an Amish community to learn how to make organic soap. The Amish use ingredients from their gardens, kitchens and barns to brew soap. The human-rights lawyer got spooked about stewing animal fats so he substituted avocado oil, castor oil, cocoa butter and palm kernel oil. He mixes them together in a big cast-iron pot heated over a wood-burning stove. He throws in natural stuff that adds fragrance, like lemongrass, cedarwood, eucalyptus, lavender, then he pours it into a wooden soap pan with a wooden lid. Next he bakes it in a wood-burning stove, lets it cool, slices it up and sells it at markets and online. He says every morning he wakes up excited about some new natural ingredient he wants to toss in his soap. I can't imagine waking up excited. One thing's for sure, sitting in a lecture hall with 300 Asians and Muslims isn't going to excite me. Why bother when they're way smarter than me and taking over the world and all that. There's this girl called YangYang at Dairy Dream who's a super-brain. She's going to university to study business and you just know where that one's going. In five years she'll own a bunch of Dairy Dreams and poor minority white trash like myself will be soaking her scoops.

I told Mrs. Freeman that the ruination of Spaceship Earth is thanks to the geniuses with post-secondary education.

'Are you suggesting,' she inquired, 'that we eliminate post-secondary education?'

'We need to learn from plants and animals,' I told her. 'Before they're all dead.'

On principle I'm against the Tim Hortons concept, the whole franchise thing, plus they don't buy fair-trade coffee, meaning little kids are picking the beans. But their soup's alright and affordable. Rossi's in a state because Kirsten's crowd threw clumps of wet toilet paper at her. 'Why would they do that?' she asks, looking like the JK kid I remember. We used to pretend to be pioneers and shoot horse thieves.

'Maybe they didn't like your tank top,' I say.

'What's wrong with my tank top?'

'It's a bit revealing,' Tora says. She's scribbling in her notepad again. I've quit actually reading her poems; instead I look down at the pad and picture snow falling upwards or something.

'It's no more "revealing" than Kirsten's tank top,' Rossi says.

'There's more of you to reveal,' I point out.

'It's total bull,' Rossi says, 'all that stuff about how if you've got it, flaunt it.'

I'm pretty sure there's MSG in the soup because I always get a little hyper from it. 'Did you read about that girl whose ex is posting sexually explicit videos of her on YouTube? You might want to give him a call, Ross.'

'Very funny.'

'He made it look as though she'd put them there herself. He *impersonated* her. Had her inviting any boy on the planet to enjoy her services.'

'That's heinous,' Tora says.

'Oh, the wonders of technology.' I smear butter on my roll. I always ask for extra butter because I'm a butter addict. For some reason the servers seem to resent handing over extra butter, like it's costing them personally, when we all know the Tim Hortons Corp. can spare a few slabs.

Tora hands me her scrawl. I look down at it, trying to decide which doughnut to consume. Tora wants to be a writer. She plans to go to university and take creative writing. I told her no decent writer studies creative writing. She accused me of being envious because I have no direction. She doesn't think I'm serious about the soap thing. I've actually been thinking about a mint facial soap. Mint's got anti-inflammatory properties, which would be good for zits.

'I'm going to crash Nicole's party,' Rossi announces.

I get a blueberry cruller. The dough sticks to the top of my mouth, making speech difficult.

'You've got to get over this party thing,' Tora says.

'And do what?' Rossi asks. 'Sit around writing lonely poems? No thank you.'

'You could get a hobby,' I say.

'Don't start with the pennies,' Rossi says. When we were in Brownies, I collected pennies to earn a Brownie badge. I've kept it up because I want to have a penny for as many years as possible. My oldest penny is from 1939. I like holding it and thinking about some mother holding it in 1939, listening to the wireless about Herr Hitler, worrying that sonny boy will have to go to war and get his legs blown off. I like knowing that she's dead and that her son's dead and that the penny has changed hands millions of times since then. Hands that belonged to people who were just as freaked about something or other. There's always something to freak about but the penny keeps going.

5

A cop comes to our school to talk about Youth Violence. He's short and losing his hair and talks really loudly even though the microphone's set up. He keeps popping it on words like *purpose* and *protect*. His name is Power. *Inspector* Power. He says there have already been twelve homicides in our area this year. 'If you live by the sword, you will die by the sword,' he warns the assembly of head-and butt-scratchers. 'Lay down your arms,' he says. 'The families who live here have good hearts and desire peace and just want to raise their families.'

Ms. Brimmers – Drew's replacement – stands gazing at Inspector Power, getting creamy about the man in the uniform. Brimmers is very serious about her job because it's her first gig as principal. Occasionally she smiles, which is truly scary because her lips curl back rodent-style and her nose wrinkles. Unlike Drew, she's always looking over her shoulder, watching for knives.

'Shootings are a symptom of something else,' Inspector Power says. 'You need to acquire the social skills that enable you to resolve incidents in a peaceful manner.' He pops the mike on *peaceful*. 'You've got to start thinking about compassion.'

I guess nobody's told him that violence buys status, not to mention stardom. It's not like anybody's forgotten the Columbine boys – heck, they're so famous a video game was named after them. Maybe Inspector Power hasn't noticed that, even in the movies, the good guy ends up blowing everybody's heads off in order to protect the families who desire peace and just want to raise their families. If you look at history, all the killings are supposed to be about protecting somebody or other; from the Romans on it's just one big disembowelling process in the name of defence. No different from gang wars. That's another problem I have with Shakespeare, he makes battlefield stuff look noble when the fact is, it's just more slaughter for no good reason. And while his Henrys and Richards are plotting inside their castles, peasants are being burnt out, raped and pillaged on a regular basis. Over and over again the most ruthless despot wins. I guess there are a few exceptions, Hitler for example, but he still managed to kill six million Jews. Gandhi never lifted a sword but who wants to starve themselves and sit around in a diaper spinning cotton? And anyway, a bullet got him in the end. Meanwhile India and Pakistan are back to wanting to nuke each other, and the Middle East is one big ticking bomb. Somebody should come up with an advertising campaign that makes killing a sign of weakness. A campaign that makes *not* killing sexy, that makes guns look like crutches for cowards who lack social skills, that makes living and dying by the sword something to be ashamed of. Maybe somebody could design *We Wun Without Guns* T-shirts, or *Don't Slice, Be Nice* hoodies, *Bombs Are for Buttheads* baseball caps. I'm no advertising wizard but it must be possible. Advertisers can make us do anything. The hitch is violence sells. And there's nothing like a war to keep the corporations happy.

I've been reading about Genghis Khan because I'm obsessed with conquerors and monarchs. I like knowing that, even with all that power and cash, they were still dragging their asses and not exactly excited about getting up in the morning. Mostly they fretted about who was out to get them or betray them and, of course, which of their many enemies must be incarcerated or slaughtered. Anyway, for centuries old Genghis has been made out to be this Mongolian psycho killer. Well, it turns out he wasn't half as gruesome as all those Vikings and William the Conqueror. Educated people resented that this labourer – Genghis – turned out to be an amazing warrior leader, but the academics made him out to be a ruthless murderer while the likes of the Plantagenets and Alexander the Great got special treatment. None of them conquered half as much land as old Genghis did. Old Caesar doesn't even compare. But they were of noble birth and thus got noble treatment. That's what I mean when I say the people with post-secondary education are bad for Spaceship Earth. You can't believe a word they're saying.

Inspector Power says he knows that we carry weapons to look tougher, to show that 'Don't-f-word-with-me image.' The crotch-scratchers snort.

'I understand,' Power says, 'that many of you carry knives to protect yourselves. But rest assured that any weapon you carry can be turned against you.'

Ms. Brimmers is nodding so much I keep expecting her to get dizzy and pass out.

'Rest assured,' Power repeats, 'that on the whole, our schools are safe, our suspensions and expulsions are down, but there's no denying that we're seeing more guns, and more knives.'

It kills me the way they go on about weapons. Sick people can make weapons out of anything. Plastic box cutters go unde-tected by the security system, and if a box cutter isn't handy, they'll shove toilet paper down your throat and choke you to death. Weapons aren't the issue. Sick minds is the issue. Violence isn't freaky. Violence rocks. They beat up on someone to prove they're the big man. If the cops catch them, even better. A crim-inal record is a badge of honour with these losers.

I keep thinking about that John Bull guy organizing the peasants after the Black Plague wiped everybody out and there was a labour shortage. Suddenly peasants could demand pay for sweating blood for some noble. John Bull demanded to meet with King Edward II who was fourteen or something. The peasants had no bone to pick with the boy king, they were happy to support him as long as the nobles paid them for their labour. Edward agreed to meet with John Bull to discuss the matter and old John Bull showed up on a mule to explain the situation. Edward, sitting on his über-purebred, said, 'Fine.' John Bull sat there stunned on his mule for a minute. When he said, 'Thanks,' and turned around to go deliver the good news, one of Edward's henchman lopped off his head. Two weeks later the hormonal king ordered a proclamation saying the peasants would remain slaves and should expect *even worse* treatment than before John

Bull got them thinking they might be human. I don't see this being any different from the corporations controlling Third World labour. All those educated CEOs exploiting the peasants. *We're* exploiting the peasants because we buy all that crap they make for a dollar a year.

Power tells us to say a prayer or at least bow our heads in memory of the twelve homicide victims in our area already this year. This guy kills me.

Kadylak's diarrhea from the chemo is worse. She's got sores on her mouth, anus and vagina. Peeing is torture so she's refusing liquids, which is a concern. She can't concentrate on anything. I try reading to her but she's not listening. I get her a freezie, pick up the remote and surf, but there's nothing she wants to watch. I turn it off and listen to the whirr of the hospital for what feels like a couple of hours.

'God is bigger than a tree,' she says.

I don't argue.

'God is a spirit,' she says. 'Bigger than the universe. They teach us that in church.'

Her sheet and blanket are in a tangle at the foot of her bed. 'Are you too hot?' I ask. 'Or do you want me to straighten these out?'

'Is it time for me to go to heaven?'

'Definitely not,' I say. 'It's just the chemo. It's always like this.'

'It wasn't this bad before.'

I don't tell her it was but didn't seem as bad because it was her first and second time. By round three you're familiar with the suffering, you wait for it, fear it. I tell her about the kids in the out-patient clinic who come in for maintenance, who've gone through what she's going through and have no cancer. Kids with new hair who are back at school kicking balls around.

'Do you want to go to the playroom?' I ask, trying to change topics. She doesn't answer, just stares up at the bird mobile her dad hung up for her. She loves birds.

'Why's my mum always crying?' she asks.

'She's sad because of all the chemo and the pokes you're getting. She knows you're hurting.'

I saw her mother on the way in. She was scurrying to her night cleaning job. She looks about ninety.

'There's a blue jay's nest in our backyard,' I say. 'You can see the chicks poking their heads up and squawking any time one of their parents is around with food. It's like they're squealing, "Me, me, me!" You'd think they'd be quieter so no predators could hear them.'

'What's predators?'

'Animals who eat them.'

'The babies don't know that they can be eaten,' Kadylak says. 'That's why they don't keep quiet. They don't know that they can die.'

I stroke her forehead until she goes to sleep. I know she'll wake up in agony in a couple of hours and no one will be here. She'll rock and rock, calling for her parents. I tuck Mischa the bear into her arms.

Now that she doesn't have a day job, and when she isn't ambushing felines, Drew waters the plants every two seconds, rotting the roots. She's slouched at the kitchen table surrounded by dead vegetation. 'Maybe they need plant food,' she says. She's still in Damian's PJs. Her only contact with the outside world is the newspaper. She reads every single page, which is enough to stop anybody going out.

'Maybe you shouldn't read that all the time,' I say. 'It's all under corporate control anyway.'

'One of those fucking cats killed a bird,' she says. She's eating peanut butter again. 'It was flapping its wings but was too injured to fly.' She stares at the sandwich. 'I didn't know what to do. So I did nothing.'

'Chasing the cat off would have lengthened its suffering,' I say.

'I want to *kill* those cats. When I'm dead those fucking cats will be shitting and pissing on my grave.'

'I don't think it's legal to bury humans in backyards.'

'Fucking vermin. The basement stinks of cat. It seeps through the foundation. I'll be trapped underground, steeped in cat piss.'

'I thought you wanted to be cremated.'

The cats are her world now. Her enemies. All her life she's protested against violence. Now she wants to slaughter felines.

'There's some wacko in Calgary,' I say, 'skinning cats and ripping out their entrails.'

'Do you have his number?'

'Remember,' I say, in an effort to change the subject, 'how Taliban women's bones get all soft from never going outside? That's what's going to happen to you.'

'I go outside.'

'To put the garbage out and chase the cats.'

'I'm taking time off, alright, give me a break. For the first time in my life I'm resting.'

Call that resting? Pacing, plant-killing, cat-chasing?

'Nobody's saying go back to work,' I say. 'Just go outside for more than two minutes.'

This is a switch because she used to be the one telling me to get off my ass. I start making a peanut butter sandwich.

'How was school?' she asks. What she wants to know is did anybody ask about her. I don't tell her nobody asks anymore, except old Blecher who makes Drew's skin crawl. She actually said that: 'Blecher makes my skin crawl.'

'We had an assembly with a cop,' I say. 'He told us if we live by the sword, we'll die by the sword. Oh, and Mr. Zameret had a stroke.' Zameret's one of the geography teachers. When he isn't talking about tectonic plates or something he's washing his hands. He says he never gets sick because he washes his hands all the time.

'Is he going to be alright?' she asks.

'He's a total vegetable. He was lying on his kitchen floor all weekend in shit and piss. The other teachers thought it was weird that he was absent since he's never sick. Brimmers sent Coombs over to check on him. The police had to break down the door.'

Drew drops her head into her hands and starts convulsing.

'I didn't think you liked him,' I say.

'He has no one to look after him.'

Who does? Is she imagining I'm going to stick around to change her diapers?

She puts the kettle on for the thousandth time. 'He'd made big plans for retirement. Florida, golfing, the whole bit.'

'Good. Means he's got cash for a nurse.'

'Sometimes, Lemon, you are so harsh.' She wanders off with her kettle on the boil. She'll forget about it. If I don't turn it off, the house will burn down. Which might be alright.

So I'm up in a tree, which was peaceful until a group of crystal-meth abusers showed up. They don't notice me, which is why I sit in trees. Nobody ever looks up. Most people trudge through life staring at the sidewalk. I recognize one of the druggies, she used to be one of those artsy types who's always doodling in little notebooks. She's really skinny now because 'tina'– I love it that they give this lethal drug a girl's name – makes you lose your appetite. Tina is cheap and causes weight loss, which makes it real popular among teenage girls. The hitch is it's highly addictive so pretty soon you start stealing to pay for it. Anyway, this artsy girl, Shannon, couldn't cut it academically. She dropped out and started staying out all night, only showing up at her parents' to steal techno-gizmos she could sell. I know all this because Shannon's mother kept expecting Drew, the school principal, to do something about it. Drew sicced old Blecher on Shannon, which probably made drug abuse look pretty inviting.

Shannon and company must be coming off a high because they're pretty aggressive, pushing and shoving and talking dirty. Larry Bone, dullard extraordinaire, says he has more sketch but tells the girls they have to suck him off to get it. He orders them to wear lip gloss so they all scramble around in their purses and start lubing their lips. Glossed up, they get on their knees in front of Freakboy. I look away, through the leaves at a horizon that's tainted brown.

Shannon's mother blames her daughter's new 'friends' for her drug addiction, calls them 'wolves' and 'downright evil.' I don't know how she fits herself in the picture, what with your mother supposedly being the strongest influence in your life and all that. I look down and there's the artiste with her mouth around Bonehead's joint. Her mother told Drew that Shannon had been 'bright' and 'bubbly' and 'effervescent' before she came to our school. When Drew asked me about Shannon, I told her that having to be bright and bubbly and effervescent would make anyone a junkie.

Bonehead looks skyward and spies me. I stare back at him, forcing him to look away. He loses his erection and starts taking it out on Shannon, slapping her head and calling her nasty names. She falls back on the grass and he starts climbing the tree. 'It's the dyke!' he shouts and they all gather around with potholes for eyes. I imagine myself sacrificed, ripped open, burned. I start singing 'Rule, Britannia!' really loud, with a British accent the way Mr. Swails sings it in history class.

Rule, Britannia, Britannia rules the waves,
For Britons never never never shall be slaves.

Usually my outrageous singing gives egregious assholes pause, but Bonehead starts grabbing at my feet while the others hop around, anticipating bloodshed. I yank myself higher into the tree, singing even louder, but he keeps coming.

Rule, Britannia, Britannia rules the waves,
For Britons never never never shall be slaves.

My impending death makes me try to think of all the things I'll miss when I'm dead, but I can't think of any. Bonehead's breaking branches, *hurting* my tree. This, more than anything, ticks me off and I jab my army boot into his face. He releases his grip to grab his schnoz and squeal. His body makes a convincing thud as it hits the ground. The formerly effervescent Shannon searches his pockets for his stash then makes a run for it. The other junkies chase her. I swing out of the tree monkey-style and beat it.

6

I do Drew's banking, anything she can't do online. The ATMs are down so I wait in line with the Third Worlders who've all got babies and toddlers fussing and grabbing. These aren't the Third Worlders crowding the lecture halls to become doctors and engineers. These are the ones married to the guys operating the car wash. I know this sounds racist but these women are pushy. If you wander slightly out of line, they get right in there and nab your spot. I'd never make it in the Third World. Weak whiteys get trampled. Which is appropriate if you consider how we've treated them over the centuries. You can't say we're not getting what we deserve. You can't exploit somebody's land and resources and expect them to love you. What makes me nuts is the slavery over there. Women and girls being owned by some psycho who cuts off their clitorises and rapes them. Even some male slave got his balls cut off for allegedly making eyes at the master's wife. Although it's not like we don't have slaves over here, indentured labour and all that, scuzzbags trafficking women and children.

The teller hands me the cabbage and I join the automatons pounding the pavement. It kills me how they all check out their reflections in store windows, just kind of glance casually, as though they're not worried their asses look fat. What are they *seeing* in that reflection? Pants too tight, flab spilling over? Are they thinking, 'If I just suck it up and run those extra forty Ks I'll look like Brangelina.' There must be a lot of 'sort of' qualifying going on. 'I sort of look slim in these pants.' I, personally, get seriously depressed when I look in store windows. I walk stooped, for starters. I'll think I'm walking straight then catch sight of myself and see that I'm hunched like one of those little Chinese ladies carting jumbo packs of toilet paper on their backs. You know they've spawned forty kids and live on rice in a house with eighty grandchildren. Mr. Swails had us reading about China when it turned communist. What a screw-up that was, nationalists and communists cutting off each other's heads, coolies turning on foreigners, raping and pillaging just like white people. Everybody was starving and barbecuing the cats and dogs. Chinese ladies hobbled around on bound feet. They'd endured years of pain and deformity to establish status and suddenly they were a joke. Crippled, they couldn't defend themselves, which was unfortunate because everybody was angry and looking for somebody to kick around. It'll be no different for us when we hit the wall.

My plan is to die ignorant. I don't see how knowing the details of *Homo sapiens'* demise is going to improve my quality of life. It's like the kids with cancer on their third round of chemo. They were better off ignorant. By round three they know what's coming and it scares the shit out of them.

Blecher's eating little cheese triangles again. 'Did you see the girl who won Miss Universe?' she asks me. 'She's from Toronto. She said she always strives to maintain a positive attitude. She's studying computer technology.'

'Who isn't?' I say.

'It's a growing field.'

One of these days the tech world's going to short-circuit and we'll be surrounded by computer geeks who won't know how to grow food or make soap or talk to people.

Blecher leans toward me, still chewing. 'Limone, do you *want* to graduate from high school?'

I don't react, stare at the teddy-bear music box on her desk.

'Because if you want to graduate, you're going to have to apply yourself. I was talking to Mr. Huff and Mr. Lund and we're all agreed that you are *not* meeting your potential.'

That's sweet, the three of them worrying about me. The only reason they bother is because I'm the stabbed principal's daughter.

'We've had an idea.'

She's waiting for me to ask what. The bear has red lips, human lips. Freaky.

'We thought you could write a play. Mr. Huff would make it part of your English grade and, if you got some students to perform it, Mr. Lund would make it part of your Drama grade.'

'I don't know how to write a play.'

'Of course you do. You think of a situation, then write things for your characters to say.' She struggles to open a packet of crackers, goes at it with her teeth. The packet explodes, ejecting cracker bits office-wide. This distracts her. I jet out of there.

Doyle's wearing a T-shirt with *Back Off 200 Feet* printed on it. 'We need more fruit salad,' he tells me. We don't, but he enjoys watching me gash myself dicing pineapple. 'You going to Nicole's party?'

'Negative.'

'Everybody's going.'

I don't react, run water over my strawberry-stained fingers while some little kid and his mother check out the flavours. 'May I help you?' I ask.

'Give us a minute,' she says. 'He might take a while to decide.'

'No hurry.'

She looks embarrassed and I realize that the kid is retarded or mentally challenged or whatever you're supposed to call it. His tongue lolls as he peruses the flavours and I just know his life is never going to get better than this. He'll just get older and uglier and freakier. This makes me so sad all of a sudden I can't breathe. I have to *force* myself to breathe. Other customers butt in, the usual suspects demanding bigger scoops, dips, sprinkles, hot fudge. The boy watches my movements, his eyes bugged with expectation. I don't want him to decide because once he decides I'll have to make it for him and there's no way it'll be as good as he expected.

'Have you decided?' the woman asks. She can't be his mother because she looks as though she wouldn't mind if he got hit by a bus. Maybe she's a social worker. The boy's oblivious, awash in his ice cream fantasy. Meanwhile a dragon mother keeps breathing fire at her twin girls who have horsey faces and nasally voices. The mother orders frozen yogourt, which is a serious drag because I have to use the compressor to mash the berries into the yogourt. They want different flavours, meaning I have to clean the frigging machine each time. My mentally challenged boy watches. Maybe he's better off with limited brain power, spared the knowledge of all the horror in the world. What's a competent mind give you except fear and despair?

When you work in ice cream, you're constantly sticky, especially your forearms, touching the sides of the tubs every time you scoop. So the money gets sticky, and the cash drawer and every other surface you touch. When you're not serving, you're supposed to wipe things down. Even after I've finished the yogourts for the dragon mother, my challenged kid hasn't made up his mind. Not wanting to pressure him, I start wiping things down. His social worker keeps checking her watch. Doyle, who's had his finger up his nose in the back, reappears.

'Any time you don't have customers,' he tells me, 'you should be wiping things down.' I wag the J Cloth in front of his face. He's got a zit beside his proboscis, one of those evil ones that you know is full of bile.

'I think he's decided now,' the social worker says.

Because he's a little cross-eyed, it's hard to tell which flavour the boy's looking at. I aim my scoop at the Pralines 'n' Cream but he shakes his head as if I'm about to snuff him. I head for the Wild Berry Swirl. This seems to work except that, after I scoop, he's pointing at the Double Chocolate Chip.

'Does he want a double?' I ask.

'Alright,' the social worker concedes, not looking too happy about it. Maybe it comes out of her expenses. Even after I scoop the chocolate chip, he's pointing at the Black Cherry.

'No, Alberto, that's enough,' the social worker says.

I worry that missing out on Black Cherry is going to scar Alberto for life or something. I check over my shoulder to make sure Doyle's in the back then quickly cram a scoop of Black Cherry on top of the Chocolate Chip. 'Third scoop's on the house,' I mutter to the social worker who smiles for the first time. Amazing how when you save somebody a buck they become your best friend. I hand the cone to Alberto who actually says, 'Thank you.' Not many kids say thank you these days. He's got this aura about him. They walk away, slowly because he's loaded down with the cone. And because he's wearing a leg brace. I get so sad again I can't stand. I squat on the footstool Doyle bought for YangYang because she can't reach the cabinets.

'Did you charge for that extra scoop?' our hero demands.

I stare at his festering boil.

'You can't go giving extra scoops,' he warns. 'If Mr. Buzny saw you doing that, you'd be out on your ass.'

I start wiping again. Alberto is just a tiny figure now, limping toward the exit.

When Doyle was chasing me, before I pretended to puke on him, he'd walk me home after late shifts because a girl was raped behind the dumpsters. Rumour has it she did everything the rapist ordered because she was scared he was going to kill her. It pissed him off that she was a virgin and didn't know how to give blow jobs so he forced his penis into her anus before he shoved it into her vagina. He penetrated her in various orifices nineteen times before he let her go. The cops still haven't charged anybody. They can't figure out why she didn't struggle.

So walking alone at night is no picnic. Particularly after shoving my boot into Bonehead-the-junkie's face.

I hear a crashing sound and jump about ten feet before I figure out it's raccoons going at garbage bins. I walk faster, even though I'm in no hurry to watch Drew losing her mind and bone density. I try not to think about what happened to Alberto after he finished the ice cream, when his hands and face were sticky and he had nothing left to dream about.

7

It's dead quiet in the house, which means she could have offed herself but I'm in no mood for discovering the body. I keep thinking about those babies in the foundling hospital in England in the eighteenth century. Some lord got sick of stepping over dead babies in the street so he guilt-tripped his rich cronies into coughing up for a foundling hospital. Starving women lined up to surrender their babies. The hitch was there wasn't enough room in the hospital for all the babies. The women had to pick balls out of a sack to determine who got to leave their babies behind. A green ball meant you could hand your baby over immediately, never to be seen again. A red ball meant your baby was put on a waiting list, and a black ball meant your baby was back on the street. The mothers whose babies got in always gave the babies something to remember them by. It was usually a bead bracelet or a cheap charm or something, but some of the women were so poor all they had was a ribbon or a nut. They'd poke a hole through the nut so the baby could wear it as a necklace. The ghouls who ran the hospital never gave the trinkets to the babies. The kids never knew that it was hard for their mothers to hand them over, that they were loved and mourned. Half of them died in the foundling hospital anyway. A couple of hundred years later those nuts with holes in them are in a glass case in a museum. You have to pay to see them.

This is one of the problems I have with my biological mother wanting to see me all of a sudden. She left me no sign.

I check the mail since Drew doesn't bother anymore. Bills, and the usual organizations asking her to send cabbage to help them save the world. No love letter from my devoted bio mum. That's what would happen in the movies. *Dear beloved daughter …*

I grab some saltines and crack open a book about the Reformation for some light reading. All that killing over religion makes no sense to me. I guess the point is it wasn't about religion but control. Look at old Cromwell, what a power junkie he must have been, the Lord Protector. What a wank. You have to wonder how the people put up with all that crap without TVs to distract them. Nowadays, with the one-eyed monster they can slip anything past us.

I like history, except for the fact that we don't learn from it. I might even get a decent mark if it weren't being taught by Mr. Swails. He thinks he's an actor and is always pretending to be James II or something. He loves doing French accents, especially Mary Queen of Scots who was raised by Frenchies. He does a virgin queen version of Elizabeth as well as a dried-up-old-hag Gloriana. I figure he's a cross-dresser. Anyway, it's hard to get the facts straight with old Swails prancing about. All those wars and beheadings, forming and dissolving of parliaments. Swails gets giddy when he talks about the beginnings of democracy and all I can think is, what's changed? The rich still get richer while the rest of us work for them. Maybe machinery doesn't chew up our limbs as often, and we get days off. And at least kids don't go down the mine, or become blind working long hours in factories without artificial light. Of course Third World kids go down the mine and become blind working long hours, but they don't count.

Our galoot of a neighbour is at his drum set again, thumping along to tunes from the seventies. He's an NFL flunky turned personal trainer. I don't know who he's personally training because he seems to have an abundance of time on his hands. He's got four kids and a mute wife plus a Rottweiler he hits with a shovel, which stops the dog barking for about two seconds. The personal trainer never walks the dog, just lets it dump in the yard then shovels the doodoo into the schoolyard across the street. I should report him but fear repercussions. Which is what's wrong with the world, I guess, all of us fearing repercussions.

After my persecuted-Jewish-girl phase, I got hooked on African-American slave stories. I'd always imagined lynching like in the movies, hooded Ku Klux Klan members carrying torches, dragging some black guy out in the dead of night and stringing him up. The fact is, up until the fifties, lynchings took place in broad daylight on weekends. Bus tours were set up so the out-of-towners could catch the action. Children were let out of Sunday school early so they could enjoy the show. Usually, after they beat the shit out of him, they'd tie the 'nigger' behind a wagon or a car and drag him around so the whole town could gawp at him. He only got lynched after he'd been tortured and spit upon. Some ninety-three-year-old man who escaped lynching because somebody, some *white* person, finally shouted that he was innocent, was quoted as saying the men in the Klan robes tormenting him were his neighbours. He recognized them through their masks. Neighbours he'd helped because he was a wizard at fixing lawn mowers.

It's not like I feel good about not reporting the personal trainer. But the way I see it, all the authorities would do is ask him if he shovels dog feces into the schoolyard. He'd say, 'Heck, no,' and they'd get back in their government cars.

The thing about history is that it shows you that stuff keeps repeating. It looks different because of technology and all that, but it's the same stuff. Like all the privatization that's going on. Pretty soon we'll be buying air from the corporations who are polluting it. That's after we bail them out, of course.

I close the window but I can still hear the drumming. What keeps a noddy like that going? Waldo, the security guard at the mall, works out about eighteen hours a day. When he isn't pumping iron, he's hanging around the counter asking for 'free licks.' According to Waldo, life's one big disappointment. He's always yammering about how he got ripped off or let down by somebody or other. After boring me for an hour with the details of his disillusionment, he'll say, 'But hey, what're you going to do? That's life.' Which is a valid question, what *are* you going to do? Sit around eating crackers? Which is what I'm doing. Stuffing entire crackers in my mouth and sucking the salt off them.

Alberto with no more ice cream is probably in bed in a group home. Who takes off his leg brace and tucks him in? Does anybody read him a story? A social worker was stabbed by a kid in a group home. Everybody thought they had a good relationship because they walked in parks and the kid confided in her. The social worker thought the kid was making progress. You have to wonder about that, what we *think* we see versus what's really going on. Which is another reason it's hard to believe in anything. The way I see it, man came up with the God concept because he was sick of being disappointed in man. God doesn't disappoint because he lives in your head, so you can make him into anything. Believing in God has to be better than sitting around eating crackers, thinking about dead conquerors and monarchs.

Rossi fakes orgasms because she wants the boy to feel good.

'That's like lying to yourself,' I said.

'It doesn't bother me.'

'How's he supposed to learn to give girls real orgasms if everybody's faking it to make him feel good?'

'That's not my problem.'

'It's everybody's problem. Fake orgasms, fake smiles. How are they supposed to know the difference?'

She flicked her hair the way she does when she thinks I'm being juvenile.

'It's no wonder,' I said, 'when girls say "no" guys keep shoving fingers into them.'

'Gross, please, spare me the details.'

'They figure "no" is just token resistance.'

'One day, Lemon, you'll grow up and we'll talk.'

I witnessed non-consensual sex while I was sitting in a tree last week. This boy pushed a girl on the grass and his hands were under her shirt and down her pants and she was saying 'no' and he kept at it. I wanted to shout at her to grab the dweezle by the balls and give them a good twist. She just lay there, probably because she didn't want him calling her frigid or a dyke. What's sad is these girls grow into women who fake it. And the dweezles grow into men who think that women who don't let them do whatever they want and look ecstatic about it are bitches. People call me a bitch because I ditched Doyle. The one time I let him put his fingers up my snatch, all I could think about was when did he last wash his hands? When it started to hurt I told him I had to piss, which put a hold on the groping. Next I made like I had major menstrual cramps and had to locate some Advil.

I've been thinking maybe I should write that play, not to please the crawlers who'll probably give me shitty marks anyway, but to shed light on this crucial topic: the perils of faking it. I mean, if you fake it long enough you must lose sight of the real thing. Faking gets you places but then you have to lie there with your legs over your head *ooh*ing and *aah*ing for like, forever. Maybe you stop *expecting* to feel anything. Maybe it becomes normal to spend all your time making somebody else feel good.

8

Old Huff has us reading *A Midsummer Night's Dream* again. I'm doing Helena who's got to be one of Shakespeare's all-time most boring characters. Personally, I think the bard must have had a problem with women because they're all either chasing after some guy, doing flirty-flirty with some guy or trying to get some guy offed. Then there's the saintly, virginal types who don't have a live nerve in their bodies.

'Who can tell me something about Helena and Hermione's relationship?' Huff queries. Everybody tries to look busy because nobody wants to tell him anything.

'They hate each other,' Kirsten says. 'That's obvious.'

'Why is it that obvious?' I ask.

'Yes,' Huff says, 'why is that obvious?'

Kirsten twirls her hair, thinking hard. 'They want the same guy.'

'Is that a reason to hate somebody?' I ask.

'They're rivals, duh,' Kirsten says.

'Do we always hate our rivals?' Huff inquires. 'Don't we respect them?'

'Not if they're after your guy,' Nicole explains.

'What if the guy *lets* the girl go after him?' I ask. 'Shouldn't he take some responsibility?'

'He's a *guy*,' Kirsten says as though this explains everything.

This concept that boys are ruled by their gonads really irritates me. 'How does his being a guy free him of responsibility?' I ask.

'That's obvious.'

'How is that obvious?'

'He's a guy,' she says like I'm stupid.

'Hermione doesn't hate Helena at the beginning,' I say. 'Helena hates Helena.'

'Why does Helena hate Helena?' Huff asks. As usual he's leaning on the back of his chair, looking as though he's about to make some profound statement. He never does.

'Why does anybody hate themselves?' I ask.

'Interesting question,' Huff says. 'Why does anybody hate themselves?'

Megan, this fat girl, says, 'Because their parents don't love them.'

Everybody tries to absorb this. Huff narrows his eyes to suggest that he's in deep contemplation. Being parentless, I can't comment.

'Do we know that Helena's parents didn't love her?' Huff inquires.

'She's *totally* ugly,' Kirsten explains. 'She hates herself because she's ugly. That's obvious.'

'Who says she's totally ugly?' I ask.

'*She* does,' Nicole says.

'No, she doesn't, she just says she isn't short and cute like Hermione.'

'Beauty is in the eye of the beholder,' Megan says, which is truly outrageous as she never says anything. Personally, I think if *you* don't think you're beautiful, nobody else will. I know this from experience as I happen to think I'm hideous even though this Greek plumber who shows up for Cookies 'n' Cream tells me I'm 'gorgee-ous.' He says it repeatedly, licking and dripping, 'You are a gorgee-ous girl. Howcome you not married, what's a-matta with boyz deese days? They got no cocks?' When I tell him I'm only sixteen, he does this Mediterranean shrug like there's no better time to get hitched. The point is, him telling me I'm gorgee-ous doesn't make me feel any less hideous.

'You're suggesting that she suffers from low self-esteem,' Huff says.

Low self-esteem is a term used to excuse rudeness, laziness, meanness. Any time there's a problem at school the likes of Blecher blame it on low self-esteem. I bet Blecher figures old Hitler suffered from poor self-esteem. The rude, lazy and mean types don't get any less rude, lazy and mean after Blecher's pep talks. The old sense of entitlement kicks in. They want it all, and everybody knows the fastest road to power and riches is guns. Guns are a big self-esteem booster.

'She's got a crush on a guy and he hates her,' Kirsten says. 'That would depress anybody.'

'Why?' I ask. 'I mean, why would you want somebody who hates you? It seems to me, if you had half a brain, you'd go read a book or something.' That's another thing I can't stand about Shakespeare. He's always making people chase after people who hate them.

'It's not about brains,' Nicole says.

'That's obvious,' Kirsten says.

What they mean is it's about sex, something I – a frigid dyke – wouldn't know about. Huff's getting a little red around the ears with all this hormonal activity. The bell goes. I beat it.

Rossi won't come out of the bathroom because she's discovered that Kirsten and company have been texting about her, describing demeaning sexual acts she allegedly performs to try to be popular. They say she'll let a guy shove anything up her snatch, including small animals and snakes. I tried to make like this is so ludicrous it's funny. I did a fake laugh – me who despises fakery – hoping to keep Rossi from taking the slander too seriously. Ha ha ha. That's when she went into the bathroom. I can't see her taking pills or anything so I'm not too fussed. Her mother yells at us from the bedroom again. It's not actually yelling. She's not mad at us, she's just worried because there's nothing in the fridge for us to eat. *She* can't eat because she's got a serious stomach problem and doctors had to cut out most of her stomach. All she can eat is special gruel in cans, which means she forgets to buy real food on the way home from her bank job. After standing all day, she lies on the floor in her bedroom and rests her legs on the bed so the fluid drains from her swollen feet back into her body.

'It's okay, Mrs. Barnfield,' I shout back. 'We're eating Triscuits.'

'Isn't there some cream cheese in the fridge?' Mrs. Barnfield yells. 'I thought for sure we had some cream cheese.'

'It's okay, Mrs. Barnfield. Get some rest.' I don't tell her about Rossi locking herself in the bathroom because she's got enough problems. There's been another bank merger and people like Mrs. Barnfield are getting downsized. Already the bank has cut back on her benefits, which is a major problem because she has to take all kinds of expensive drugs for her stomach problems. Her husband's no help since he's dead. He was a video poker addict who took off for South Carolina where they used to have video gambling machines in every convenience store and gas station. When he couldn't get any more cash from his credit cards, he locked himself in his car and set it on fire. So Mrs. Barnfield and Rossi haven't had it easy.

I'm thinking of making Rossi the star of my groundbreaking play. I started writing it last night when I couldn't sleep courtesy of the personal-trainer drummer. My main character's name is Lillian and she's been laid off from a bank and dreams of starting a hat-making business, only she keeps getting sidetracked by a soap opera called *Truly Loved* starring liposuctioned model types who jump in and out of the sack.

'I never for one second forget that I'm dying,' Tora says. I'd forgotten she was there. That's how she survives in school. Nobody notices her.

Lillian, my main character, hadn't known that soap operas are about beautiful people humping. So there she is surrounded by hat felt and feathers, getting distracted by naked men and women going at it between the DustBuster commercials.

'I wake up,' Tora says, 'and I know it's only going to get worse.'

'What?'

'Everything.'

'Maybe you're depressed,' I say. 'Maybe you should go on one of those drug trials they're always advertising. The ones beside the ads for premature-ejaculation recruits. They pay you for that stuff, all you do is take the drugs.' I've considered applying only I don't think I'm actually depressed. Sometimes I want to kill people but I don't think that qualifies as clinical depression. Athough it really got me down when I read about the British giving the Indians bits of blankets infected with smallpox. There was old King George stuffing himself with pheasant while the Indians were opening gift boxes stuffed with contaminated blanket.

'You should come out, Ross,' I say through the door. 'You don't want to worry your mum.' She doesn't answer. I've looked in their medicine cabinet. There's only Tylenol in there, and nasal spray. Mrs. Barnfield keeps her heavy-duty medications in the kitchen. Melody Pasternak tried to kill herself with Tylenol and ended up barfing black stuff for days. Rossi knows this so I can't see her trying it. Melody even wrote a suicide note about how she couldn't stand the loneliness and how Byron Whitehead had broken her heart. Byron Whitehead is supposed to be an intellectual, he edits the school paper and writes really fascinating articles about scientific studies nobody gives a goose's turd about.

'Ross,' I say. 'There was this woman who lived in the eighteenth century. Her name was Mary Wollstonecraft and she was fed up with women having to follow men around all the time. And she was fed up with old Rousseau who wrote about how women should be breeding and breastfeeding. Basically she was fed up with dickheads telling women how to be women. This was way before the suffragettes or anything, I mean women weren't supposed to even have brains before the nineteenth century. Anyway, Mary wrote a book about women's rights, insisting that they should be equal to men's, and that it was high time girls stopped being raised to think that the most important thing in life was to please men. That's how people thought in those days, that a woman's duty was to please some dolt. Pretty soon everybody was saying nasty things about Mary because she was challenging the status quo, so there she was, all alone in some attic, writing down what was important to her.'

I don't hear anything in the bathroom. I try to remember if there are razors in there. 'Ross ... ?'

'What's your point?' she says.

'Just that you don't have to care what people say. People always talk. Words are wind, Ross, one big fart.'

'I'm not like you. You don't care about anything.'

I don't argue. Like I said, the only time I've been heartbroken was when my hamster died.

'What happened to her?' Rossi asks.

'Who?'

'Mary what's-her-face.'

'Oh, well, she met some painter she had the hots for but he was already married. She asked his wife if she could move in with them but the missus wasn't too wild about that idea so Mary took off to France thinking there'd be some radicals there. She wanted to educate French women about how they didn't have to be doormats. The hitch was, the French Revolution was getting going and they didn't like freethinking women there either. Pretty soon those French Revolutionaries were talking about sending her to the guillotine. Fortunately she met some American adventurer she went nuts over and he told her to go to Scandinavia to educate women because the Swedes wouldn't cut her head off. So off she goes on her good mission, spreading the equality word. When she gets back to London she finds out that the adventurer's been banging boots with some tart. Mary got so depressed she walked around in the rain, figuring if her clothes were soaked she'd sink in the Thames. She didn't, though, a boatman pulled her out.'

This doesn't seem too smart, actually. If you want to sink, use rocks. Maybe Mary Wollstonecraft didn't want to drown. Maybe her dunk in the Thames was a cry for help.

'Then what happened?' Rossi asks.

'She left him and met some other guy she respected and trusted and who respected and trusted her. They got married, even though neither of them believed in marriage, and they had a baby.'

'And they lived happily ever after,' Tora contributes.

'No, actually. The placenta got stuck in her uterus and some doctor shoved his arm up her and tried to yank it out but it broke into pieces and got infected. She died two weeks later.'

'That is a horrible story,' Rossi says, flinging open the door. 'Why would you tell me such a *sick* story?' She looks really annoyed, which is a healthy sign.

'It's a true story.'

'So let me get this straight,' old Tora says. 'She was this feminist type but she got married.'

'Being a feminist doesn't mean you don't marry.'

Rossi grabs the Triscuits from me and starts chewing. 'They've started a virtual sex network.'

'Who?'

'Kirsten and Nicole. They told me I could join, then they go spreading this smut about me.'

'You want to masturbate in front of your cell so some football player can masturbate in front of his cell?'

'Don't use that word.'

'Think it through, Ross. What do you think Kirsten and Nicole are going to do with recordings of you fingering yourself?'

'I don't know how you can not care that nobody likes you.'

I don't actually think it's that nobody likes me. I'm just this bump on the road they step around.

'You're a fucking freak, Lemon! Nobody can stand you.'

This hurts. Not the *fucking freak* part but the fact that she's using it against me. I know she's been humiliated and all that but I still don't think I deserve to be her hostility sponge. I grab my backpack and slam the door behind me hoping she'll come running out to apologize.

Maybe I won't make her the star of my play.

I convince Kadylak to go to the playroom to build a Lego house. She's not talking much and her mouth sores are worse. A boy I don't recognize keeps slamming things around. His mother's there but it's pretty obvious she's one of those types who let their kids rule once they get cancer. When I ask him to keep it down, he looks at me like I'm some kind of serf. That's the way it's going to go, I figure. Back to serfdom. Once people get wiped out by debt and have to surrender their techno-gizmos. The upside is that it might mean revolution. Although it's hard to think of a revolution that ended up helping anybody in the long term, what with absolute power corrupting absolutely and all that. You just have to think of old Stalin, Mr. Genocide. They always say he was a ladies' man which is hard to compute. Imagine banging old Joe while famine victims are eating babies.

'We forgot to put in a door,' Kadylak says.

'Do we need one? If we just use windows we wouldn't have to answer the door.'

She stops building and looks at me. 'Why don't you want to answer the door?'

'It's usually somebody selling something.'

'Like what?'

'Religion, natural gas.'

She thinks about this, scratching under her head scarf. Her mother makes her wear Ukrainian headscarves, sending the message that she can't stand to look at her bald. Kadylak hates the scarves because they itch and are always sliding off her head.

'I think we should have a door,' she says. 'Someone nice might visit.'

And who might that be? I can't remember the last time some-one *nice* visited. Drew had this boyfriend for about ten minutes who had a motorboat. He got her water-skiing, which she seemed to think held meaning. She'd come home pink from sun and beer. He used to refer to her as his 'smart lady.' When he dumped her, she said she knew all along he was an idiot.

'If someone nice wanted to visit,' I say, 'we could throw down a rope from one of the windows and they could climb it. It would be a kind of test. Only the people who were really deter-mined to see us could come up.'

Kadylak fondles Lego pieces, trying to work this out. She doesn't like disagreeing with anybody. She's one of those people who'll say it doesn't hurt while you're stepping on her fingers. Meanwhile Wacko Boy flings Nerf balls around. His mother sits on a kiddie chair with her arms tightly crossed, holding herself together, while her eyes recede into her head. This happens to parents whose kids have cancer. They stop seeing anything except the cancer. They don't even see the kid.

'I think we should have a door,' Kadylak declares and starts to pull down a wall. I want to hug and kiss her, because she's so brave, so willing to believe that someone nice might visit. I don't hug and kiss her because I'm afraid it might freak her out. Her family isn't very demonstrative. I help her take down the wall. Her father shows up just as she's fitting in the door. She doesn't see him because she's busy constructing. He stands watching her, his white T-shirt and pants smeared with paint. He's pretty stoic so I can only imagine what's going on in there. When she sees him, she lights up like a firefly and flits toward him. He lifts her up and holds her to him, hard. They don't move. I can see her knuckles whitening where she's clinging to him. Both of them have their eyes closed tight, shutting out the pain.

9

Another sparrow has been mauled by the cats. Drew was holding it in her hands to keep it warm because she'd read somewhere that you have to keep them warm after they've been traumatized. This meant Drew couldn't do anything but sit around holding the oiseau for a few hours. She told me to mash banana for it, and offer it sunflower seeds. It wouldn't eat anything. I put water in a bottle cap but it wouldn't drink. It just stared at us with tiny tortured eyes. At one point it chirped and even hopped around the kitchen for two seconds but it was obvious it couldn't fly. I read somewhere that you're not supposed to handle birds because their bones are so fragile they break. I didn't mention this because Drew had already handled it and I didn't want her thinking she'd hastened its demise. I started thinking about what I wanted to do to the cats, burn them or club them to death or shove them in a box and drop them in the lake. Drew kept holding her finger against her lips to remind me that we had to be quiet around the bird. That's when I left. I couldn't stand watching it die.

For this reason I am up a tree minding my own beeswax. To my dismay, Larry Bone and a few other cretins have shown up for a fist fight. Ever since they saw some movie with Brad or somebody forming a club where guys go at it bare-knuckled, Bone and company have been doing it. The more blood the better. They video the squirmishes and post them on YouTube with Bonehead giving a play-by-play like some sportscaster. The school knows about it but there's nothing they can do because it's off the school premises. Normally I wouldn't sweat witnessing the dullards playing gladiators. But it's a little different now that I've kicked Bone in the face. If he sees the 'fucking freak' he might just haul me down by my boots and swing at me. So I do my stick-insect impression while some kind of cyclone is whipping around inside me. Slade the blow-job freak seems to be top dog at the moment, dancing around, flashing his paws. I don't know how long these dolts can keep at it. A couple of them already have bleeding faces. The majority clutch their hands after a few jabs, no doubt trying to compute why it hurts when it looks like such a blast in the movie. My mind's not actually scared of these halfwits but my body's telling a different story. Some kind of animal thing. It wants to take off but my mind advises it that they'll swarm me on sight. And of course I need to whiz.

A wannabe steps into the action. I've seen him before, genuflecting in front of King Jake – the rap-addicted future insurance salesman – who is not actually fighting himself but allowing his majestic presence to heighten the stakes. 'You can do it, man,' he tells the wannabe, I think his name is Walter, who looks ready to crap his pants. He hops around Slade who lets him flail for a few minutes before he starts slugging him. The actual sound of flesh hitting flesh is different from the movies, messier with more tone modulation depending on which part of the anatomy's getting pounded. Obviously the head sounds sharper, bone to bone, but the torso, particularly the gut, sounds dull. In movies they slam baseball bats into sides of beef for the fight effects. Most of these boys are more flab than meat.

Walter buckles and Slade slams the side of his head. Walter keels over and lies there.

'Get up, man,' King Jake commands but the boy doesn't move.

'Fuck,' the ever-articulate Slade comments. 'Get the fuck up.' He nudges Walter with his Nike. The other geniuses crowd around and I consider making a break for it but the cyclone in my body has cooked me to the point that I feel ready to pass out, to drop from the tree like some kind of overheated iguana.

'Fuck this shit,' Slade announces. He and his close companion, who always wears a dog collar, leave the scene of the crime in disgust. The other cretins, led by King Jake, also disperse, muttering *fucking this* and *fucking that.* Only Walter the wannabe remains, inert on the grass. I have pissed my pants, can feel the wet spreading. I try to picture myself rushing to Walter's rescue. Maybe he has a cell and I can call 911. The cops will appear and applaud my good deed, despite the piss stains and odour. The boy will live because of my self-possession in an emergency situation. Even Blecher will be impressed and will get off my case regarding my lack of enthusiasm. 'You saved a life, Limone, that's more than most people do in a lifetime.'

Walter still hasn't moved. It could just be a concussion. One of the supremo girl jocks gets concussions on a regular basis. When the teachers ask her questions she says, 'I don't know, miss, I've got a concussion.' The hitch is, if I help the boy out, word will spread that I witnessed the event and Bonehead and company will have another reason to tan my hide. Best to remain invisible until some good Samaritan notices the fallen boy. But they don't. They scoop their dogs' shit but they don't see Walter. Or if they do they assume he's drugged out, passed out, homeless. Just another body to ignore in the jewelled city.

The tree branch has numbed my ass. I no longer feel hot, only cold, stone cold. I shake a chilled leg and command it to reach down for a limb. Slowly, iguana-style, I crawl down the tree. With both feet on the ground I look at the fallen boy. Then I walk away.

Avoiding base camp due to my deranged, plant-killing stepmother, and hoping dried piss doesn't stink, I wait while a Tim Horton serf stiffs me on butter again. 'You forgot the *butter,*' I say. Usually I'm nice about it, say *please* and all that, but I'm tired of this game. 'Butter!' I almost shout, pointing at my mini-baguette. The skinny-assed one slaps a packet on the counter without looking at me. What happened to 'Have a nice day'?

I try not to think about Walter growing cold on the grass among the goose turds. I try to think about the play. Old Lund, my drama teacher, stopped me after class to ask about it. I told him I'd started writing it.

'What's it about?' He always stands with his gut sticking out and his fingers and thumbs touching each other. He's got one of those skinny beards that follow his jawline. He's an amateur actor and shows up in Shakespeare plays in church basements.

I didn't want to tell him that my play is about people faking it so I said it was about this downsized teller who makes hats and watches soap operas. He looked disappointed. I think he was hoping for a musical.

'You need conflict,' he said. 'Conflict is the essence of drama.'

'Oh, she's conflicted,' I told him.

'Are there other characters?'

'There's her boyfriend who's already married and wants nooky all the time. And her girlfriend who's always buying stuff.'

I could see old Lund was getting worried. He started feeling his beard.

'She can't figure out why people don't act like the hard-bodied crowd on TV,' I said. I was thinking about the part I wrote where the podgy, married boyfriend starts feeling Lillian up. She says she doesn't want nooky because she's having her period and he says, 'Not again,' and starts laughing like this is hilarious.

'It'll probably have a wedding at the end,' I said, 'or a blood-bath.' I didn't tell him Lillian starts faking it so hard she doesn't know she's faking it because I knew this would be too complex for the old duffer. He looked at his watch. It was after three-thirty and he wasn't getting overtime.

'Keep me posted,' he said, grabbing his fanny pack and hustling me out of there.

I keep telling myself Walter can't be dead. I'm starting to feel like Tess of the d'Urbervilles, waiting for the coppers to come for me. 'I'm ready,' she said when they showed up. What a sick puppy Thomas Hardy must have been, all those victimized, idealized women sitting around waiting for some guy to show up. Old Tess condemning herself for being aroused before the libertine raped her.

Beside me two wizards are saying rotten things about their ex-wives.

'Women want to change you,' the one with hippo nostrils says.

'You got that right,' the one with Donald Trump hair agrees.

'They won't take the whole package,' the hippo-nostriled one says.

'No kiddin'.'

The first wizard starts talking about how corrupt our government is and how he's going to get rich because he's got a theory like Einstein's except that nobody's listening to him because they're all corrupt just like the government.

The bird's still alive. Drew's made a nest with a dishtowel in a bowl. The bird's lying in it, breathing fast.

'I wish it would close its eyes,' she says.

'It's too scared.'

'Please don't leave without telling me where you're going.'

'I didn't think you'd notice, what with the bird and everything.'

'It's dying.' Her skin's pasty from being inside all the time and her lips are shrinking. It's the first time we've talked half-normally for weeks and I wouldn't mind asking her what she really thinks of me, if she even wants me in her house. It's not like she's legally bound to look after me. But she's stroking the bird's head again. The fact is if I mention Damian and the divorce and his lousy settlement, it'll blow our cover. We've been pretending it's normal for the betrayed wife to shelter the swain's adoptee.

I hide in my room, turn on the radio and listen to the all-news station. No mention of a murder in a park. I start working on the play. I get Lillian to watch one of those motivational speakers who proclaim that you can do anything if you think positively. I make her chant things like 'Change Means a New Beginning,'

'God Never Closes One Door But He Opens Another,' 'Every Cloud Has a Silver Lining.' The kind of bunk that Zippy used to prattle before she figured out that nobody gave a fuck. In my experience it's the positive people who rip your guts out, smiling of course. I figure they get burned out being positive and have to lash out. I had this functions teacher, Mrs. Rathburn, who was ultra-positive and never let on that most of us were morons. She even made me think *I* wasn't a moron, told me about my potential and that all I needed was 'to develop good study habits.' Then she went and told Drew that I was a hopeless case, that she'd never taught anyone so 'learning-resistant.' Drew passed this on because she wanted me to start 'playing' to my 'strengths' instead of my 'weaknesses.' Anyway, next day old Rathburn was all smiles as usual and I almost got sucked in again. Those positive people can dupe you. You sit there knowing they despise you but they're smiling and telling you how special you are, and so you want to believe them. Especially since nobody else is telling you you're special. What should have tipped me off about old Rathburn is that she's nice to everybody, *everybody* is special. So that hurt for a few days, thinking I'd had a relationship with this teacher who'd understood me and would help me blossom into a brain surgeon. But I got over it. You don't have to be a math genius to make soap.

So that's how Lillian's feeling about the bank layoff. She thought she knew her boss and that he valued her for her hard work. She figured her job was secure because she wasn't one of those types who grumbled when the bank started charging monthly premiums for health benefits. Even when a petition goes around, Lillian refuses to sign it. If you look at history, the people who accept shittier conditions, less pay and all that, always get shafted in the end anyway. The company store always wins.

I make Lillian's shopaholic friend, Courtney, show off the cute outfits she buys. She talks about her gingivitis and how much the periodontist is costing her. She says a guy from high school visited her mother to get Courtney's number. Courtney's mother says the guy's done really well selling Astroturf but

that he looks a little different than he did in high school. Courtney says, 'How's he look different, I mean other than what you'd
expect?'

'He's losing a bit of hair,' her mother says.

'That's okay,' Courtney says, 'nobody's perfect.'

'You might not recognize him,' her mother says.

'How bald is he, Ma?'

Meanwhile old Lillian can't believe she has to sit around
listening to this twaddle that isn't anything like what the half-
naked toy boys and girls are saying on *Truly Loved*.

Speaking of toy boys, I figure my biological father had to be
a stud with gonads for brains. I don't have a problem with this
like I have a problem with my mother dropping me in the
Walmart toilet. Maybe because he's never come looking for me
like she has. He's probably got a plumbing business and a wife
who's constantly whining that he doesn't spend enough time
with the kids. The last thing he wants is another junior. Plus he
may not even know I exist. I have to admit, I wouldn't mind if
he was a super-nice guy who, when he finds out about me, sends
me a few Ks or something. Enough to set me up in the soap business. I'd like him to look like the dads in the Father's Day ads:
salt-and-pepper hair, a big warm smile. Or like Ryan O'Neal in
Paper Moon. Zippy bought me that movie and told me my daddy
was probably just like Ryan, that he probably didn't even know
I existed. She said if my real daddy saw me he'd fall in love with
me just the way Ryan fell for Tatum. I got pretty obsessed with
this movie until Tatum wrote a tell-all book about how Ryan
slugged her after she won the Oscar, and how he let his drug
dealer molest her, and how Melanie Griffith, one of his wives,
dragged her into an orgy when she was twelve. Pretty soon
old Tatum was addicted to cocaine and heroin and trying to
kill herself.

Drew's calling me, which is unusual these days. I consider
pretending to be asleep but figure if it's the cops wanting to grill

me about the murder, they'll find me anyway. At least in custody I won't have to worry about Bonehead seeking revenge. 'What?' I shout back.

'Can you come down here?'

Maybe I should pack a few things, a toothbrush, something to read, A Tale of Two Cities, which has to be one of Dickens' biggest snore fests even though it's got that famous line in it. There's already been a wedding so I figure a funeral's next. I really admire Dickens because he woke people up to child labour and all that, but I think he must have gotten burned out getting paid by the word, writing all those weddings and funerals.

'Lemon?' she calls again. 'Come and meet Vaughn.'

Egads, I totally forgot about the tree saver. He's probably all hair and body odour. Best to delay contact for as long as possible. What makes him think there's any point in saving trees? Nature reserves are only protected as long as Big Business isn't interested in drilling or clear-cutting or developing. So Thor can save a tree while he's squatting on it but he'd have to be pretty deluded to think the tree's days aren't numbered.

'Lemon?'

I haul my ass to the kitchen.

'This is Vaughn,' Drew says.

As expected, he's got messy hair and clothes and a backpack that's been around the world a few times. I make a peace sign.

'Same to you,' he says.

Drew's clutching a bag of birdseed she must have dug out of the broom closet. I can see she wants to get back to the bird. 'This is Lemon. Could you make him comfortable? I think there's clean linen in the closet.' There isn't because she doesn't do laundry anymore.

'Follow me,' I tell him, heading back upstairs, hoping he isn't noticing my fat ass. I scrounge around for sheets and towels. Vaughn doesn't say anything, which I find unnerving. Most people gab. He helps me make the bed. He doesn't smell, which suggests he knows about showers. I try to fold the sheet neatly back over the blanket the way Drew does but it looks crooked.

'Don't worry about it,' Vaughn says. He has green eyes; I've never seen truly green eyes before. His skin's weathered from exposure, making the whites of his eyes look really white and the green of his irises even greener. I see trees in them, ponds and frogs, moss.

'Do you want a cup of tea or anything?' I ask.

'I'm alright, thanks.'

'The bathroom's the first door on your right.' I stand around feeling retarded, which is unusual for me. There's something about him I can't figure out.

'Thanks for all your help.' He offers his hand for me to shake. It feels rough, ripped up by tree bark. It makes sense that he has nothing to say to me. He probably figures I'm a mall-hopping teenager, contributing to all that tree-killing.

'Good night,' he says.

'Hasta mañana.'

10

The bird's dead, of course, with its eyes still open. Vaughn tells me as soon as I come downstairs but I want to be sure so I watch it for a long time. I decide we should bury it before Drew wakes up. As usual our alcoholic neighbour to the north is sitting on his lawn chair in his Jockeys nursing a Heineken.

'You don't want to go putting that in the ground,' he advises. 'Could be diseases on it.'

'We're not going to leave it here,' I lie. 'This is just temporary, we've already notified the authorities.'

He nods approval in that Cardinal Richelieu way of his. He had a wife once. Every few hours he shouts that he wants to fucking kill her. She seemed nice enough, mowed the lawn and didn't overload the garbage bin. His Eminence stuffs it with little plastic bags, forcing the lid to remain open, allowing the critters to spread debris all over our lawn. It used to drive Drew nuts. Now, like with most things, she doesn't seem to notice.

Vaughn's a good digger, must have strong arms due to tree climbing.

'Go deeper,' I tell him, wanting to avoid future exhuming by the cats.

Vaughn made porridge for breakfast and offered me some. I enjoyed it, can't remember the last time I had it. He even washed the dishes, spoke maybe two words. There's no question he's been spending way too much time with squirrels. Rossi phoned to say she was sorry about calling me a fucking freak and all that but I wasn't too interested. *Sorry* is one of those meaningless words people toss around before they kick you in the head again.

Saturdays I work an eight-hour shift at the mall, actually nine hours if you include the lunch break for which I do not get paid.

I've never figured that one out, it's not like you get to *enjoy* lunch hour, there's no time to go anywhere unless you have wheels. You're stuck on a plastic chair in the food court watching people gorge. And of course, slobs stare at you. A lubber with his gut hanging out and his legs spread is currently ogling me. I pretend to be engrossed in *The Mayor of Casterbridge*. It's not like I'm this huge Hardy fan but Drew has the whole set, read it in college. When I asked her if she knew what a dirtbag old Thomas was to his wives, she said that geniuses' personal lives shouldn't colour how we perceive their work. She has a point, since most geniuses are dirtbags to their wives.

She has a few thousand books she read in college including a shelf dedicated to Extraordinary Women. That's how I know about Mary Wollstonecraft. Last night I was reading about this Gaskell woman who wrote a book before old Dickens got rich talking about workhouses – while he was being a dirtbag to his wife. Gaskell's novel described life in industrial Manchester. She actually hung out with all these starving, sooty-lunged workers and wrote down how they talked. Meanwhile old Victoria was getting it on with Albert and having forty kids so she wasn't too worried about her starved and overworked subjects. It turns out that in Manchester there were these girls who worked in match factories to try to keep themselves fed. The hitch was some chemical in the matchstick solution gave them 'phossy jaw,' which translates into hideous, permanent facial deformity. Another Extraordinary Woman, her name was Annie Besant, found out about this and made it her business to let the public know that the matchstick girls were being poisoned. She handed out pamphlets at the factory door and convinced the girls to protest by not going to work. The factory owners eventually caved and stopped using the chemical that caused phossy jaw. Personally I think it's a little outrageous that old Dickens gets all the credit for exposing the workhouses when Gaskell was ahead of him. What nobody remembers is that these Extraordinary Women were speaking out before they had *any* rights. In those days, if a woman got married, she had to hand everything over to the husband. And it was legal for hubby to beat her. If she took off, she lost all rights to her children and former property. Her signature on legal documents meant squat. If she refused to spread her legs for hubby, he could take her out for a buggy ride and drop her off at the asylum. Before old Jean-Jacques Rousseau made breastfeeding fashionable, well-to-do women weren't even allowed to nurse their babies. The infants were handed over to wet nurses or fed water with bread in it. That's why so many of them died.

The ogling lubber is joined by another podger. They swill Diet Coke and start gabbing about computer games. They're all excited about some game that lets you kill people within an eight-metre radius. 'And,' the first podger enthuses, 'you can do a two-handed kill!'

Meanwhile, in *The Mayor of Casterbridge*, old Thomas has Elizabeth-Jane pining for some Scottish guy. The Scot gets all hot for another woman and marries her. Poor old Elizabeth-Jane keeps pining for him while her father – who isn't her father but she doesn't know this – keeps trying to think of ways to get rid of her. Maybe she'll end up dead like old Tess. Or married to some sheep farmer.

Doyle can't stop holding forth about some car he wants to buy. He asks if I think Rossi would go to Nicole's party with him. I know she'd jump at the chance but wish to shield her from this humiliation. I look busy serving a bunch of Jehovah's Witnesses. They all say they want regular-sized cones then get hissy when I don't mash another scoop on them. 'You ordered regular,' I remind them. They pay me individually with lots of dimes and nickels and pennies. It gets sticky going into the till, which will drive old Buzny wild.

I saw Walter the wannabe in the cafeteria eating poutine. He looked alright but nobody was talking to him. His lower jaw was so swollen he couldn't open his mouth properly. He had to eat the fries one at a time like a little old man missing teeth. He

71

caught me staring at him and flipped me the finger. It was good to see him, though, alive and all that.

Doyle's adjusting his underwear again. He thinks no one notices, that he can just grab his crotch and scoop ice cream in one fluid movement.

When I was seven, scooping ice cream was my dream job, my ticket to limitless cash and Chunky Monkey. You have to wonder how many other dreams will turn rancid once you're up close to them.

Some couple is taking two hours to pick flavours. He's your basic designer-T-shirt workoutaholic. She's wearing a mini-skirt and stilettos and can't keep her hands off him. The workout-aholic pays no attention to her, just keeps staring at the tubs of ice cream like he's about to make the decision of a lifetime. You just know that before he got her in the sack he had his hands all over *her*. Now that he's had her, he's more interested in Peanut Butter Chip. Meanwhile she's scared of losing him so she keeps sticking her hand down his pants. You see this all the time, dudes being hot for tomatoes until they've nailed them a few times. Then the ownership thing kicks in on the part of the female. With the chase over, she's got to keep her feelers on the meatloaf, even if she doesn't want his tongue down her throat. Which is totally different from most mammals. Most species let the stud get his rocks off then ditch him and go find a cave somewhere. This makes sense rather than trying to hold on to the peckerhead. Although I still like to believe that true love is possible, especially if one of the parties dies young. A dead lover can keep you truly loved your entire life. Look at old Victoria.

I'm going to call my play *Truly Loved*. Old Lillian's going to endeavour to live the passion enjoyed by the humping toy boys and girls on the tube. Faking laughs, orgasms and interest until, crushed by the dull realities of life outside the box, she will lash out. Maybe she'll blow up the bank or something. My email is cluttered with butt-scratchers who want to be in the play. Yesterday they wouldn't have noticed if I got hit by a bus.

My plan is to make them perform demeaning acts, not unlike those allegedly performed by Rossi. My plan is to audition and reject them.

Vaughn's never heard of Bob and Bing's road movies.

'*Road to Morocco*?' I inquire. 'You've never heard of *Road to Morocco*?' I start singing the *Road to Morocco* song, bopping around the way Bob and Bing do on the fake camel. Vaughn's drinking tea made from tree bark or something.

I fit *Road to Bali* into the player. I figure if Treeboy can't handle it, he can go meditate or something. I'm not used to having a stranger around the house, particularly a mute. I wish he'd go save the oak in the backyard.

He doesn't laugh once, not even when the octopus squirts black ink in Bob's face. When it's over, I look at Vaughn and realize he isn't even watching. He's staring off into some forest.

'À demain,' I say.

He looks as though he'd forgotten I was there. 'Good night.'

I'm woken by the two of them talking. Drew's a little testy due to Vaughn's silent owl treatment. I creep to the head of the stairs to hear better. It turns out a friend of his, another tree sitter, got killed by loggers. They chased him up a tree with chainsaws, lopping off the lower branches. When the chainsaw got too close, he leapt into another tree, so they sheared the bottom limbs off that one too. Trapped, the guy clung to the tree with no water or food for forty-eight hours. The whole time the loggers and forestry thugs were shouting insults at him, shining lights and blaring music. The tree sitter finally passed out and fell sixty feet, slamming into some limbs before crashing to the ground. Besides all the broken bones, his head was split open and his lungs punctured. All the forestry department said about it was that it was unfortunate and something they'd hoped wouldn't happen.

'I should have been there,' Vaughn says.

'What could you have done?' Drew asks.

'Created some diversion. He would have made it down.'

'You don't know that.'

'We're supposed to watch out for each other,' he says as though she's a right-winger who can't possibly understand.

A monstrously gloomy silence ensues until she says, 'You mustn't go back. It would be suicide.'

Vaughn doesn't respond and I know his tree-coloured eyes are focused above and beyond her.

'It was an 800-year-old Douglas fir,' he says. 'You can't replant a 1000-year-old forest. We're destroying something we don't understand.'

If you think about it, those trees have witnessed every ruthless, selfish, greedy, destructive human act since whitey started having his way around the place. Maybe that's why whitey's determined to cut them down. The trees know too much.

I offer to make them pancakes. They don't look too interested. I dollop and flip batter anyway. 'How about some sightseeing?' I say to Vaughn, determined to cheer him up now that I know about his personal tragedy. 'A stroll down Yonge? It's the longest street in the world, you know.'

He gives me the tree-frog stare.

'Or we could shoot up the CN Tower.' Right away I deduce that concrete towers aren't too inviting to tree sitters. 'What about the island? We could rent bikes and pedal around. There's lots of trees there.'

'Lemon,' Drew intervenes, 'I'm sure Vaughn has other things to do.'

'Not really,' he says.

'It's fun on the ferry,' I say. 'You can pretend you're on a voyage.'

He cuts into a pancake with his fork. He's forgotten to put syrup on it. I pass it to him. 'It's real syrup,' I say, 'from trees.' He forks a piece of pancake into his mouth. Guess it's against his principles to eat maple syrup. Maybe taking sap from trees is like sucking their blood. I'll have to avoid the *tree* word in future. Like I avoid the *cancer* word at the hospital.

He looks goofy on the bike. The rentals have thick tires, upright handlebars and cushy seats. They're the only style of bike that doesn't hurt my butt. But old Vaughn must be over six feet and his knees jut out as he pedals. He seems oblivious to how hilarious he looks. He may be the one person in existence who doesn't check out his ass in store windows. We sit in the grass and stare at the lake. I try to get a conversation going, ask him about the tree life, but it's pretty obvious he doesn't want to talk. The water looks like it does in postcards. 'It's a picture-perfect day,' I say, sounding demented. I'm only yammering because he isn't. It's like I have to prove I have a brain. Which is pretty sad considering I don't even know if old Vaughn can tell a brain from a kidney. Just because he's quiet doesn't mean he's deep. I shut up, lie back and watch a plane and wish I were on it, going anywhere except where there's war and pestilence, famine and ecological disasters.

Unable to sleep with visions of a murdered tree sitter in my head, I worked some more on *Truly Loved*, got old Lillian, fuelled by the motivational speakers, to rally the deadbeats at the bank to protest. Half of them are being transferred to a new location in Oakville. Most of them don't have cars, which means a two-hour commute to and from work on public transit. But management says that's where the jobs are if they want them. Plus they're extending branch hours, which means some shifts will start at seven in the morning. Nobody objects because they know there's a bunch of the downsized in Oakville who'd be grateful to get their jobs. Lillian starts jumping up and down beside a plastic plant, chanting about self-respect, solidarity, human rights and union busting. Nobody's too interested. The manager gets the security guard to take her out.

Vaughn looks unconscious and it occurs to me he might be dead from all that tree-related sorrow so I say, 'Yo, Vaughn.'

'What?'

'Just checking.'

'What?'

'If you're dead.' Immediately I regret saying this with his friend being dead and all that.

'I'll keep you posted,' he says.

It's pretty obvious he has no time for plebs who aren't sitting in trees and I can respect that. I'm thinking maybe Lillian, after the big disillusionment, could become a tree sitter. After she blows up the bank.

11

Old Blecher asks me if I think I'm doing what God put me here to do.

'He didn't put me here.'

Personally I think we'd be a whole lot better off if we dropped the God concept. Without the God concept, we'd be equals. Nobody could make deals. Old Swails was telling us about Martin Luther figuring out that the Catholic church was all about making money. Priests would show up in villages and say, 'Buy this bit of parchment with Latin scribbled on it and your grand-daddy will not burn in Eternal Damnation.' The people were dirt-poor so buying religious junk meant no bread for their children. Martin Luther said, 'Forget all the junk, I'll translate the Bible for you and you can practice your faith without worrying about what the old cardinal has to say about it.' Was the Vatican ever pissed. Old Swails was jumping around pretending to be the cardinal, shouting in an Italian accent. 'Thisa heretic MUSTA BE BURNED!'

'Let me put it differently,' Blecher says. 'Do you find purpose and meaning in your daily life?'

She's giddy because she just got certified as a Life and Career Coach by the Institute of Life Purpose. She thinks people are going to pay her to ask them profound questions like 'Do you have clear goals and direction?'

She pulls the lid off a yogourt and licks it. 'Do you feel that you're making a positive contribution to others?'

'Negative.'

'Do you feel good about yourself?'

'Negative.'

She digs around in the yogourt with a plastic spoon. 'You know what I think? I think you're holding yourself back from living your life's purpose.'

Last week in Sociology Mrs. Freeman was talking about the Underground Railroad. She asked if anybody knew what it was. Kirsten said it was a railway that went underground. Nicole said it was a series of secret pathways. Mrs. Freeman went gospel as she bellowed that it wasn't like that at all, that it was the slaves just following the gourd. Then she started singing 'Follow the Drinkin' Gourd.' One of Drew's Extraordinary Women books is about Harriet Tubman, the escaped slave who went back to the south hundreds of times to rescue more slaves even though she'd been beaten and raped by her masters since she was seven years old. She'd decided she'd rather die than live in slavery. She ran barefoot through woods and swamps with bloodhounds and shotguns chasing her. Big rewards were offered for her capture. She made it though, and soon after started risking her life on a regular basis heading back south to lead more slaves to freedom. Hearing about Harriet Tubman exhausted me. I had a stash of mini-marshmallows in my backpack. I kept eating them to keep my strength up.

Harriet Tubman was someone with a life purpose.

'What if you have no life purpose?' I ask.

Blecher spoons yogourt into her yob. She's acting a little aloof because I caught her reading a *Double Digest Archie* comic hidden inside a *National Geographic*.

'I mean,' I clarify, 'don't you think it's possible that some people don't have a life purpose?'

Harriet Tubman lived to be ninety-two. No way do I want to live to be ninety-two.

'Your life purpose reflects your deepest values,' Blecher says.

I can't even think of my shallowest values, never mind my deepest ones.

'Living your life purpose,' Blecher says, 'requires being clear and aligning yourself with your spiritual nature, moving past your inner blocks.'

I listen for the lunch bell. I only came here to get away from Bonehead and company who have taken to calling me a bull dyke and braying in my direction.

'Inner blocks can defeat us all,' Blecher says. She taps her temple and her gut in case I don't know the meaning of *inner blocks*. 'You are your own worst enemy,' she adds.

'Can you give me some examples of people with life purposes?' I ask, stalling for time. 'I mean, I can only think of dead ones.'

Blecher rips a granola bar wrapper with her teeth.

'Harriet Beecher Stowe would be a good candidate,' I say. 'But she's dead.'

'Harriet who?'

'She wrote *Uncle Tom's Cabin*.'

'Haven't read that one.' She starts chomping the granola bar.

'It was the first novel to really expose slavery in America,' I explain, knowing she's bored out of her mind. 'She wrote it long before old Mark Twain figured out to write *Huckleberry Finn*, which is everybody's all-time favourite novel. Personally I think the last third needs work. Everybody talks like old Mark was the first one to point the finger at slavery, but the truth is it was Harriet. You have to wonder how much longer it would have taken to get the Civil War going without Harriet blowing the whistle.'

Blecher crumples up the granola bar wrapper and pitches it at the trash can, missing it, of course. With her mouth full of oats she can't speak, which is a plus. She holds up a finger to indicate that she will offer words of wisdom after she gets the fibre down. Fortunately the bell goes.

Rossi corners me at my locker. 'I said I was sorry,' she says.

'Don't sweat it,' I say.

'Doyle invited me to Kirsten's party. Do you mind?'

'Not at all.'

'You guys aren't going steady or anything?'

'Negative.'

She stands gnawing on a Bic. Under all that sparkly eyeliner I see the kid I used to know and I feel so sad. Because she was my best friend and we had answers and now we don't know *anything*.

'Everybody thinks it's really cool that you're writing a play.'

'Who says I'm writing a play?'

'Did you really kick Larry Bone in the face?'

'I didn't kick anybody.'

'He says he's going to whip your ass.'

I walk away from her, to my biology class where I can get some sleep.

'Come over later?' she asks.

In chemistry Doyle blows up something that singes his eyebrows. Conkwright starts yelling at him. Conkwright's one of those Scottish types who came here at age two or something but still speak with a Scots accent. 'Just what do ya think yarr dooin'? D'ya want to buurrrn the eyeballs oot of yarr head?' He gets all red and starts blowing spit. Conkwright has this idea that he's sexy. He wears shirts unbuttoned to his chest and wraparound shades even when it's raining. The girls think he's hysterical and call him Cockwrong.

I finished *The Mayor of Casterbridge*. It ended with a wedding. Somebody had to kick off, of course. In this case it was Elizabeth-Jane's fake father, who'd figured out he loved her even though she wasn't his daughter. She continued to think he was her real father, but her real father showed up and the fake father told him that Elizabeth-Jane was dead. Then the Scottish guy bumped into her real father and sent for her. This caused the fake father to take off in shame with a couple of farm implements. Meanwhile the Scottish guy and Elizabeth-Jane started rutting because his wife died. The fake father returned for Elizabeth-Jane's wedding to the Scottish guy, but chickened out when he saw how happy she was with her real father, and left a bird in a cage for her. The bird died, of course, because no one fed it. A servant told Elizabeth-Jane that her fake father had left it for her, so she ran around looking for him. She found him dead in some old barn, but didn't sweat it because she was so happy with the wedding and her real father and all that. Happy happy happy. Meanwhile old Thomas was beating his wife.

Speaking of the Underground Railroad, Mrs. Freeman is descended from slaves. Her great-great-grandfather had to choose a last name when he showed up in New Brunswick so he called himself Free Man. She goes to church on Sundays and sings. She says all ancient cultures involved singing, which was why people didn't kill each other all the time. She tried to get us to sing 'Will the Circle Be Unbroken,' which has a nice melody. I enjoyed singing it, especially the part about there's a better home a-waiting in the sky, Lord, in the sky. Which is pretty outrageous considering I don't believe in heaven and all that. I was just about the only one singing. Me and an Italian guy called Rudi who's auditioned for *Canadian Idol* about five thousand times.

Anyway, Mrs. Freeman actually gives me decent marks so I don't mind helping her out once in a while by singing or answering questions. Today she's talking about the Holocaust, a subject on which I'm an expert. 'Did you know,' I ask, 'that the Nazis ordered all the Jewish boys in Berlin to change their name to Israel and all the Jewish girls to change their name to Sara?' Mrs. Freeman looks as though she doesn't know, which surprises me since she's the teacher. 'Also,' I elaborate, 'after they banned Jewish kids from school, they killed their pets. Nazis showed up and took the kids' pets from them and killed them.'

This gets a reaction from the simpletons, which is unusual. Normally it takes the sound of gunshot to get their attention. Even Kirsten stops painting her nails. 'No way,' she says.

'You mean like,' Nicole clarifies, 'Nazis just showed up and like, took their pets?'

'Before they took their parents,' I say. 'And before they took them. Just about every Jew in Berlin ended up in death camps. There were about fifty thousand of them.'

The bedlamites' eyes glaze over again at the mention of death camps. They're not too interested in dead Jews, just their pets.

'What have we learned from the Holocaust?' Mrs. Freeman sings out.

Nobody's got an answer for that one. Most of them go back to gaming on their cells. Somebody's blares Beyoncé.

'Turn that thing off!' Mrs. Freeman bellows.

'We learned that hatred is taught,' I say. 'Little Aryan boys and girls didn't hate Jews. They were taught to hate them in school. They had these picture books about poisonous mushrooms, how you could tell the poisonous ones from the edible ones. The poisonous ones were supposed to be Jews. They showed creepy illustrations of Jews with stringy hair and big noses.'

Mrs. Freeman has a worried look about her. I don't know if she's fretting about the Jews or me. I keep talking because I think it's important that people know this. 'Somebody *drew* those pictures for those schoolbooks,' I explain. 'Some rat-brained artist was *paid* to pollute those little kids' minds about Jews. I mean, how could you live with yourself after that? And why wasn't that artist put on trial? When you think "evil Nazi" you think of Goebbels or Mengele or Goering but what about the guy who drew the poisonous Jewish mushrooms?'

No response from the scratch and moaners. Bonehead belches. The bell goes. I jet out of there.

12

After Zippy stiffed me on a second hamster she bought me two guppies. I stared into the tank for hours trying to bond with the fish. I didn't know their genders but decided to call them Caesar and Cleopatra. I went to bed determined to be happy about the guppies. They weren't furry and you couldn't hold them but at least you didn't have to clean the cage. First thing in the morning I got up to feed the guppies and do more bonding. One of them had jumped out of the tank and was dead on the floor. I dropped to my knees and howled because already I'd been imagining the good times my guppies and I would have, how they would be *special* guppies, how I'd train them to chase a floatie or something. Zippy bustled out in her fluffy bathrobe. 'What in God's name ... ?'

'Cleopatra killed herself!' I wailed. 'She didn't want to be stuck in the tank with Caesar. She'd rather be *dead* than be with Caesar!'

Zippy sat on her pouffe feeling, I'm sure, that she'd failed me again. 'We'll get another one,' she said.

'I don't want another one! I don't want this one. This one's a *murderer*!' The killer fish was glob-globbing at me.

Zippy gave the guppy to a neighbour. Their cat ate it.

So I'm planning to put the guppy suicide in the play. Because Lillian's under the illusion that she's getting her life together by going into debt buying all this stuff to fix up her place. She wants it to look like a beach house she saw on the Decorating Channel. She's hanging up Mexican blankets. The guppy suicide would definitely add conflict. Lillian would feel responsible. Your guppies don't just suddenly jump out of the tank for no reason.

'Limone,' Mr. Biggs says, 'h'what can you tell us about the human genome?' He's one of those types who puts an *h* before *wh* so *what* sounds like *h'what*. He's not even Spanish.

'Well,' I begin, digging through the messy files in my brain, 'isn't a genome part gene and part chromosome?'

'Anything else?'

'What else is there?'

Mr. Biggs has a butt that sticks out and little ballet-dancer feet. 'I see you're making notes,' he says. 'Would they, by any chance, pertain to our class today?'

'They're for Mr. Lund, actually. Sorry.'

'H'why would you be making notes for Mr. Lund in my class?'

'Sorry.' Usually if you say *sorry* enough times and avoid eye contact they lose interest. But Biggs is a closet case and hates girls, particularly girls who don't act girly. He's always making comments about my boots and 'bag-lady attire.'

'Sorry isn't good enough,' he says. 'Do you have *any* intention of passing this course?'

'Not really.' I try to look meek. 'I don't think I'm cut out for biology.'

'Then h'why did you take the course? Can you tell me *h'why*?'

'I thought it might be interesting,' I say, 'dissecting and all that. I thought we'd be doing more dissecting. Aren't we supposed to be dissecting cats?'

His reptile lips pucker, he who probably dreams about shoving his noodle into choir boys. 'H'why don't you to go down to the office and tell Ms. Brimmers that you have no intention of passing this class?'

I remain inert, hoping he'll get distracted by a sudden storm or something.

'Leave now, please,' he says, pointing at the door. All the goons, who have no intention of passing the class either, cackle.

Ms. Brimmers wears carefully tailored suits in corporate beige or grey that show off her slim figure. The statement is *I dress like a professional but really I'm a sex goddess*. I want to ask her if she's banged boots with Inspector Power yet. She had him cornered after his speech, kept sliding her jacket back so he could admire her sex-goddess hips.

'We need to talk,' she says, resting her tailored glutes against her desk. I spread mine on a chair that feels about to swallow me. 'We all believe in you, Limone.' This is a lie. They pay attention because I'm the former principal's daughter – the principal who is supposedly on temporary leave.

'You have some issues with authority,' she tells me. 'Why is that?'

'I don't have issues with anyone.'

'You're a bright girl. Why are you jeopardizing your future?'

What future? Like yours? In little suits and pantyhose shuffling paper and beating up on teenagers? Kissing ass at the school board? What future, when a species is becoming extinct EVERY FIFTEEN MINUTES? I stare at the fuzzy-leafed plant on her desk. Maybe Lillian should get a fuzzy-leafed plant. They must talk about foliage on the Decorating Channel.

'You need to demonstrate a commitment to learning,' Brimmers says, and I wonder if she fakes orgasms, *ooh*ing and *aah*ing to make the schlemiel feel good.

'Are you even listening to me?' Brimmers asks.

'Of course.'

'You have a very poor and disrespectful attitude.'

'I'm really sorry.'

'Saying you're sorry isn't good enough. How do you explain this behaviour?'

'I think I'm a little depressed right now.' Teen depression gives the stiffs pause because they figure you're suicidal and nobody wants to be responsible.

'Are you taking drugs?'

'Negative.'

'How's the play coming? Mr. Huff and Mr. Lund are very excited about it.'

The bell goes and I'm hoping she's got places to go, people to see. 'It's going great,' I say. 'I think I've found my life purpose.'

'I'm very glad to hear it.' She glances at the clock. One of the secretaries tells her Mr. Somebody's on the phone. 'I have to take this call,' she tells me. 'I don't want to see you down here again. We all understand that you're experiencing stress at home but there are limits to our patience.' She picks up the phone. 'I look forward to seeing the play. What's it called?'

'*Truly Loved*.'

'A love story, how nice.'

A toilet cubicle provides sanctuary. I lock it and stand on the seat, becoming invisible.

Kirsten storms in and starts touching up her face. Nicole trails her. I watch them through the crack in the door.

'Feel my ass,' Kirsten says. She often commands people to feel her ass and tell her how toned she is.

'There's like, no fat,' Nicole says.

'She's pissing me off. I'm a slow burner but when I get mad I go straight to rage.'

'Doyle invited her,' Nicole says. 'It's not like she's crashing.'

'She's a whore. I want to hurt her so bad, shove her tits down her throat.'

'There's somebody in here,' Nicole observes.

'Who?'

I jump down and flush the toilet.

'It's Limone,' Nicole says. She recognizes my boots. I open the cubicle and try to look busy washing my hands.

'You tell your friend to stay away from Nicole's party,' Kirsten orders. I've never been able to compute how somebody so bossy can be popular. Do people *like* being bossed around? Is that what made old Adolf prom king? Or Winston? Mrs. Freeman was telling us about the bombing of Dresden. Even though the war was won, the Brits wanted to test their bombs so they dropped them on civilians in Dresden. All the POWs who weren't killed were freed to dig ditches for dead Germans. Everybody makes old Winston out to be a hero but what about Dresden?

'She's not my friend,' I say.

'Since when?'

'She thinks I'm a freak.'

Neither of them say *damn right* because I'm supposed to be writing a play and there might be a part in it for them.

'Do *you* want to come?' Nicole asks. She has this imbecilic habit of sticking the tip of her thumb in her mouth and resting it on her lower teeth. 'You're welcome to come if you want.'

'I'll take it under advisement,' I say and scoot.

Rossi's watching a show where people undergo plastic surgery to look like somebody famous. They're operating on a woman who wants to look like Cher, which is pretty wild when you consider how much reconstruction Cher has had.

'That's heinous,' Tora says. She's doing homework, which drives me nuts. She's always going on about how she hates life and school, meanwhile she's averaging 98 percent. You just know, after she figures out that Creative Writing is a waste of time, she'll become a shrink or something.

'Did you girls find something to eat?' Mrs. Barnfield shouts. She's on the floor with her legs on the bed again. The bank warned of more layoffs. Mrs. Barnfield says she's not worried because she has seniority, but you can tell she's worried out of her mind because she's verging on comatose. Rossi says she's not even swallowing her cans of gruel.

'Rossi, sweetheart, are there any more Triscuits?'

Rossi doesn't answer her mother – she rarely does – so I shout, 'We found Bits & Bites, Mrs. Barnfield.'

I haven't told Rossi about Kirsten wanting to shove her tits down her throat. But it seems pretty obvious it would be better for all concerned if Rossi doesn't go to the party.

'I want to be reconstructed to look like Tatiana,' she says.

'Who's Tatiana?' Tora asks, solving equations at record speed.

'Are you serious? She's like, only the most gorgeous super-model in the entire world.'

The plastic surgeon starts marking up some other woman's face with felt marker. I read more of *The Great Gatsby*, which is another novel about some guy mooning over a girl he can't have.

'I don't know how you can stand to read all the time,' Rossi says.

'So, are you seriously going to the party with Doyle?'

'You have a problem with that?'

'No problem. He's pretty revolting, though, seriously.'

'What would *you* know about revolting?'

'He shoved his tongue down my throat and his fingers up my snatch.'

'Ouch,' Tora says.

'That's called sex.'

'Remember that boy in JK,' I ask, 'who got you to take off your underpants and put on his?'

'No.'

'Sure you do, he was this four-year-old pervert. Doyle reminds me of him.'

'What was his name?' Tora asks. 'Maybe it *was* Doyle and he changed his name in shame.'

'You guys are so totally uptight. Like, why don't you just *grow up*?'

'Are you going to let Doyle ding you?' I ask. I almost call her *old sport*. Gatsby's always calling everybody *old sport*. Which gives you an indication of just how deluded he is.

'Is that any business of yours?' Rossi demands.

'I think he's counting on it. Price of admission.'

'Lord preserve us,' Tora says.

Rossi sighs wearily and stares back at the blood and gore on the one-eyed monster.

'*I've* been invited to Nicole's party,' I say.

'No way.'

'I'll take you if you're determined to go.' I know some karate moves and could probably protect her.

'No way did they invite you.'

'They invited her because of the play,' Tora the future shrink says.

'They'd call us dykes,' Rossi says.

'Let 'em.'

'Anyway, I'm going with Doyle. He's taking me in his dad's car.'

'Don't let him do any racing,' I say. 'A couple of geniuses raced their parents' Mercs and smashed a taxi, killing the driver. He was from Pakistan, two days short of becoming a Canadian citizen. He'd been sending money to his wife in Pakistan and was planning to bring her over.'

'Why are you telling us this?' Rossi demands. 'That is so *totally depressing*, like, why do you repeat stuff like that?'

'Cautionary tale,' Tora says.

'The cops found a car-racing video game in one of the Mercs,' I elaborate. 'Some game where you race through city streets smashing into other cars. One of the rich boys is black, meaning nobody can pin the tragedy on poverty and race. It could be anyone, anywhere.'

'What's happened to the youth of today?' Tora says while solving another five-page math problem.

'If the politicians and corporate kings can bomb, steal, destroy *entire* cultures and ecosystems, why should we behave ourselves?'

'Where are our moral leaders?' Tora says.

'Seriously, it's not like hard work pays off. Ooops, there goes your pension you've been paying into for thirty years.' I grab another handful of Bits & Bites and toss back a couple of Cheerios. 'It's way more fun to race in cyberspace. When that gets boring, do it for real. Kill a Paki.'

Rossi's riveted to the tube where a surgeon is marking up a woman's ass. 'Oh I so totally want to get that done,' Rossi says. 'Like, just get my ass lifted. I so want J. Lo's ass. Like, before she got pregnant.'

I'm making eighteen slushies for a Brownie troop. I was a Brownie but couldn't conform. All that pledging to share and be a friend, meanwhile those girls would rip your face off. I was constantly on the outs, partnerless, the last one to find a spot in the circle. I enjoyed earning the badges, doing the research on the Huron or something. The other Brownies exchanged secret notes while I presented my project on the three sisters – corn, beans and squash – that the Huron cultivated. They lived in longhouses where the women ran things because the men were out hunting. The women decided who could marry who and who should be banned from the longhouse. They wouldn't put up with deadbeat husbands, would order them out into the cold to freeze to death. The downside was that the women died around forty from inhaling all that smoke from the fires.

The Brownies are squabbling about flavours and grabbing at each other's slushies.

'So what's with Rossi?' Doyle demands.

'What do you mean?'

'Does she do it with dogs?'

'Did she do it with you?'

'Very funny.' He's got the mop out and is pretending to clean the floor. 'They're saying some pretty perverted things about her.'

'Consider the source.'

'Why would they lie about that shit?'

'Why lie about weapons of mass destruction? To get a war going, clever clogs. Kirsten hates Rossi, wants her obliterated.'

'Why?'

'Hmmm, let me think. Could it be because she's drop-dead gorgeous and Jake's been sniffing around her?'

'They say she's the latest go-to girl.'

I ignore him. Think about Gatsby chasing Daisy, getting them all to drive to town for drinks. It's stinking hot and air conditioning hasn't been invented yet. They're lying around on couches drinking G&Ts and complaining about the heat. Gatsby's making moony eyes at Daisy, and wife-beater Tom's getting miffed. Old Jay's got this idea that little miss Daisy is going to run off with him but Tom knows better. His wife's a spoiled brat who likes her comforts and her shitcan marriage because she expects nothing from it. Expectation kills you every time.

'You shouldn't be reading at work,' Doyle says.

'I already wiped things down, old sport.'

'Did you check the napkin dispensers?'

'Bing bing bing.'

'Has Rossi said anything about going to the party with me?'

'She said she's going to the party with you.'

The old guy in the Speedy Muffler cap presses his crotch against the counter. I don't ask what he wants, just get it for him but at the last minute hand it to Doyle and say, 'I've got to whiz.' Sorry to disappoint, old sport.

I see Larry Bone ordering from Wok About and think maybe I should let him whip my ass later. Just another teen murder. They're talking about getting gun-sniffing dogs at our school. Not enough money for textbooks but, hey, let's get us some gun-sniffing dogs. There's progress for you.

Bone's by himself for a change, looking half-normal, digging in his pocket for cash to pay for his lo mein. I almost feel bad about kicking his face in. I pass the woman who orders smoothies from me. She always looks nervous, fidgeting with her purse or her cell or something. And she wears hats, which is unfortunate. Nervous people in hats should be avoided. She smiles anemically at me. 'G'day,' I say. I hate retail. All these parasites think they know you just because you happen to know their favourite flavour.

The washroom's crowded with smoking girls. They mess with their hair and faces. I gag from second-hand smoke while I wipe somebody else's piss off the seat. How is it okay to spray piss all over the seat?

The nervous woman in the hat is at the sink dabbing at strawberry smoothie on her blouse. 'I had a bit of a spill,' she says.

'It happens.'

'Do you enjoy your job?' she asks, forcing a howdy-doody, brain-damaged smile. 'I've always thought it would be wonderful to work in an ice cream parlour.'

'They're taking applications,' I say.

She holds her hands under the dryer for about six hours, gawping at me the whole time. I don't know if she's gay or what but she totally creeps me out. I wipe my hands on my pants. The mall's blasting that Joni Mitchell song about how if she had a river she'd skate away on it. Roger that.

13

In the early nineties some Russian construction worker was digging around birch trees when he stumbled on the missing Romanov's bones. He said he heard a crunching sound and knew it meant either coal or bone. First he dug up a chunk of pelvis then a piece of a child's skull. The archaeologists swarmed the place and declared it was obvious that Alexei and Maria didn't die peacefully because their remains were very damaged. They'd been beaten and kicked around, their bodies doused in acid and burned. I know the Bolsheviks hated the Imperial family because they'd been living off the serfs and all that, but I still don't think that justifies a blood fest. That's what I mean when I say revolutions turn rotten. You don't wake up a family in the middle of the night, drag them to the basement and blast them. Alexei was only thirteen. Czar Nicholas – imperialist tyrant that he was – had already abdicated, everything had been taken from him, it wasn't like he was a threat. The soldiers totally humiliated the family; they couldn't even take a piss without a soldier watching. They transported them to Moscow in peasant carts. This was after they'd killed Rasputin, the empress's guru and confidante. So she was seriously wrecked, sitting on straw while poor people threw rotten food at her. Same old mob story.

It's like with David Weiss getting swarmed. They wanted his binders because he'd written all these notes for a test they had to take. Weiss is obsessive about his binders, labels them, has inserts with different headings, carries them everywhere. He wants to be a chemical engineer. They pushed him to the floor and started kicking him. When they 'wind' people they kick them in the gut until they start to vomit or cough blood. Weiss clung to his binders for protection but the thugs kept at it, busting his nose and glasses. They started dancing around, mocking the way he had to squint to see. It's hard to actually witness swarmings because the person getting beaten is on the ground, surrounded. So you can't say you *saw* the whole thing. Mostly you hear it. The corridors are too crowded anyway, people just step around it. He didn't return to class, must have made a break for it when the security guard was getting his ketchup chips. Usually you have to get buzzed out.

Anyway, they called him *Jew Boy* and all you can think is, can't we get beyond this? Nobody will report it, of course, including moi. Snitching means you're next. Even the teachers turn a blind eye because they're scared the thugs will key their cars.

The paper had a picture of the Romanovs sitting on the roof of their prison house in Siberia. They weren't permitted outside. The only way they could get fresh air was on the roof. They looked so forlorn up there, staring at the camera. You just know Nicholas knew they were doomed. The Bolsheviks even shot their servants.

Drew's spooning peanut butter out of the jar, doesn't even bother with bread anymore. Maybe she's starving herself to death, punishing herself for failing to problem-solve. This would mean I'd have to look for new digs, go live with Damian and the tomato. I don't want this.

'There's some kind of fungus on peanuts that's bad for you,' I tell her. 'Maybe you should try varying your diet.'

'Anything happen at school?'

'Negative. Did you go out?'

'I sprinkled cayenne pepper. It's supposed to burn their eyes.'

'Whose?'

'The cats.' She spoons more peanut butter.

'Is Vaughn around?'

'I thought I heard him come in. The hospital phoned for you. A girl was asking for you.' That must be Kadylak. It's too late to call back. I try not to worry about her, seek refuge in my room and listen to Mr. Sinatra telling me he's got me under his skin. Meanwhile he's being a dirtbag to his wives.

When Gatsby and Daisy drive back in his fancy white convertible, she smashes into the floozie Tom was dinging. The floozie, thinking it's Tom in the convertible coming to rescue her from moving to the prairie with her gas-pumping husband, rushes into the road. Daisy doesn't stop the car to see if they can help the floozie. She keeps on driving and Gatsby keeps on swooning over her. With a dead woman in the road. No wonder Zelda went nuts. Although they say Scott rescued her when she tried to throw herself in front of an express train. So maybe he did truly love her.

I try to concentrate on the play, get old Lillian into kinky underwear she bought online because the vamp on the soap was wearing it. Her beau, pretending to be Speedy Gonzales, chases her, shouting, 'I'll catch you, pussy gato! Arriba, arriba!' They keep tripping over her newly purchased consumer goods. Lillian starts swatting him with towels and calling him *old sport*. He's digging it but pretty soon it's obvious that towels aren't enough and he has to get thwacked with an umbrella. It's all about feeling, this beating up. When you're kicking the shit out of somebody, you're hoping to *feel* something. When you don't, you kick harder.

'Phone for you,' Drew says without opening the door. We have this thing about respecting each other's privacy. We respect each other so much we're total strangers.

'Did you hear about Weiss?' Rossi asks.

'Yeah.'

'He's in the hospital with a concussion, a broken nose and busted ribs.'

'At least he's not dead.'

'Nobody saw who did it.'

You just know Gatsby isn't going to report Daisy's hit and run. He'll take the rap and go to prison for her. She'll be drinking mint juleps and getting swatted by hubby while old Jay plays blushing bride.

'How's the play coming?' Rossi asks.

'Bitchin'.'

'Is there a part for me in it?'

When you consider that ass-kissing makes the world go around, and that there's no way *you* can kiss ass, you know you're going to be cleaning toilets for a living. Then all of a sudden you're writing a play and everybody wants to kiss *your* ass and you can't stand that either, and you realize it's a lose-lose.

'My mother freaked in the hairdresser's today,' Rossi says. 'She said they made her hair orange but it's the same colour it always is. I'm a little worried about her.' I don't tell her it's obvious her mother is dying. I don't tell people when stuff is obvious. They hate you for it.

'I've got to get back to writing,' I say.

'You are *so* lucky you have talent,' she says. Kiss, kiss.

Vaughn's on the deck, ready to howl at the moon. 'Ding ding ding,' I say. Don't know why I'm bothering, just that I'm feeling scared. Not of Bonehead particularly. Nothing that specific.

'What's up?' he says.

'What do you make of that tree?' I ask, immediately regretting that I used the *tree* word again.

'Very nice.'

The personal trainer drummer is thumping along to Led Zeppelin. Treeboy doesn't seem to mind. I consider telling him that the guy thumps his dog with a shovel but decide this might not be a conversation starter.

'I sit in trees sometimes,' I blurt. 'You see all kinds of stuff. People forget you're there.'

'That's one of the problems,' he says.

Thump thump thump.

'They found these wild boys in B.C.,' I say, dismayed that once again I'm babbling around this guy. 'They were raised in the remote wilderness and have never been to school or watched TV or anything. The Salvation Army gave them fifty bucks for food and the boys said it was far too much. Can you imagine any so-called civilized kid refusing fifty bucks?'

He shakes his head.

'All they eat is raw eggs, fruit and vegetables. Any money they're given they spend on bags of marked-down produce. They're emaciated.'

'They would be wise to go back into the woods,' Vaughn says, sliding open the glass doors. 'Good night.'

I don't think he likes me.

Our librarian's alright. She's got a wandering eye, which can be a little distracting, but she takes an interest if you're a reader. She's nuts about Austen, though, and the Georges. When I asked her if any of those women ever wrote a book that wasn't about some woman pining for some guy, she looked about to cry for a second. That's what I mean when I say it's best not to mention stuff that's obvious. 'Have you read Catherine Cookson?' she asks me. 'You should, being such a history buff. She tells a good story. Very feisty heroines.' I take the book from her. It's called *Tilly Trotter*. I can't see myself enduring a heroine called Tilly Trotter. However, I don't want to make Mrs. Wartowski cry. She called *The Great Gatsby* a must-read classic. I don't tell her how grossed out I was about Daisy riding into the sunset with her stinking rich husband, leaving her toddler and the roadkill behind. And old Gatsby lying around in his pool waiting to get arrested. I was glad the gas-pumper shot him. Put him out of his misery.

I return F. Scott's masterpiece. Mrs. Wartowski smiles, which is a little unsettling because she has a couple of brown teeth. 'Romantic, wasn't it?' she asks.

'Absolutely,' I say and take off with the Cookson.

I don't know who came up with the idea that kids are safer in schools than on the street. You can escape on the streets, climb a tree or something. Here you're trapped. Somehow Bonehead's got hold of my email address and has been texting me ugly threats. Fortunately, I rarely check my mail because nobody I want to know has my address.

Anyway, my method for survival at school is to keep a low profile, but suddenly, thanks to Huff and Lund, I'm this impresario. Both crawlers cornered me outside the cafeteria. 'How's the dramatist?' Lund inquired.

'Can we have a read any time soon?' Huff wheedled.

I can't see them tolerating Lillian charging around in a thong, thwacking Mike with rolled-up newspapers. I thought newspapers was a nice touch because that's how you hit your dog. Mike's becoming an abuse junkie. He says he's never felt so *alive*. And Lillian is getting off on beating him. She has power for once. She's like those kids who shoot up the cafeteria. It's not the bullies who commit mass murder. It's the wussies who've been kicked around.

'Can you give us a timeline on it?' Lund asks, fondling his beard.

'Not really.'

'It's doing wonders for the school community,' Huff says. He had me reading Puck today. Talk about an ass-kisser. If I were Oberon I'd swat him. I guess old Will knew a thing or two about ass-kissing, otherwise he wouldn't have survived all those rabid reformists.

One of Bonehead's missives says he's going to fuck me blind. It's got me a little tense, I have to admit. I'm pretty sure he's all talk, though, old Larry, just your regular loud-mouthed junkie.

Harry Houdini's real name was Weiss. Ehrich Weiss. His mother never hugged him because she wanted him to be strong. Just before his dad kicked off, he told Ehrich – who was twelve or something – to be the man of the house. Ehrich worked his butt off in factories, taking all kinds of abuse. It was his brother, Theo, who got into the magic tricks. The hitch was there were a gazillion magicians in vaudeville. Nobody was too interested. It wasn't until Ehrich started drowning himself in milk cans that people took notice. And pretty soon that wasn't enough, he had to be tied up and thrown in rivers or jails, hung upside down in straitjackets. People were only interested if it looked like he was doomed. Meanwhile he was missing his dead mother and trying to contact her through mediums. When he figured out they were all fakes, he sued them till he went broke. His wife married the bottle because Harry was always nearly killing himself. One night some borderline cases came backstage and punched him in the gut when he wasn't prepared for it. Usually he'd let people belt him to prove he was superhuman, it was part of his act. The punch ruptured his appendix but he didn't know it and had a high tolerance for pain. The following night in the Chinese Water Torture Chamber he was too weak to climb out and started smashing his head into the glass. His wife broke the glass with an axe. All he talked about in the hospital was that the trick didn't work out and nobody would respect him anymore. He was disgraced, he said, he would never again be able to make money as a magician. His last words were 'I can't fight this.' So there you go, someone who fought everything, all his life, ends up dead at forty-two. I'd rather make soap.

David Weiss didn't cry out when they were kicking him but you could hear the breath being forced out of him, and the puking. I should be nicer to him. I avoid freaks, being a freak myself. A posse of freaks is a serious target. When he comes back to school, I'm going to be nicer to him, maybe sit beside him in biology, copy his notes on the human genome.

Kadylak's sucking on ice to cool the chemo sores in her mouth. The social worker just left. Kadylak doesn't trust her. The social worker's always nodding at her. She even nods at Kadylak's parents when they try to speak English. I guess social-worker school taught her that nodding conveys empathy. Anyway, Kadylak hates it and goes mum when she's around. I read her some of *Tilly Trotter*, which she enjoys because it's all about a spirited orphan farm lass. Kadylak loves descriptions of countryside since she's never seen any. She closes her eyes and you just know she's skipping in the buttercups. A creepy guy called Hal wants to court Tilly and turns nasty when she tells him she's not interested. He stalks her, which causes Kadlylak's eyes to pop open and I'm not sure I should keep reading. 'Keep going,' Kadylak insists. Her mother's sick with the flu, so sick she can't get out of bed and go to her jobs, which is why Kadylak called me last night. Not only is the chemo killing her, she's dying of loneliness.

'She should stop going out,' she says.

'Who?'

'Tilly. She shouldn't go out with Hal around.'

'She can't stay in the cabin with the old folks the whole time, she'd go nuts. Besides, she has to chop wood and stuff, do chores.'

'I wouldn't go out,' Kadylak says. 'I'd hide.'

'For your whole life?' I immediately regret saying *whole life* to a child with cancer.

'The farmer can do her chores.'

'He's got his own chores. Besides, she doesn't want to be dependent on anyone.'

'If she goes out, Hal will hurt her.'

'Maybe the farmer will save her,' I suggest. 'It's pretty obvious she's nuts about him. Maybe they'll get married and live happily ever after.'

'The frog will turn into a prince.' She's on drugs and can't keep her stories straight.

'Something like that.' I read until she dozes off. I hold her hand, which feels puffy and hot from the poison inside her. I think of all the kids I've seen who've gotten better. I decide I'll save money so we can take a bus into the countryside. I'll find a B&B on the net that's a working farm. I'll watch her eat two helpings of scrambled eggs. I'll show her farm animals and fields, and at night we'll lie in the grass and look up at the stars and sing 'Will the Circle Be Unbroken.'

14

Damian had this idea that I should go out with him and his latest tomato to celebrate his birthday. This required that I procure a gift. I spent about four hours in a store that claims to do fair trade with Third World artisans. The salesgirl ignored me, yakked on her cell and checked herself out in the mirror about five hundred times. She was wearing high-heeled pointy boots over tight jeans. Looking sexy is the important thing, doesn't matter if it cripples your feet. I pocketed a couple of hand-painted spinning tops. I don't normally steal but I wanted to hurt this girl.

Damian unwraps the set of ebony elephants that I did, in fact, pay for. 'They're from India,' I explain.

'Very nice.' Damian hands one to the tomato. She doesn't look too interested, puts it down and starts picking at her fake red fingernails. I spin one of the tops on the table and watch it whiz around. The tomato and Damian feign amusement. 'How do you like dem apples?' he says.

'It's bad news for elephants these days,' I say. 'They're acting like humans, raping and killing rhinocereses.'

'Excuse me?' the tomato says.

'It's called hyper-aggression, caused by humans poaching and culling them and taking over their habitat. Baby male elephants witness their mothers and sisters getting slaughtered and suffer from post-traumatic stress disorder. So they run around raping and pillaging.'

'I thought they were supposed to be gentle creatures,' the tomato says.

'They are, until they're traumatized and starved. Humans get pretty savage when we're traumatized and starved, not to mention overcrowded. We're all vertebrates.' The tomato attempts to look like she knows what *vertebrate* means. 'You see,' I continue, to demonstrate my superior intelligence, 'normally mothers and sisters shape the brains and behaviours of infant males. Being orphaned compromises their neurobiological development.'

'Since when did you become an expert on elephants?' Damian asks.

I just stare at him because I make it a policy not to answer really stupid questions.

'Anyway,' he says, 'they're very nice.' He means the ebony elephants. He'll probably stash them behind his inflatable doll or something. I'm sorry I gave them to him. He doesn't deserve them.

'Goldie wondered if you'd like to go shopping with her,' he says, 'find some new outfits.'

I grab the top and spin it again. It's pretty fantastic, I have to admit, bright colours swirling. I have to remember to give them to Kadylak.

'You're developing a nice figure,' Goldie says. 'You should show it off.'

'Why?'

They look at each other then back at me in a carnivorous manner. 'Aren't you interested in boys?' she asks, wrapping her claws around her wineglass.

'Should I be?'

Old Damian snorts. 'Do you prefer girls?'

'Hamsters.'

'You're something else,' Damian says. 'Isn't she something else?' The brain surgeon nods.

'It never hurts to look attractive,' Goldie says.

'Marie Antoinette endured four-hour sessions with psychotic hairdressers and had to sleep with her head on a wooden block so the glued-on hair wouldn't get mussed.'

'Why?' the simpleton inquires.

'So she'd look attractive.'

'Isn't that the one who got her head cut off?' Damian the history scholar asks.

'If she'd stuck with being an ornament,' I say, 'she might have become popular. Let that be a lesson to us all.' I wink at the tomato. 'Stick with being an ornament.'

Damian gulps more vino. '"Let them eat cake." Isn't that what she said?'

The tomato starts fiddling with his hair.

'Let them eat cake,' he repeats with a flourish of his hand. He and the simpleton chuckle and snort together.

'The poor people hated her because she did dumb-ass things like getting the heads of her dogs carved onto armchairs,' I explain. 'The reality is, she didn't know any better, nobody'd educated her in anything except looking pretty, etiquette and horseback riding. After they chopped off Louis's head they let her rot in the Bastille for months. She watched two of her children die there.'

'That's tragic,' the tomato observes.

'They say she was composed when she was carted to the guillotine, except she stepped on the executioner's toe. "I'm sorry, sir," she said, "I didn't do it on purpose."'

The tomato appears moved, even goes so far as to hold her painted claws over her mouth in shock.

'One thing about you, Limone,' Damian says, 'you sure know how to kill a party.'

'Is this a party?' I ask. 'Did we sing "Happy Birthday" yet?' I start singing 'Happy Birthday' really loudly, causing heads to turn.

'Cool it,' Damian commands, reaching across the table and grabbing my wrist. He's always grabbed my wrist when he's pissed at me, dragging me to my room or the car, slamming the door on me.

'Hands off, old sport,' I say.

Possibly mildly embarrassed at having revealed his inner beast, he releases his grip. 'Sorry. Let's just try to have a nice dinner, can we do that?' Goldie nods but I just stare at him wiping sweat off his forehead with his napkin.

'How's your mother?' he asks.

'Which one?'

'Drew. Has she gone out yet?'

'To chase cats. And squirrels. The squirrels keep going at the birdfeeder. She chases them with a broom. And barks at them. And the cats.'

'A woman with a PhD,' he says. 'Whoever would have thunk it?' What keeps *him* going? Banging demoiselles? How can he stand it? And what about her, what's her raison d'être? Pleasuring her sahib a few times a week? 'How's it feel to be fifty-two?' I ask.

'Fifty-one,' he says, 'don't rush me.' Goldie starts fiddling with his hair again. 'It feels terrific,' he says, 'never better.'

'Why?'

'What?'

'What's terrific about being fifty-one?'

'Less responsibility,' Damian says. 'Here you are, almost grown up. Soon you'll be off to university, making your own life.'

University. The great panacea.

'It's exciting,' he says, even though it isn't.

'What are you going to study?' the brain surgeon asks.

'The human genome.'

'Really? That's fascinating.'

Damian wipes his snout. 'Your real mother seems mighty keen to meet you. She even called *me*.' He's waiting for me to ask why but I don't. 'She sounds nice.'

'That's exciting,' the tomato says, 'finding your real mother.' She says *exciting* exactly the way Damian does.

'Where's *your* mother?' I ask her.

'Hamilton.'

'Do you ever see her?'

'Sometimes, at Christmas.'

'So your real mother lives an hour away but you only see her sometimes at Christmas. That's exciting.'

'Don't get snarky,' Damian says, which he always does when I state the obvious.

Rossi's life purpose is to get a job at H&M. I go with her to fill out her one hundredth application. After she fills out the form she looks for something to spend her mother's hard-earned cabbage on. 'I need a top for the party,' she says.

I'm so sick of hearing about the party – who is or isn't going and with whom – I try to think of a compelling change of topic.

'Too bad you can't poison people these days,' I say.

Rossi keeps flipping through racks at high speed.

'Before autopsies,' I continue, 'everybody was getting poisoned. Royalty was always ordering servants to sample food to make sure it wasn't poisoned. Imagine being the servant, getting a bite of a decent meal for a change then waiting to see if it'll kill you.'

Maybe Lillian could slip something into the bank manager's coffee while she stops by with Timbits for her former co-workers. They'll act happy to see her even though they don't want her around because she reminds them of what shit-eaters they are. She'll personally deliver the poisoned coffee to the boss. Or maybe she'll jet up to head office and chase after the CEO with an arsenic-laced Timbit. I like endings where everybody dies. Shakespeare had that right. The vengeful and the avengers, all toast.

All the tops look shrunken. Rossi tries one on anyway.

'It looks too small,' I say.

'It's supposed to look that way. I'm not sure about the colour, though. Do you like the pink better?'

She always asks my advice before ignoring it.

'It's too small,' I repeat. I don't want her falling out of a toddler shirt at the party.

'That's the style, Lemon, get a grip.'

I try to remember her old body. The body that could do walking handstands. She tries on a toddler miniskirt and gets pissed when she can't zip it up. Maybe Courtney, Lillian's shopaholic friend, could try on toddler clothes. Courtney's one of those pretty, skinny women everybody hates. Lillian spends way too much time envying her. Envy is the sorrow of fools. Some ancient Chinese guy said that.

Mr. Paluska is playing cards with Kadylak. With his free hand he's massaging her feet. I don't want to interfere so I take the book cart around to some other kids. They all have private rooms because infections can kill them. The conscious ones get pretty excited when they see me. It's not like they're all saints, some are just plain mean. But overall, potentially fatal illness seems to make people nicer. Too bad we can't compute that we're all going to expire sooner or later so we might as well behave decently. I was up a tree the other day and these two suits were arguing over a parking spot, actually screaming at each other. The suit who screamed the loudest got the parking spot. Which makes you wonder about world politics.

This girl called Molly, who was probably alright once but has been spoiled rotten and thinks I'm her servant, is trying to get me to go downstairs and buy her some fries. The steroids make these kids crave salt and therefore junk food. Of course the corporations are more than happy to comply. We've got Burger King, Pizza Hut, KFC, right here in the hospital, all providing excellent nourishment. 'My mom would get me fries,' Molly says. 'You're mean. I'm going to tell my dad.' The room is packed with stuffed toys her parents and their associates have given her. It's scary, actually, all those staring eyes. Just one stuffed animal would perk up Kadylak. I shove a penguin into the book cart while Molly's sulking.

I see Mr. Paluska in the corridor in his paint-splattered T-shirt. He's got young Marlon Brando shoulders from heaving paint cans around. I liked that movie. Of course I had to run around shouting 'Steeeeelllllaaaaa!' for a couple of days. Vivien was pretty convincing in it, probably because in real life she was finding out that Larry was a queer.

'Can you go see her?' Mr. Paluska asks.

'Of course.'

'She miss her mother.'

'I know. I'll go right away.'

'Thank you.' He grabs my hand and holds if for a second and I feel ready to pass out because *no one* holds my hand. He lets go almost immediately, probably because I look stunned or something. My hand just dangles there in a cold wind.

'Now my other children sick,' he says. 'Whole family sick.'

'I'm so sorry.'

He shrugs and heads for the elevator. I watch his shoulders.

Kadylak's lost more muscle mass and has trouble walking. I wheel her into the playroom. She wants to play house, invite me over, serve me plastic pies and cakes. She goes nuts when I give her the penguin, holds it against her face and kisses it. Of course I'm worried Princess Molly's going to show up and snatch it from her.

'What are you going to call it?' I ask. 'Is it a him or a her?'

'A her,' she announces. 'I'm going to call her Sweetheart.'

'That's a nice name.' The whole time I'm thinking how sick it is that I've been ogling her father's body.

'She's going to sleep with me, beside Mischa.' Mischa the bear is losing fur.

'I'm sure they'll get along great,' I say.

'Can you read me *Tilly*?'

So Tilly goes to the village and on the way back Hal is waiting for her with a net. He and his neanderthal cohorts drop it on her from a tree. She struggles to escape but just gets more tangled in the ropes. Kadylak looks worried out of her mind, gripping a piece of plastic cheesecake. 'Maybe I shouldn't read anymore,' I say.

'Please read.'

Hal starts ripping up Tilly's petticoats while the other goons cheer him on. All of a sudden, you'll never guess, the farmer shows up.

'I knew it!' Kadylak says.

The farmer carries her in his arms to the old folks' cabin. He says he's going to protect her from now on, but we all know he's got cows to look after.

'He should shoot Hal,' Kadylak says.

'Then he'd go to prison.'

'He could say it was an accident.'

'That doesn't always work out.'

A couple of pages later, Hal and company have torched the cabin and the old folks have died from shock or whatever. Poor Tilly sees the smoke and charges up the hill.

'Where's Simon?' Kadylak demands. Simon's the farmer.

'He's shearing sheep or something.'

'He said he would protect her.' Which makes me think of all the times I've told Kadylak she's not going to die and she's believed me. We start out small, believing everybody, and then we grow up and figure out everybody's full of it.

15

Waldo, the security guard, is hanging around the counter talking about two boys who spilled lighter fluid on a girl and set her on fire. 'Like, can you get your head around that one, like what kind of psychos would do that?'

'Maybe they saw it on a reality show,' I say. Doyle's slamming around the scoops and buckets because he gets jealous when I talk to Waldo. When Waldo isn't around, Doyle scoffs, 'What's it take to get a job as a security guard?'

'So this woman's walking along the beach and finds a bottle,' Waldo says, and I feel a joke coming on.

'What kind of bottle?' I ask, feigning interest to annoy Doyle.

'Any kind, doesn't matter. The thing is, there's a message in it. So she gets it out and it says if she rubs the bottle, she'll get a wish. So she rubs it and a genie pops out and the woman says, "How come I only get one wish, you're supposed to get three?" "That's the deal," the genie says. "One wish."'

You have to wonder why it's always guys telling jokes, and how they don't notice nobody thinks they're funny. I keep looking fascinated to aggravate Doyle who starts cramming napkins into the dispensers.

'So the woman says,' Waldo continues, '"I wish for world peace." The genie goes, "Well, that's a little hard because there's wars all over the place." The woman says she'll write a list for him and he can sum up all the war zones in one wish. He says he doesn't know if he can do that, that's a mighty big wish. She writes it out anyway – it takes a couple of hours – and shows it to him and he says, "No way can I pull this off, you're going to have to think of another wish." So she says, "Okay, how about finding me a good man who's not afraid of commitment, who's got a decent job, who'll share the housecleaning and cooking and take the garbage out without me nagging him?" The genie looks real worried for a second then he says, "That's a really big wish. Can I see that world peace list again?"' Waldo sucks on his slushie, I do a fake hahaha laugh to bug Doyle. 'Shouldn't you be doing the rounds?' he says to Waldo. He's staking out his territory. Soon he'll be raping rhinoceroses.

To my horror, Damian and the tomato appear, arm in arm. 'Look at my hard-working girl,' he says. 'I like the hat.'

'What are you doing here?'

'We just saw the most amazing movie,' the tomato says, and I fear she's about to tell me about it.

'What'll you have?' he asks her.

This shuts her up; she'll be choosing a flavour for a couple of hours.

'Drew isn't returning my calls,' he says. 'Is she alright?'

'Swell.'

'Has she gone out yet?'

'Line dancing.'

'Really?'

'She's met some pilot who takes her flying. She loves it.' A smattering of jealousy purples the old lothario's face.

The tomato, finger in mouth, pulls him to her side. 'I can't decide whether to go soft or hard.'

'Less chance of botulism with the hard stuff,' I say.

Damian fishes a piece of paper out of his pocket and hands it to me. 'Your real mother's number. You took off so fast I didn't get a chance to give it to you.'

'I think I'll have the Cherry Cobbler,' the tomato announces, clapping her paws together. I stuff the paper in my pocket and grab a scoop.

Rossi's completely freaked because she masturbated on her cell and now Kirsten's broadcast it worldwide.

'Why did you send it to her?' I ask, swallowing a Timbit. I ordered ten to share but, of course, I'm eating them all.

'She said she was only going to show it to the guys we know,' Rossi says. 'Like, the ones going to the party.'

'Did you get a list?' Tora asks. She's got her laptop out and is working on her essay for Swails.

'What do you mean, did I get a list?'

'Get it in writing,' Tora says.

'Is that supposed to be funny?'

'Why are you so desperate to be mated?' I ask.

'I'm not desperate.' She's got zits on her chin, a sure sign of desperation. 'That bitch is sewering me.'

'Maybe you shouldn't go to the party,' I suggest.

'And let her get away with it? No way. I'm going.'

'How does your going stop her getting away with it?' Tora the future shrink inquires, still tapping on her computer.

'I'm going to hold my head high. I've got nothing to be ashamed of.'

A young woman struggles through the glass doors on crutches. She's missing a leg below the knee. I'm used to seeing limbless people in photos from Afghanistan or Iraq, victims of land mines. But this amputee shocks me because she's white and smiling and talking cheerfully to another young woman who has both legs. Girls' night out. Smiling and talking cheerfully with just one leg. I wait for Rossi to notice her but she doesn't. I start reading a sports section that's lying around, not because I'm interested but because I don't know what to say to Rossi and I finished *The Mayor of Casterbridge* and haven't gotten my glommers on a new tome yet. Tora's no help because she's busy getting another 100 percent. Some Chinese basketball player is over seven feet tall. It turns out his parents were both tall and 'encouraged' by the Chinese authorities to copulate. They didn't marry for love but to produce a giant for the Chinese government. The giant was treated by a special doctor who fed him bee pollen and caterpillar fungus to make him grow even bigger. Now he plays for the NBA but he's scared to go out of his room when he isn't playing basketball because if he gets into any kind of scandal, the Chinese government will chew him out, not to mention the NBA and all his corporate sponsors who've got million of dollars tied up in him. So the giant sits in his room playing computer games while the other players party.

'I can't believe you guys don't care about what's happening to me,' Rossi says.

'I do care,' I say. 'I just can't relate.'

'What do you mean you can't relate?'

'All this hoochie chasing.'

'It's not about sex,' Rossi argues.

'What's it about then?' I know it's about being popular, accepted and all that but I want her version.

'I like guys.'

Same old line.

Drew needs her teeth cleaned. She's been putting it off and now her gums are bleeding. She's agreed to go to the dentist if I accompany her, which means I get to play hooky. It takes her about four hours to get dressed. When she comes downstairs I notice her pants are hanging off her. More weight lost on the peanut butter diet. 'You should eat something now,' I say, 'because you won't be able to later.' The dentist has to freeze her entire mouth before the cleaning because Drew is super-sensitive. She doesn't answer me, just pulls on a jacket that looks a size too big.

The subway is stacked with lifers. Drew stares out the window into the darkness while I watch the great unwashed, try to figure out what head-pounding is going on in their lives. Usually you can pin it on the job. They're all working for some asshole. A bald guy in a leather jacket and square-toed shoes is reading a book called *Think and Get Rich*. Amazing how wealth goes on being the safety exit. Nobody seems to notice that the stinking rich are total screw-ups. Drew grabs my arm and hangs on to it. It starts to hurt but I don't say anything.

My biological mother's name is Constance Ramsbottom. Connie Sheep's Ass.

The dentist is one of those fakers who asks how you are even though he doesn't give a monkey's turd. He sticks needles into Drew who looks scared out of her mind. I know she hates it when dentists yabber at her so I keep him talking until the hygienist takes over. Then I turn up the volume on the TV so chair-side chatter becomes challenging. Drew closes her eyes, numbed. I surf around the soap operas; some stud's got a gambling problem and I decide old Lil could start gambling. I'm holding auditions tomorrow, even though I haven't finished the play. It's time to jerk some cretins around, Kirsten in particular. They're all going for it, haven't noticed that Lund and Huff aren't in the loop and that the auditions are in my basement. I haven't told Drew yet. I'm hoping she'll be absorbed in her newspapers, sucking back another tragedy.

The oral hygienist is talking loudly about her new Shih Tzu dog who's 'doing his business on the carpet.' Even when she lets it run around the yard it comes back in and shits on the floor. At night it sleeps beside her bed and yelps. She's going to start caging it. Somebody told her that if you cage them at night, they're so happy to get away from their shit and piss in the morning they run out and crap in the yard.

'Castles with moats,' I say, 'used to have parts jutting out so humans could crap through a hole into the moat. I don't know what the dogs did.' Even with her mask on I can see the hygienist's having trouble following my line of thinking, which is to get her to lay off poor old Drew who's too polite to tell her to shut up and clean her teeth. 'Castles without moats had shafts that would narrow into a pit. Some poor serf had to come and shovel it out once a week. There were flies all over the place. People got maw worms that would eat you up from inside. People were pulling worms out of the corners of their eyes.' The hygienist clams up.

We stop at a juice bar and I make Drew drink some carrot and beet juice using a straw. She's so pale I'm afraid she's going to pass out. I'm not used to her looking scared. 'What's it like being out and about?' I ask.

'Fine.'

It makes sense that if you stop going out it gets harder and harder to go out. I read somewhere that the way to treat phobias is with exposure. So the less Drew is exposed to the harsh realities of Spaceship Earth, the harder it's going to be for her to resume earning a paycheque. Don't like to think about what will happen when the cabbage runs out.

Maybe Lillian will stop going out, after she blows up the bank. She'll make some chatroom buddies. Tora's dad doesn't talk to his family because he's too busy texting buddies he's never met, buddies in Australia and South Africa who can't see how mean and ugly he is, and buy his line that he's a devoted family man. Likewise Lillian's chatroom buddies wouldn't know what a fuck-up she is. Nobody could trace her tales about her fabulous hat-making business and hot sex life. Maybe that's where it's going to go when the oil runs out. We'll all sit at home and spew lies into cyberspace.

16

Eleanor of Aquitane's father decided to become a pilgrim. Up till then he'd just been another stinking-rich warrior type. After some battle or other, he decided God did exist. It was Christmas and he got this radical idea to send bread and sweetmeats to his starving serfs whose feet were wrapped in rags. Next he marched off to Spain to find God, leaving his pubescent daughters to be chewed up by various rival factions. Everybody wanted to marry them because they were stinking rich. Their mother was dead, of course, dying of grief after her precious only son fell off a cliff. So old Eleanor and her sister Petronella were rattling around various castles, shitting into moats or down shafts, pulling worms out of their eyes.

Vaughn's been using my computer, connecting with other tree frogs. 'Thank you,' he says when he's finished.

'You're welcome.'

'I'm a little worried about Drew.'

'Me too.'

'She's very different.'

'She got stabbed.' On the way back from the dentist there was the usual wacko in the subway talking to himself, only this nutter kept pointing at people and saying, 'Bam. I got you.'

'She talks to *you*,' I say. 'What's she talk about?'

'You. And me. She worries about us.'

'Why?'

'She thinks we're lost.'

'Unlike herself.'

He sits on my bed, which is a little disturbing. 'Do you despise everyone?' he asks.

'Not everyone.'

'Who don't you despise?'

'You. Yet.'

'Give it time.'

'Perhaps.' He's looking in the direction of my aborted play and I'm worried he's reading it and figuring out just how sick I am.

'It gets tiring, disdaining everything,' he says. 'I used to do it, it wore me out.'

'So now you love everything.'

'Not at all. I just look at things from a different angle. There's always another angle.' He stares at a picture I cut out of the paper for my mother/daughter scrapbook. It's an African mother with AIDS holding her baby girl with AIDS. What's astonishing about the photo is they look happy even though they're dying. They smile into each other's eyes.

'If you look for the worst,' Vaughn says, 'you see the worst.'

'What do *you* look for?'

He thinks for a minute. 'Nobility.'

'You mean when you're up a tree, and rednecks are coming at you with chainsaws, you look for nobility?'

He shrugs. 'They've all got families to feed.'

'So it's okay that your friend fell down and broke his back?'

He blinks a few times then stares into oblivion again. I don't buy this saintly shit. He's as angry as the rest of us.

The rival factions try to kidnap Eleanor and force her hand in marriage. She longs for Daddy-O but he's headed for Spain in peasant clothes. After walking for a week he runs out of bread and decides to eat a fish some fisherman is hawking. After frying it up and gulping it down he pukes his guts out. The enlightened king manages to scribble a note to his daughters telling them he thinks he didn't cook the fish enough, and that if they read this letter it means he's dead from rotten-fish poisoning. He tells them they mustn't worry because his death will bring him closer to God. Eleanor inherits his massive fortune and becomes even more marketable as a wife. Her evil elders marry her off to Louis the Fat's son who's devout and thinks laughing is a sin so you can imagine what a riot he was. Eleanor, accustomed to dancing, sun and sea, soon discovered that damp old Paris was no party town. Just like Marie Antoinette, she was scorned for being different. Unlike Marie Antoinette, she didn't take shit from anybody. She put up with Louis for a few years then had the marriage annulled. She married Henry II and went off with him to the crusades to kill some heathens. He became King of England and she started popping babies. Some of the children died, of course, but three of her sons survived and grew into rebellious teenagers who plotted to steal the throne from Henry. The King's forces killed two of the treacherous sons, which left Eleanor's favourite, Richard the Lionheart. Eleanor started plotting with Richard to overthrow Henry. The King lost patience with all this subterfuge and locked Eleanor up for twenty-six years. Richard the Lionheart was killed in some battle or other. You have to wonder what kept Eleanor going. You'd think if both your parents died when you were a kid and your husband locked you up for decades and slaughtered your sons, you'd want to pack it in. But old Eleanor lived to be eighty-something, which nobody did in those days. Guess she had a life purpose.

Even Bonehead shows up to audition. I keep him waiting in the rain, along with Kirsten and Nicole. I hand out pages I've format-ted to look like a screenplay so the dummkopfs will feel like they're auditioning for *Spiderman Twelve* or something. I told Drew that it's all part of a school project. She just got a *Harper's* in the mail with a headline about how nuclear energy is going to kill us so she's busy reading. But Vaughn's doing laundry, which is unfortunate. He catches a couple of thespians acting out the Mike-chasing-Lillian scene, shouting 'Arriba! Arriba!' and calling her *pussy gato*. Vaughn doesn't laugh or look askance, just does the tree-frog stare. 'Later,' I tell him, waving my hand to suggest he squat elsewhere.

I ask the simpletons if they're comfortable with nudity, which gets them all giggly and it becomes pretty obvious everybody wants to take it off. I even get them to dry hump on the mildewy basement couch. My intention is to demean them but they're having a great time. They think they're on a reality show. I give 'direction,' criticize how they look, walk and talk and they take it. I speak with authority, 'direct' Kirsten and Bonehead to fake it doggy-style. None of this makes me feel any better. I start thinking I'm no better than they are.

On the radio a Jewish woman was talking about her mother who went up the chimney at Auschwitz. When the Gestapo showed up, the mother calmly told her daughter to run, to always keep moving so the Nazis could never find her. She gave her a leather bag full of papers. She told her daughter to keep the papers no matter what. The girl refused to believe she would never see her mother again and spent years searching for her. She couldn't bring herself to open the bag and look at the papers because she feared it was a war diary and that reading it would rip her apart. Sixty years later she looked in the bag. The papers turned out to be a novel about the war. She had it published and it became a bestseller, sixty-four years after her mother wrote it. She said its publication helped her to understand what the point of her survival was. When you read a story like that you have to wonder what the point is in *your* survival.

Bonehead and Kirsten are looking at me, waiting for direction. 'Go home,' I tell them.

I sit on the mouldy couch thinking to be or not to be. I don't see how taking arms against a sea of troubles ends them. There's always more shit coming down the pipe.

'All clear?' the Tree Frog asks.

'Yep.'

He pulls clothes out of the dryer and starts folding them. I never fold, just stuff things in drawers. Vaughn has become our official laundry boy. I watch him fold a pair of my underpants, tucking in the crotch then folding the two sides. He mates socks and forms them into little balls. All this takes time, which I have.

'How did it go?' he asks finally.

'Bitchin'.'

'Do you feel any better?'

'What do you mean?'

'Than before.'

'Before what?'

'What happened here.'

'What happened here?' I know he's hoping to assist me toward enlightenment, create an opportunity for self-reflection that will make me see, from another angle, that the world is resplendent with nobility.

'You tell *me*,' he says.

'Tell you what?'

'What happened here?'

'Who's on first?' I ask.

'No, who's on second. What's on first?'

'I dunno.'

'I dunno's on shortstop. Who's on first?'

'First's on second.'

'Who's on first?'

He keeps staring at me and I consider telling him I don't need a straight man or big brother or a conscience but that would be reacting. I start singing, 'Take me out to the ball game, take me out to the crowd. Buy me some peanuts and Cracker Jack. I don't care if I never get back ... '

'I'm making frittata, do you want some?'

'Fri-who?'

'Spanish omelette with potatoes.'

'No, gracias. I've got to watch my figure.'

I resume singing, more loudly, 'Let me root, root, root for the home team. If they don't win it's a shame. For it's one, two, three strikes you're out, at the old ball game.'

He retreats and I am alone with the slings and arrows of outrageous fortune.

Kadylak's blood count is low and she has a fever. They've put her on an antibiotic drip and have stuck another needle into her to get blood samples. I tell myself not to freak because at least they're not putting her on a ventilator. When they wheel in the X-ray cart they tell me to leave. Even though Kadylak's pretty out of it, she won't release my hand. I loosen her fingers and tell her I'll be right back. I wrap her hands around Sweetheart the penguin. I stand outside her door and try not to despise everyone. Molly, the princess, is on the prowl. I try not to despise her.

'What's going on?' she asks.

'Nothing.' She knows I'm lying. Kids with cancer smell lies.

'Then how come you're just standing there?'

'I'm waiting.'

'For what?'

'Her parents are in there. I think I saw a new DVD in the playroom. Go check it out.'

'What is it?'

'I can't remember. Go see.' She schleps away, dragging her IV pole. The doctors and nurses bustle out and don't notice, me which is good because they don't want me in there. Kadylak's still conscious but fitful and seems to be looking through me, to the other side. 'Do you want me to read?' I ask.

'*Tilly.*'

A blood infection can turn septic and kill one of these kids in hours.

Simon, the farmer, is getting married and old Tilly's pretty broken up about it. He invites her to the wedding but doesn't dance with her because he's too busy shtupping his wenchy wife. Dejected, Tilly heads up the road where old Hal is waiting for her. He jumps her but she fights him and he tumbles off the road, smacking into a tree. He tells her he can't move.

'He's lying,' Kadylak says.

Hal says his back is busted. He begs Tilly to get help before nightfall because after nightfall the animals will get him.

'Let them,' Kadylak says. Her colour's getting worse, her hands are mottled; her fingers and toes turning purple. I run and get a nurse. They wheel her to ICU. Put her on a ventilator.

I'm flinging a Nerf ball around with Wackoboy when Kadylak's father shows up.

'Where is she?' he wants to know.

I explain, watch him fall back against the wall. I tell him to wait while I find a nurse. They're all busy staring at monitors. I get loud. 'He doesn't know what's going on! His wife's sick!'

Brenda, fast-moving and efficient, grabs my arm. 'Keep your voice down.' She walks me down the corridor. 'What did you tell him?'

'I said Intensive Care. I told him about the ventilator.'

'You shouldn't be discussing the patient's care with the parents.'

'He wanted to know. Nobody was around.'

'You can always find us. It's late, you should be going home.'

I leave him with her. I should be holding his hand. Kids on ventilators don't look comfortable. Beyond all the usual tubes and wires, they're getting air forced into them. The machine wheezes. Just as the air's going out and the kid starts to look half-normal, the ventilator blows another tornado into them. I try not to picture Kadylak's torment. I try not to picture her father watching her. But it's all in my head. And I forgot to give her the spinning tops.

17

'Why,' demands Mr. Lund while digging around in his fanny pack for Tic Tacs, 'did you hold auditions before we've even read the play?'

'It was just very preliminary,' I say, 'to help me with the writing process. I've hit a bit of a block.' I don't tell him I'm disgusted with myself and will never pick up a pen again.

'I've heard reports that you discussed nudity.'

'Only in the abstract, to help with character development.'

He pops a couple of Tic Tacs and fondles his beard. 'Mr. Huff and I,' he warns, 'cannot offer our full endorsement until we read the play.'

'I understand,' I say. I don't tell him I don't give a goose's turd about him or Huff or my grades. All I want is Kadylak running through fields of buttercups.

I scram to the library so the maladjusted can't ask me if they got a part.

'You must read *Clarissa* by Samuel Richardson,' Mrs. Wartowski tells me. 'He invented the psychological novel, predates Austen.' I don't want to make her cry by asking if it's about some girl pining for some guy so I just take the book and start reading. Of course it's about a virgin everybody wants to deflower. Because Clarissa's dutiful, her grandfather leaves her all his cash and property, which puts her evil siblings' noses out of joint, not to mention her nasty parents and uncle. Being dutiful and all that, Clarissa signs her cash and property over to padre. Well, the next thing you know, he's trying to marry her off to some congenital idiot who's also got cash and property. Meanwhile her sister Bella's been getting hot and heavy with a no-good rake named Lovelace. Clarissa's been watching these goings-ons and fancies him. She starts penning him amorous letters. Old Lovelace drops Bella so he can pursue this pious, chaste virgin. Stealing her virginity becomes his obsession. You have to wonder how we went from preserving our virginity at all costs to offering it to any scuzzbag just to get it over with. Nobody wants to be caught dead being a virgin these days. A hundred years ago, if you lost your hymen you pretty much *were* dead. Lovelace writes to his pal Jack about how he's going to do Clarissa, how he despises her piety and self-importance. Meanwhile he's penning her fake love letters. The whole novel is written in letters, which I guess is what's so psychological about it. So old Clarissa, on the run from her evil family and the congenital idiot, falls for Lovelace's lies about setting her up with a pious lady in London. The pious lady turns out to be the madam of a brothel, and old Lovelace is in the next room, clawing at Clarissa's door.

If I phone the hospital they won't tell me anything.

Old Swails is blaming Queen Isabella of Castile for the Spanish Inquisition.

'Excuse me,' I say, 'it wasn't like Ferdinand had nothing to do with it.'

'Ferdinand was King Consort,' Swails says. 'Isabella was the ruler.'

'He was as rabid a Christian as she was. There wouldn't have been a Holy War if it weren't for Ferdinand.'

'What brings you to that conclusion?' he says, switching to Prince Charles mode.

'Women didn't lead troops.'

'*She* planned the campaigns.'

'Yeah, but only Ferdinand was dumb enough to carry them out when they were short of cash. Genocide costs money. The Christians had blown entire kingdoms on trying to eliminate the Muslims and the Jews for centuries.'

'How does this make Ferdinand responsible for the Inquisition?'

'He was chomping at the bit even though Isabella said, "Whoa, boy, we're broke." She was supposed to get some cash when she married the creepy old King of Portugal. But King Enrique III, her sleazebag half-brother, found out she'd secretly married Ferdinand and went ballistic. He took away all the towns that were her only source of income. You'd think that would have cooled his jets but Ferdinand went on a killing rampage anyway.' This, of course, brings to mind Clarissa's situation when she refuses to marry the congenital idiot. Her father disowns her, leaving her destitute. All through history girls have been forced to marry hideous men or be left with nothing.

'Don't forget,' I say, 'Isabella was the one who sponsored Columbus. She must have had some smarts, even if she was a Jesus freak.' I have to admit, she's not on Drew's Extraordinary Women shelf, probably because of all that Inquisition torturing and murdering.

'Can we talk about something else?' Kirsten asks. 'This is like, totally depressing.'

'What do *you* want to talk about?' I ask her.

She twirls her hair, thinking hard. 'I don't see why history has to be about people killing everybody all the time.'

'What should it be about?'

'Art, and I mean, like, palaces and stuff.'

'They had to kill people to pay for art and palaces and stuff,' I explain. 'Henry VIII attacked all the monasteries so he could top up his treasury. His soldiers were raping nuns.'

'Could we stay inside one century for once?' Swails asks me. 'Last time I looked we were discussing the fifteenth.' He hates the way I jump around.

'It's all the same stuff,' I say.

I'm pretty sure old Swails is a wife-beater.

'I asked for extra butter,' I say. The attitudinal Muslim server sneers at me and I want to throw a burqa over him, see how he likes it. How are you supposed to tell all those covered women

124

apart? I read somewhere that Afghani kids cling to their mothers because if they lose sight of them they'll start chasing after some other covered woman. You've got zip peripheral vision in a burqa. The women are constantly tripping in the bombed-out streets. Plus they get headaches and chronic neck pain from the weight of the fabric.

I phoned Connie Sheep's Ass, got her voice mail. She sounds like a putz. I didn't leave a message.

'Did you study for Swails' test?' Tora asks me. She, of course, is studying.

'Negative.'

'So you don't know who Catherine of Aragon's parents were?'

'Isabella and Ferdinand.'

You have to wonder why the Muslims and the Jews, since they've both been persecuted forever, can't get it together to form an alliance and blast the Christians. If they bombed the Christians instead of each other, they could take over the world. The way I see it, Christians have been top dog way too long. Old Isabella was only obsessed with discovering the Americas because she wanted to convert the pagans to Christianity. If you think about it, all Christians have ever done is invade, spread disease and exploit people and resources. Marco Polo was different, of course, hanging out with the Mongols, learning their language. He even started bathing regularly instead of stinking up the place. He couldn't get over how Kublai Khan let religions coexist, didn't run around slaughtering people if they didn't believe in *his* god. Nobody was starving in China and the roads were paved with stones. No wonder old Marco didn't return to muddy, bug-infested Europe for twenty-five years.

I phoned Connie Sheep's Ass because I was feeling guilty about ignoring her after reading about that Jewish writer going up the chimney and her daughter carrying her papers around for sixty years. I'll get over it.

Rossi swoops to our table. 'They're Twittering that I'm having sex with Babineaux.'

'*Are* you having sex with Babs?' Tora asks.

'No way.'

'You seemed interested.'

'Particularly in his ambidexterity,' I add.

'I wasn't serious.' Rossi starts nibbling on a Boston Cream she'll puke up later.

'So, just ignore it,' I say. Cyber-bullying is pretty common. People make up all kinds of stuff.

'It could get him into trouble,' Rossi says. 'Remember when Kirsten got everybody to agree online that Ms. Egan molested her?'

Ms. Egan was gay and gave Kirsten lousy marks and sent her to the office whenever she was late, which was all the time. You don't do this to a queen bee. Even with the allegations unproven, Ms. Egan's career took a dive. There's no question Kirsten has leadership skills.

'Why don't you stop reading what she's writing about you?' I suggest.

'Because it's there. Everybody's reading it.'

'Not I,' Tora says.

'Nobody cares, Ross. You've got this idea that people give a shit. They don't. They don't even give a shit about Kirsten. They trail her because it's easy, it means they don't have to think.'

Before she became a boy toy, Rossi was an artist. Her favourite painter was David Milne and she tried to paint like him with lots of specks of colour. He did a painting the night his son was born that had huge snowflakes in it. Rossi went wild over the painting because she said it breathed joy. She said Milne was always trying to breathe paint onto paper. I got her a book on Milne, which I read since she just looked at the pictures. Old David never recovered from the carnage he saw during World War I. He was commissioned by the Brits to paint what he saw, charred bodies on tanks and all that. When he came back he moved to a cabin by some lake and never talked to anybody, only his wife and kid in the summer. He said you have to make your own small world perfect in an imperfect one. Even though he had to crap in the woods and haul water and eat fried eggs and potatoes every single day, the cabin was his perfect world.

'I hope this means you're not going to Nicole's party,' I say.

'Why wouldn't I?' Rossi demands.

'Because they're spreading lies about you!' I almost shout.

'And they've all seen your twat,' Tora adds.

'Don't use that word, that is a *disgusting* word.'

'Okay, so they've all seen your vagina.'

'Shout about it, why don't you.'

'Seriously, Ross,' I say, 'I think you want to go for damage control here.'

'If I don't show up, they win.'

'Win what?' Tora asks. 'A trip to Vegas?'

'I have my dignity,' Rossi says.

'*What* dignity?' I immediately regret saying this because the daycare kid I used to know shows up on Rossi's face. 'I mean,' I backpedal, 'dignity is something you feel yourself. It doesn't matter what other people think.'

'*You* care about what other people think. That's why you wrote the play.'

I gobble the last of my Sour Cream Glazed. 'I didn't write it.'

'What do you mean you didn't write it?'

'I quit.'

She looks as though somebody's just died. 'They all think you've written it.'

'Won't they be surprised.'

'You got them to do all that stuff to audition and there's no play? They're going to be like, totally pissed off.'

'So don't tell them. I'm not telling them.'

'What about Huff and Lund?' Tora asks.

'What about them? They just want me to do the work so they can punch out on time.'

Tora stares at me, looking like the shrink she's going to be once Creative Writing goes bust. 'You're planning to drop out, aren't you?'

'It's a possibility.'

A few weeks ago I asked Rossi why she doesn't paint anymore. She said, 'What for?'

'For yourself. Milne did it for himself. The most he ever got for a painting was five hundred bucks. Everybody was chasing the Group of Seven, they didn't give a rat's fart about Milne.'

'I'm no David Milne,' she said and I wanted to shout, how do you know unless you work at it, work at *something* besides getting butt-scratchers to notice you? But I knew I wasn't exactly a great example of a hard worker.

'Kirsten's going to murder you,' she says.

'Tell her to make it quick.'

Naturally there would be a lockdown on the day I want to leave early to check on Kadylak. Some borderline cases started brawling. The cops say it wasn't gang-related, just some boys doing the payback thing. A bystander tried to intervene and got knifed. We were slipping on his blood in the hall. I had to keep reminding myself it was real. We're not allowed to leave the classroom. It stinks of vomit, thanks to one of the concussed girl jocks. Everyone was hysterical at first, yammering on cells to anybody who'd listen, including the press, acting like it would be a miracle if we made it out alive. After calling the TV stations they called their mothers. Nicole keeps coughing and snotting in my direction. Which gets me thinking about the Black Death killing Alfonso. Isabella was next in line for the throne unless Enrique managed to snuff her. You have to wonder about all those royals smoking their siblings. Elizabeth I never named a successor because she knew it would mean the successor, or the successor's backers, would plot to kill her. Same with a husband. She figured once she'd popped a child, the husband would off her so the kid could rule under Daddy's control. What's so great about control is what I'd like to know. Why can't we LEAVE EACH OTHER ALONE?

Mrs. Freeman keeps trying to quiet the class by holding her finger against her lips and saying *sshhh*. Nobody pays any attention. Some of the simpletons are playing Monopoly, most of them are gaming on their cells or plugged into iPods. Mrs.

Freeman, clearly agitated, keeps sitting down and standing up and peering through the window on the door. She tries to get a discussion going about the American soldier who's hiding out in B.C. because he doesn't want to go back to Iraq and kill innocent people and get blown up. Nobody's too interested. 'I think it's great,' I say over the racket. 'It's not like he doesn't know what he's talking about, he was there, saw all those kids getting their hands and feet blown off.'

'But he enlisted,' Megan, the former mute, insists. 'He has to follow orders.' There's no question she's been taking SSRIs. People get aggressive on them, start spouting opinions all over the place.

'If a few thousand soldiers had stopped following orders,' I say, 'maybe there wouldn't have been a Holocaust. Soldiers are supposed to have morals and all that. They're not machines. He thinks it's an unjust war.'

'He signed a contract,' Megan says.

'So did Hitler. A piece of paper means squat.'

'I fucking got Park Place!' one of the Monopoly stooges shouts.

'Fuck you, man,' shouts another, 'I got fucking Boardwalk.'

The cheerleaders watch the coverage of our school on their cells. There are cruisers flashing and a crowd of parents waiting for their bundles of joy to escape certain death. Mrs. Freeman looks ready to pass out. She had a Black Panther boyfriend once who got shot in the face and took six days to die. Kirsten's overfed mother is on TV, wearing pounds of makeup, saying how worried she is about Kirsten. 'If the school's not safe, what is?' she demands.

I keep reading. Old Lovelace takes Clarissa to the opera. She gets all dreamy and says it's the happiest day since she left her father's house. She didn't seem too happy in her father's house so I don't know what she's on about. Lovelace escorts her to her bedroom and seizes the moment to disrobe her. She fights him off and he says she's trying his patience. He offers to marry her which is a ruse to get her in the sack. He's even got a fake licence.

So just when she thought Lovelace was cultured and sensitive, poor old Clarissa discovers that he's your regular sex maniac.

A cop struts in and stomps around in his bulletproof vest, checking us out. He takes a couple of butt-scratchers into the hall for questioning. Nicole coughs and snorts. I figure the Black Death is on the rebound with all those antibiotic-defying mutant bacteria. In the old days they shut down the towns, didn't let anyone in or out. Old Isabella was cut off from her mother again. You have to wonder about all those motherless queens. Just like elephants growing up motherless, they turned nasty. Maybe *I'm* turning nasty. I sure don't care who got knifed or if they're dead. I'm sick of boys with weapons. Join the military. Do the payback thing with a suicide bomber. Take a vacation in sunny Uganda.

18

I can tell from the way the nurses are huddled that something's up. I hoof it to Kadylak's room but of course she's not there. My legs wobble as I hover by the nursing station. As usual it takes them about an hour to notice me. Brenda looks up as though she's surprised I'm there.

'Is Kadylak okay?' I ask.

'She's still in ICU. We have a new patient for you to keep an eye on. He keeps pulling out his IV and scratching at his sutures.'

I follow her down the hall, past Kadylak's room. 'Is she still on the ventilator?'

'I don't know the details,' Brenda snips, pushing open a door and pointing to a crib. 'This is Bradley. He's eighteen months. He had a malignant tumour the size of an orange in his abdomen. It's important that he doesn't pull out his IV.' This must be why the nurses were huddled. You don't see a baby with an orange-sized malignant tumour too often. 'His parents should be back shortly. They're exhausted. I told them to grab a bite.' She marches off into the next tragedy.

I see evidence of the parents on the sofa bed: a pop novel, an Evian bottle, a hairbrush and a copy of *Sports Illustrated*. Was Dad really able to read about golf while they were cutting into Bradley? Or was it a cover because Mom was unable to converse or stand straight for more than two minutes? I've seen this before, the husband trying to keep it together while the wife flails, or vice versa. It doesn't last long. After a week or so the demands of the living take over and they start spending less time with the kid.

Bradley doesn't look too good. No doubt he hasn't eaten since the surgery and babies drop weight fast. His eyes are barely open but his little hand is working at the IV. I gently pull it away and hang on to it. He doesn't understand what's going on, and nobody can explain it to him. I'd like to tell him to pack it in because there's no way he's going to make it and the treatment's going to be brutal. He's murmuring something and I lean over to try to hear it, hoping he has secret knowledge. There must be some reason a kid this young gets blasted by cancer. Don't they say the wisest souls live the shortest lives? It's the rest of us, thrashing around year after year, who are the slow learners.

Speaking of slow learners, it was quite the scene exiting the school with all those hysterical parents about. Kirsten and Nicole painted up and headed straight for the cameras. Kirsten's mother squeezed her greasy mug in there again too. It was one big reality-show reunion. Coombs, super-jock phys. ed. teacher, started holding forth, flexing muscle, while Brimmers did PR damage control. I looked around to ascertain that Drew wasn't about. I'd thought maybe news of bloodshed would have lured her out. Mrs. Barnfield had hightailed it to the school, was clinging to Rossi, kissing her over and over and stroking her hair while tears dripped on her name tag. It's hard to think of her as 'Marg.' Marg has no idea that her baby's pink shots are being broadcast world-wide. She has no idea her baby spreads her legs for anything that walks. I want to protect Marg from the inevitable awakening. When she saw me, she started hugging and kissing me too. She smelled of those expensive medications she takes for her stomach. It was nice to be hugged.

Bradley's parents return in a spat.

'Who are you?' Mrs. Bradley demands.

'A volunteer.'

She stares at my hand holding Bradley's.

'The nurse wanted me to keep an eye on him while you grabbed a bite. He keeps trying to pull out his IV.' I want to feel sorry for these people but they have vicious faces, although they're probably just scared. Scared people turn vicious. Which is what's going to happen to the six billion of us when the oil runs out.

Mr. Bradley sits on the sofa and snatches the *Sports Illustrated*. Mrs. Bradley takes Bradley's hand from mine. 'That will be all, thank you,' she says, like I'm her servant.

'I'll be around if you need a break,' I say.

'Thank you,' she says without meaning it. To her I'm just another clueless teen, not worthy of Bradley, and she's probably right. What she doesn't know is that when she gets tired of holding his hand, when it gets too frightening for her, when he starts to look emaciated, when it's time to get her roots touched up, I'll be doing the hand holding. I can hear the Bradleys bickering through the wall. This can't be good for Bradley. I consider charging in there and telling them to zip it, but this would guarantee my expulsion from the floor. You have to wonder if Bradley's yanking at his IV because he can't stand listening to his parents squabble.

I play Crazy Eights with Molly whose father hasn't shown up. He bought her a BlackBerry and always lets her know when he's going to be late, which is all the time. When he phones he tells her he loves her and she always says, 'I love you too, Dad,' like she's on automatic. Her mother flies all over the place selling computer widgets. She texts Molly from airports and taxis.

Molly keeps changing the rules of Crazy Eights. I let it pass because she's a seriously poor loser and I don't have the energy to deal with her sulking. Wackoboy joins in with his version of the rules.

'That's cheating!' Molly shouts.

'It is not!'

'It is too!'

I redirect them to the computer games. Within seconds they're totally focused on the screens. No wonder the corporations want us hooked on media gadgets. It keeps us quiet. I dig around in my backpack for something to read and of course pull out *Tilly*, which stops me breathing because I don't want to touch it if Kadylak's going to die. I see her face all happy at the beginning when Tilly was cheerily collecting firewood. I want to see her like that again but I know the novel's going to take us dangerous places before we end up with a wedding. This can't be good for Kadylak. Especially after she's been blasted by the ventilator. I dig around for *Clarissa*. Old Lovelace convinces a couple of whores to dress up like his 'dear aunt' and 'cousin.' They talk with tony accents and call Clarissa *my dear*. They kiss her cheek and pat her hand and Clarissa believes them when they say they've come to look after her. They dope her tea and Lovelace gets her in the sack. The whores pin her down while Lovelace rapes her.

'Can we have freezies?' Wackoboy asks.

'Sure.' On my way to the kitchen I listen outside Bradley's room. It's morgue quiet in there. I push the door open slightly to make sure they're still around. Hubby's asleep but the missus looks at me. If she were a cat, she would hiss. I close the door.

I wish Mr. Paluska was here. I used to think I looked forward to his arrival because of what happens to Kadylak when she sees him, but now I'm thinking it has to do with what happens to me. Just like all those heroines, I'm pining for some guy. Only my hero's married and hardly speaks English.

I pick two freezies the same flavour so they can't argue. I hand them over then cruise the unit. Scientists are saying all the crap in the environment is showing up in umbilical-cord blood. They say they can tell from looking at the blood if the child's likely to get cancer. So this whole idea of the baby being protected by the placenta is bogus. The mother can eat right, but if she's breathing she's going to poison her kid.

The nurses are talking about some Iranian who set himself on fire in a Tim Hortons toilet.

'His wife left him,' Brenda says. 'Took the kids.'

'But why Tim Hortons?' brainless Nancy asks.

'Why not?' I say. 'It's contained. He knew the fire wouldn't spread. Plus he wanted to make news. If you want press, you've got to go public.' They look at me with who-asked-you? expressions. The Iranian's wife must have heard about it by now. She'll probably be disgraced, stoned in the streets for forcing her husband to set himself on fire.

'I guess people won't be lining up for Timbits for a couple of days,' I say. 'It won't last, though. They've got to get their sugar fix.'

I don't know why the nurses don't like me. Overall I think I behave pretty well at the hospital. Peggy, who's obese and has rheumatoid arthritis, talks to me about her cats. She moves really slowly because of her fat and all the pain in her joints so I help her carry stuff. Anyway, she's not on tonight and, without Kadylak or Mr. Paluska, it's pretty much a desert in here. If I knew how to cry I probably would, but I haven't cried since Alice, my hamster, died.

Back in the playroom Wackoboy and Molly are fighting over which DVD to watch. I do Eeny Meeny Miny Moe to settle it. In seconds they're absorbed in some Disney crap. Old Clarissa's in seriously bad shape after being raped and all that. She manages to escape the whorehouse and take refuge in a church, but a copper nabs her as she's leaving. It turns out the madam at the brothel is charging her for not paying rent. So old Clarissa ends up in debtor's prison. She keeps writing letters, though. And praying.

'There you are,' Treeboy says, blinking in the fluorescent lighting. He looks too woodsy for these pastel walls. 'We've been looking for you.'

'Who?'

'Drew and me.'

'You mean Drew left the house?'

'No, but she's been calling around.'

'Well, you found me.'

'Could you come home?'

'Why?'

'Because she wants to see you.'

'Why?'

'Because she's worried about you.'

'Just call her and tell her I'm alright.'

He sits on one of the kiddy chairs, meaning his knees are up around his ears. 'I'll wait for you.'

'I'm not leaving.'

'Okay.' He'll sit there for hours like some kind of spider. One thing about tree sitters, they're in no hurry.

Molly drags her IV over to him. 'Are you Lemon's boyfriend?'

'I'm her friend and I'm a boy.'

'She's gross. You'd have to be totally desperate to be her boyfriend.'

'I am totally desperate,' Vaughn says.

'Why?'

'Don't like the way things are going.'

'What things?'

'Most things. How are things going with you?'

'I've got cancer.'

'What's that like?' I can see she's a little uncomfortable under his tree-frog stare, which is unusual for Princess Molly.

'Nobody likes you when you've got cancer,' she says.

'Why not?'

'You smell bad and sometimes you barf. And you never know when you're going to have to go to the hospital again so nobody wants to be your friend.'

'Why not?'

'Because you might die, stupid.'

'We're all dying.'

'Not right away.'

'*You're* not dying right away, are you? Do you want to play checkers?'

I leave them to do the rounds. Most of the kids are unconscious or watching TV. A few parents skulk about. The younger children can never understand why their parents don't take them home. It wrecks the parents every time the kid asks. They stop asking after a while.

I untangle the lines of a sleeping teen who reminds me of Faith who died of septic shock after a nipple piercing. Drew called a school assembly in her honour and everybody pretended they gave a buzzard's ass when the fact is Faith was low on the pecking order, Kirsten's errand girl. In elementary school Faith was the only person who didn't say it was retarded when I galloped around on my imaginary horse. I even told her my horse's name, Feodora, and colour, palamino. Faith imagined her own silver horse and called it Star. She galloped around with Feodora and me for about five minutes before she decided it was boring. She hitched Star to a parking sign and went chasing after the popular girls. Even then they were sending her on errands, telling her to give notes to so-and-so, or tell so-and-so 'she's not my best friend anymore.' Faith sometimes made it to best friend for a day but it never lasted. Anyway, you have to wonder about the nipple piercing, if she did it because Kirsten told her to. Or because she thought it might turn on some yokel. Anyway, she's dead and forgotten. Except to her parents who must wonder how their beloved daughter could die from a nipple piercing. Unless, of course, she was driving them nuts. Dead, she can shrink back into the baby pictures, be forever adorable and free of piercings.

No action coming from Bradley's room. I push open the door a crack even though I know it will piss off the missus. She's unconscious on the armchair while old Bradley's working on his IV again. I gently take his hand and wrap it around a teething ring.

Vaughn and the two kids are kneeling on the floor. At first I think they're praying but then Wackoboy shouts, 'Bug!'

'What kind of bug?' I ask.

'Tiny,' Molly says.

I kneel beside them and see nothing except specks in the linoleum until Molly points out the bug. It's less than crumb-sized, grey with white spots. It's slowly, deliberately working its way around some building blocks. 'How does it think it's going to get out of here?' I ask.

'Bugs don't think,' Wackoboy declares.

'Wrong again, son,' I say. 'Ants have bigger brains in propor-tion to body size than humans. I bet this bug has a humongous brain.'

We watch it heading in one direction then being obstructed by a block and changing tactics.

'It keeps going,' Vaughn says. 'It'll keep going until it can't go anymore.'

'Then what?' Molly asks.

'It'll die.'

'I don't want it to *die!*' she blurts with more emotion than I've ever heard from her.

'We'll take it outside,' Vaughn says. 'Set it free.'

'The windows don't open,' I point out.

He finds a piece of scrap paper and waits patiently for the bug to crawl on it. He cups his hand around the paper and the bug and heads for the elevator. The kids scramble after him, dragging their poles, keeping their eyes on the bug. If Vaughn hadn't been here, they probably would have stomped on it.

'I shall return,' he says, winking at me as the elevator doors close.

'Talk to me,' he says. We're sitting in Tim Hortons, hoping for a fire. Beside us are two forty-something men who think they're sex gods. They check out every woman in the joint. 'So this bank teller,' the paunchier one says, 'asked me to go for a coffee.'

'You're kidding,' the other Adonis responds. 'She asked you for a coffee? Really? That's awesome.'

'Why?'

'That's the first step, I mean *coffee*, that's like the first move. After that, I mean, not that day but next time it's like, *showtime*.' Both sex gods are wearing leather bomber jackets to hide their Molson tumours.

Vaughn's still staring at me. He can stare all he wants. I snuck into ICU. She didn't even look like Kadylak. Illness wipes out personality. You're just more diseased flesh. One of the Holocaust memoirs I read said that when you're dying of starvation, nothing matters except the next piece of bread. You don't even see the corpses around you, you step on them, chasing that next piece of bread. Cancer's like that. After a certain point nobody sees you anymore.

'How's your friend?' Vaughn asks.

'What friend?'

'At the hospital. Drew says there's a girl there who calls you.'

'She's in ICU.'

'I'm sorry,' he says and he actually looks it. Most people say *sorry* while they're thinking about what movie they're going to rent or something.

'What'd she look like?' the sex god who wasn't invited out for coffee asks.

'Brown hair, five-nine, which is short for me.'

'You're kidding? Five-nine is short for you?'

'She was all over me. Must've seen those cheques rolling in.'

'Let's go,' I say. We walk home and, I have to admit it's alright having a man around. You breathe easier and don't jump at every sound. Maybe women put up with crap from men because they want bodyguards. I'd like to get in touch with that bank teller, warn her that next time is Showtime.

Drew jumps up when she sees me. 'I've been so worried,' she says. She hugs me which is completely weird since we don't hug. We're all jutting bones, jabbing each other.

'It was pretty lame,' I say. 'No Columbine.'

'Thank God for that,' she says, which is pretty outrageous considering she's an atheist. 'Do you want some tea or hot chocolate or anything?'

'I'm pretty whacked.' I'm not up for sitting around being thankful that I'm alive. Kadylak's dying and I can do shit about it.

19

No one's returning my calls to the hospital. I could go down there again but Brenda, the catfish, will probably boot me out. Volunteers aren't supposed to get involved with the patients. I turn on the radio. Some fashion columnist is talking about what a crime it is that manufacturers produce knock-offs of designer clothes. You can buy a knock-off of an Yves Saint Laurent fourteen-thousand-dollar jacket for two hundred bucks. 'It's a *crime*,' she keeps repeating. I want to be this woman, sweating about knock-offs and this season's skirt lengths. She says everybody's wearing wide belts – *everybody* – and fitted jackets with frayed edges. She describes a 'fabulous skirt' she's planning to buy after the show. She talks as though this will be an accomplishment. Two seconds later some weary aid worker comes on to discuss impoverished women in India shoving wood and anything else they can find up their vaginas to plug their menstrual bleeding. If they're lucky enough to get work as labourers, they don't drink or eat all day because they can't shit or piss in front of the men. So they get urinary-tract and bladder infections and there are no antibiotics to treat them. 'Women die from these easily treatable diseases,' the aid worker says. Meanwhile drug companies are raking in the dough. You'd think a couple of global corporations could spare a few million Kotex and a few million cheap pills. But hey, I shouldn't be thinking about this. I should be shopping for a fabulous skirt.

Clarissa's writing letters to her parents to beg for forgiveness. You have to wonder what kind of sick puppy Samuel Richardson was, writing a heroine who spends 24/7 praying or begging forgiveness from her abusers. Although I guess that's pretty standard, the persecuted seeking approval from their persecutors. All those

Jews obeying the Germans, trying to please the borderliners so they wouldn't plug them with bullets. In one Holocaust memoir this baby, whose parents were plugged with bullets, was hidden by goy Poles. She was taken to the Poles' flooded basement. Waist-deep in sludge, the Pole's son held her to his chest. Years later he told her that his parents had instructed him to drown her in the sludge if she cried because if the Nazis found out the goys were hiding a Jew, they'd all be killed. She didn't cry and they took her to a convent where she lived till the war was over. Grown up and supposedly recovered in Canada, she couldn't remember anything about the convent or what had happened to her parents. Her daughter became a psychologist and took her mother back to Poland to the convent. It turned out a ninety-four-year-old nun remembered the woman as a child and had never stopped loving her or thinking about her in sixty-something years. The psychologist figured that her mother had been able to survive the horror of the war because she'd been loved unconditionally by the nun. Even though she'd blocked the nun out with all her other war trauma, the security that love produces stayed with her. After she'd been reunited with the nun and her childhood, she stopped having nightmares about the war. You have to wonder if all children were loved, I mean *really* loved not just owned, controlled, spoiled and gloated over, we'd have a better world.

It's party day. I'd pass but I'm worried about Rossi. I watch her apply five pounds of makeup. Mrs. Barnfield's constipated again and spending six hours on the toilet, which creates tensions over bathroom usage.

'George II *died* trying to force a crap,' I whisper to Rossi. 'Seriously, I'm worried about her. It's not healthy. And anyway, why's she trying to poop when she's hardly eating?'

Rossi doesn't respond, has that lean and hungry look she gets after she's been making herself puke. She's trying on toddler clothes. 'Do I look fat? Honestly, do these jeans make my ass look fat?'

'Try a wide belt and a frayed jacket,' I suggest. '*Everybody* is wearing them this season.'

Mrs. Barnfield exits the washroom looking less tense, which is a good sign. Plus she starts cleaning her kitchen cabinets. She's one of those types who takes everything out and actually wipes the shelves. 'You look beautiful, angel,' she says to Rossi. She's always telling Ross how great she looks. I get the feeling she loves her unconditionally, which makes it hard to understand why Rossi is so messed up. Unless it has to do with her dad being a video poker addict and all that. He was never around, which might explain Rossi's need to get attention from anything with a penis.

Mrs. Barnfield's all excited because Rossi got invited to a party finally. 'I used to *love* parties,' she says. 'I was a real party girl.'

'Were you into disco?' I ask.

'You bet. You should've seen me in my platform shoes.'

Rossi turns her back on her mother and sticks out her tongue like she's gagging.

'What colour were they?' I ask.

'Hot pink,' Mrs. Barnfield says. 'With gold stars on the platforms.'

'Wow,' I say. 'They'd be worth serious coin these days, I bet.' I like Mrs. Barnfield and can't figure out why Rossi's so mean to her all the time.

'We wore halters and bell-bottoms and sweated like pigs,' Mrs. Barnfield says.

'Pigs don't sweat,' Rossi says.

'And we drank sodas,' Mrs. Barnfield says. 'And maybe a little rum and Coke but *no* drugs. Don't do drugs tonight, angel, okay? No E, isn't that what they're all doing? A girl had a heart attack taking E.'

Rossi leans into the bathroom mirror to line her lips.

'You look absolutely gorgeous, honey. Do you need some money? Take a cab home, okay?' This is another thing that blows my mind about Mrs. Barnfield, she's always forcing cash on Rossi. Even when we were little and I was getting fifty cents a week, old Ross was walking around with a wad. 'Do you know this boy she's going with?' Mrs. Barnfield asks me.

'Doyle? Yeah.'

'Is he nice?'

'He's alright.'

'He wasn't one of the boys responsible for the lockdown?'

'Nope. I work with him at Dairy Dream.'

'Oh really? He's got a job then, that's nice.'

'His dad's a dentist.'

'Really?' Mrs. Barnfield's eyes go all dreamy as she works out the daughter-married-to-dentist fantasy, the big house, the Mercs, the grandkiddies. Poor Mrs. Barnfield. 'Well, I won't wait up,' she says. 'I know you're a big girl now but please, angel, don't be too late. Give me a smooch.' Rossi allows her mother to kiss her cheek before she takes her cash.

Doyle's not too happy to see me. 'What's *she* doing here?'

I lounge in the back seat. He just got his licence and drives around for hours in his dad's guzzler.

'She was invited,' Rossi says. 'We might as well give her a ride.'

'You've done something different with your hair,' I tell him. He ignores me, plays gangsta rap, bopping to the beat. I'm thinking about my depression because that's got to be what this is. Some psychologist is saying that King Harold was depressed *before* he lost the battle of Hastings to William, the Norman invader. They're saying being branded a heretic by Rome depressed Harold. He supposedly suffered intense feelings of guilt and loss, which was why he sucked as a leader. *I'm* suffering intense feelings of guilt and loss about everything – Kadylak, Mr. Paluska, my mothers. I even feel badly about duping Lund and Huff, and about not giving a goose's turd about anything that's going on around me. You're supposed to care about stuff in your immediate vicinity but I'm sitting around worrying about girls from Thailand being sold as cash crops, being shipped in airless containers to New York brothels. I worry about women being burned because their dowry money isn't enough, or because some hothead husband decides they've been unfaithful, or getting stoned to death for not wearing a burqa. But boys killing boys in my neighbourhood? A knifing in the school that's got everybody in a flap? It happens.

Speaking of consumer goods, Nicole's house is full them. Doyle and Rossi lose me ASAP. I go for a whiz, spend some time examining the bidet, making the water squirt. Maybe it feels good having water squirt up inside you, maybe Nicole and her ma get off on it. I consider trying it but somebody's pounding at the door. I go look for food, eat some pizza and tacos. Nobody notices me, which is good. I lean against the wall and watch the ritual. Girls run their fingers through their hair, boys ogle. Girls gossip and slander and say *like* every second word. Boys talk tough, say *like* every second word and *fucking* every three seconds. Beside me some wizards are talking about sports, how some fucking team is losing all its fucking players. 'It's a fucking tragedy,' the shaggy-haired one says. Another genius can't decide whether or not to buy the new Nintendo, 'Like, what if the fucking thing goes on sale? Last game I bought, the fuckers put it on sale like, the day after. Fucking rip-off.'

One of the artsy-crowd queers is saying, 'Let's go get matching sweaters,' in a squeaky voice to anyone who'll listen. He's one of those types who survives by acting brain-damaged. He only gets invited because he provides freak-show entertainment.

I eat more tacos, wishing I'd brought a book. The music's slamming my brain around, making me think about George Eliot putting leeches on her head to get rid of headaches. It's hard to imagine old Marian, her real name, reaching into a jar and grabbing the bloodsuckers then plastering them on her forehead. Meanwhile she was writing about all those beautiful pining heroines. Old Marian hooked up with a couple of serious dweezles in her own love search. You have to wonder if it was because her mother liked her pretty sister better, and of course her brother who was numero uno and could do no wrong. Not only was Marian ugly but she didn't go to church. When her mother died Marian felt so guilty she started going to church with her father and wiping his snot till he kicked off. Then there was nobody to love her, which is why she went after putzes. Finally she found a guy who was as ugly as she was but he was already married. He told her she was brilliant and hid the crappy reviews from her. He decided he couldn't live without her so he left the wife and kiddies and shacked up with Marian. A lot of people weren't too happy about this, especially the gentry types who'd freaked when they found out George Eliot was a woman. If she'd been a nice little church-going Victorian lady, they might have been able to handle it but there was old Marian, living in sin and refusing to go to fancy dress balls.

'Have you seen Rossi?' Doyle asks.

'I thought she was with you.'

'So did I.' He frowns into the crowd. 'They're all looking at her on Jake's cell. Maybe she took off.'

'Are you worried about her?'

'Shit, no, I hardly know her.'

'Did you bump uglies yet?'

'What?'

'Isn't that why you brought her? To get into her thong?'

'You are so bitter.' He grabs some Cheezees and merges with the dancers.

Queen Kirsten and King Jake start swapping spit on the couch and everybody else partners up. I look for Rossi, squeeze past overheated bodies, beer cans and cigarettes, spot Larry Bone and his junkies huddled over a coffee table snorting powder. Taylor in the dog collar grabs my ass but I keep moving. I see girls pushed up against the walls and I try to figure out if they're enjoying it. They probably don't know, have been faking it so long they're not even inside their bodies. Maybe it's like that for the boys as well. They're scared shitless they won't be able to get it up so they rush the process just so they can announce they fucked somebody. I push open sliding doors and step onto the deck.

Butt-scratchers crowd around the gazebo, whooping and hollering. I sprawl on a lawn chair and look for stars. It's always a challenge in the city, but sometimes I can spot the Dippers. On camping trips Drew used to show me constellations but I've forgotten most of them. She pointed out the North Star at the end of the Little Dipper's handle and said it led slaves to freedom. When I asked her what happened on cloudy nights, she said some of them were given compasses by abolitionists. Alexander Ross posed as a birdwatcher so he could hang around plantations and guide slaves north. It's nice to know there were whiteys risking their lives to help slaves. Levi Coffin got them into boats so they could cross Lake Erie. I think about this when I get really depressed about white people. But then, of course, escaped slaves weren't exactly welcomed in Canada. If they got work at all, they were paid shit wages and their kids weren't allowed in white schools. Yep, nobody was too excited about all those darkies comin' to town.

Somebody starts shrieking down around the gazebo. It's customary for ditzes to screech at parties so I don't sweat it. I smell weed and notice a few saggy asses passing around a blunt. Some wizard says, 'Harsh toke, dude.' I think about old Clarissa writing letters in prison. Lovelace tries to visit her but his former pal, Jack, scares him off with his sword. He tells Lovelace if he tries to approach Clarissa again, he'll skewer him. I figure Clarissa and Jack will get hitched, although she's stopped eating, which could present a problem. She's still begging for her father's forgiveness.

I stare at the sliver of a moon and try to believe that Kadylak's off the ventilator, sitting up in bed sucking on a freezie, that Mr. Paluska is massaging her feet.

The screaming gets a little scarier. I'm thinking maybe I should call 911. Best not to get involved. I grab more pretzels, suck the salt off them. The stink of pot is making me queasy and the music's getting louder. Soon the neighbours will call the cops who won't show up. The screaming stops and after a while the crowd leaves the gazebo so I figure I'll go chill in there, it's screened, which means no bugs. It's pretty dark but I sit on one of those built-in benches and return to my Kadylak fantasy. I watch Mr. Paluska's muscles again, imagine touching them, feeling them around me. My eyes adjust to the dark and I notice a heap of something in the corner. I figure it's a pile of canvas or something but then it starts to move and I jump about six feet thinking it's hiding a giant rat that's about to claw me to death. It stops moving and I decide the second-hand weed smoke is making me hallucinate. After a couple of minutes of serious staring, I realize it's a body. I get ready to bounce out of there but then the body starts making wounded noises. 'Are you alright?' I ask it. It doesn't answer so I move a little closer. It's a woman and she's naked. 'What happened?' I ask. She's in a fetal position with her hands over her head. I recognize her perfume.

'Don't let anybody in,' Rossi whimpers.

'What happened?'

'They took my clothes.'

'Who did?'

'Don't leave me, okay?'

'I should get help.'

'Don't get help. I'll *kill* you if you get help!'

'What did they do to you?'

'Just help me find my clothes.'

'I can't see anything. Let me get a flashlight.'

'No!' she shrieks like I just burned her. She starts crawling around, sniffling, searching for her clothes.

'Did they rape you?'

'Shut up,' she says.

'Was it Jake and the football boys?'

'Nobody raped me, alright, forget it, just help me get my clothes.'

'They're not in here, Ross. They took them. They want you walking around naked. It's a big joke.' She gropes like the blind.

'Where's your cell?' I ask. 'We should call 911.'

'Are you kidding? No way are we calling anybody. Shut up about this, alright, just help me find my clothes.'

'They're not here, Ross.'

She starts to sob, brutal, choking sobs like when she was six and her bike got stolen.

'We'll call your mum,' I say, 'and she'll bring you some clothes.'

'Don't call my mum!' she snaps. 'Anyway, they took my cell.'

'So what are we supposed to do?'

'Find my clothes.'

The deck lights flash and the crowd starts whistling and stamping their feet. King Jake shouts, 'Let's get this show on the road!' They're all there, Kirsten, Nicole, the wannabes. Larry Bone. Rossi crouches under a bench and it dawns on me that we're about to die horrible deaths, that they'll burn our faces with cigarettes, kick the shit out of us then douse our bodies in lighter fluid and set us on fire.

'The dyke's in there with her,' Bonehead announces.

'Fucking lesbos,' Taylor in the dog collar concludes. 'What they need is a corrective experience.'

I have no problem with death if it's over fast, if I go where Kadylak's going.

'Yo, ho, show us your tits!' Slade the blow-job freak shouts.

'We want pink shots!' they all chant.

'Yo, bitch, show us your gash!' Bonehead bellows.

Rossi's shaking and sobbing and I know she's destroyed, that she'll never be the same, that her days will be filled with fear and shame. I look around for a weapon, grab a seat cushion and push open the screen door. They all hoot and holler. 'Where are her clothes?' I demand.

Jake acts surprised. 'She's got clothes?'

'The skank's got clothes?' Slade echoes.

'Where are her clothes?' I repeat.

Kirsten, doubtless the mastermind behind all this, smirks and twirls her hair.

'What's the slut need clothes for?' Jake says. 'She looks better without 'em. Anyway, there might be some good men here who haven't fucked her yet. Although that's hard to imagine.'

All the hatred, the rage, starts sizzling inside me, burning my arms, my legs, my face. I climb down the steps, seat cushion in hand, wanting to terminate this asshole, spit bile into his eyes. 'Where are her clothes?' I shout. He keeps acting ignorant and his followers do the same. They should be thrown in toxic pits, smothered in landfill. 'You are *sick*!' I scream.

'I'll tell you what's sick,' Queen Kirsten shrieks, 'is some bitch saying she's writing a play and getting everybody to fake-fuck in her basement. *That's* sick. That's fucking mental. You're a fucking sick mental case!'

'A virgin too,' Jake surmises. 'Nobody'd fuck anything that ugly. Five bucks to the first guy who fucks her.'

Bonehead starts coming at me with druggy eyes. I throw the seat cushion at him, which gets a laugh. Somebody grabs me from behind and I'm slammed into the ground and they're yanking at my clothes, unzipping my pants and chanting, 'Fuck the dyke up the ass,' and all I know is I'd rather be dead then ripped open by these goons. I start kicking and jabbing and biting and smacking my head into their stinking flesh. 'Kill me, you fucks!' I'm shouting. 'Kill me, you fucking losers!' I taste blood and figure my nose is bleeding. What's weird is I'm not even scared really, I *should* be scared but it's a fight I've been waiting for. I've been wanting to hurt these degenerates for so long. Some of them back off, stunned. 'She's a fucking animal,' they gasp, grabbing at my legs, but I'm super-energized and they're canned. Bonehead's got his hands under my shirt, twisting my breasts. I slam my forehead into his nose and he yowls. Taylor in the dog collar grips me in a headlock, choking me. Slade rips my underpants and I can feel night air against my snatch.

'Whaddayaknow, the dyke's got a slit,' Slade announces. I try to kick the side of his head but two other football players grab my thighs and split me open. Goons grab my ankles and yank off my pants while Taylor breathes barbecue chips and beer on me. Slade starts shoving a beer bottle into me and I can't kick, can't move for fear of breaking the glass. Taylor is licking my face. I hear Kirsten say, 'There's no business like show business.'

149

Bonehead pulls out his dick and tries to push it in my mouth. I clench my teeth but the stink of him is making me sick. I start choking on vomit because there's no way I'm opening my mouth. Then somebody else is yelling and swinging a golf club around. The halfwits cover their heads. 'Leave her alone!' the guy shouts and I realize it's Doyle, all six feet four inches of him. He looks scared out of his mind, like he can't believe he's swinging a golf club around. He's taken off his T-shirt and tucked it into his jeans. He throws it at me. 'Get Rossi,' he says. I roll over and puke on their Nikes before grabbing my pants. I scramble into the gazebo. Rossi's still under the bench sobbing. 'Ross? We've got to get out of here.' I shove my legs into my pants then pull her out, pushing her head through the T-shirt like she's a little girl. 'It's going to be okay,' I tell her. 'We're getting out of here.' I fit her hands through the armholes. She's mute, in shock or something. The T-shirt, being Doyle's, is long and covers her ass. Printed on it is *I hope you like animals because I'm a beast*. I grip Rossi's hand and lead her outside.

'Take it easy, man,' King Jake says to Doyle who's still whipping the club around. 'We were just foolin' around.'

'Yeah, we were just jokin',' his subordinates insist, crowding around us.

'Back off!' I scream.

Doyle pushes through them and puts his free arm over Rossi's shoulders. Holding her between us, we walk around the house to the street. They don't follow. They're defeated, for now.

20

'We should go to the police,' I say, shaking even though I'm not cold. Rossi's in the back with me, trying to blend in with the upholstery. 'If you ever want to press charges,' I say, 'you have to go to the police now.' She doesn't respond so I nudge her. 'Ross?'

'I'm not pressing charges.'

'You might change your mind later, and you'll need evidence.'

'I'm not pressing charges, alright.'

Doyle glances over his shoulder. 'Where should we go?'

'To the police,' I say. 'I'll stay with you, Ross. You won't be alone.'

'All cops do is ask questions like "What were you wearing?" Unless you're dressed like a church lady, they figure you asked for it. I was drunk, Lemon, and I thought it would be fun, with Jake anyway. I wanted to piss off Kirsten.'

'It's still rape, Ross. I heard you screaming.' While I was sitting around sucking on pretzels.

'Cops make you stand naked on a piece of paper while they stick swabs in you. They don't even let you piss. Forget it. I just want to shower.'

'So where are we going?' Doyle asks.

'Lemon's. Is that alright?' She still looks like the kid whose bike was stolen, except there's makeup smeared all over her face.

'If you shower before the police examine you,' I say, 'those shits will get away with it and they'll gang-bang some other girl.'

'Forget about it, alright. Girls like me always lose at rape trials. The horny judge'll say I deserved it.'

She's got a point.

'Alright,' I say, 'let's go to my place.' Chances are Drew and Vaughn are asleep. She can use the basement bathroom.

Doyle stops in front of the house but doesn't get out. 'I'll see you later,' he says.

'Sure,' I say, although I don't want him to go, don't want to be alone with the rape victim. 'Thanks.' He shrugs, not looking too excited about being a hero.

She showers until the hot water runs out. Vaughn comes down to find out what's going on. I tell him my friend got raped. He doesn't seem surprised, gives me the tree-frog stare.

'What happened to your face?' he asks.

'You should see the other guy.'

'Do you need help?'

'With what?'

'Anything.'

'She'll freak if she comes out and finds you here.'

'I'm gone.'

'Don't tell Drew.'

'Of course not. You should put ice on your face.' He goes back upstairs.

Rossi exits the bathroom looking like a peasant woman who's popped sixteen babies that all died. I hand her some of my clothes, expecting her to say, 'No way I'm wearing this shit.' But she puts them on. She looks different without makeup. Washed out.

'Want some tea?' I ask.

'Whatever.' She sits on the couch that Kirsten and the gang were fake-fucking on. Kirsten has a point, I mean what kind of sick mental case pretends to write a play so she can get people to fake-fuck in her basement?

It's while I'm waiting for the kettle to boil that my legs quit. Whatever's been holding me up is gone and I'm squatting on the floor looking at the grime you can't see when you're standing, the grime hidden under the lip of the counter and the drawer handles. The grease stuck to the oven door and the side of the stove. The dust collecting under shelves and around the garbage can. The inevitability of more grime and grease and dust accumulating sickens me and I have to lie face down on the grimy floor, bond with it, accept it, I who have sexual fantasies about the father of a dying child; I who get people to fake-fuck in my basement; I who let my friend get raped. I'm Clarissa in prison, penitent, waiting to die, only I'm not going to be partying with God, I'm going to dissolve into more grease and grime.

'Lemon?' It's washed-out Rossi, shivering. 'Are you alright?'

'Sure.' I manage to sit up by clinging to grimy and greasy drawer knobs.

'Why are you on the floor?'

'I slipped.'

'We should phone my mum. Can we say I'm staying over?'

'Of course.'

I watch her dial and listen to her lie. I picture Mrs. Barnfield relieved that her daughter is snug at her girlfriend's house. I see her turning off the TV and swallowing her meds. With her baby safe, she can sleep now.

The couch is a pullout bed. We find the sleeping bags and crawl into them. I'd like to talk the way we used to during sleepovers, convinced we'd gab all night but then suddenly waking to find it morning.

'Are you asleep?' I ask after what feels like hours.

'No.'

'Are you okay?'

'I'm cold.'

I slide over so we're back to back, warming each other.

'Nobody's going to touch me now,' Rossi says. 'Not even Doyle.'

I shoved his T-shirt in a Ziploc bag and stuffed it in the freezer because I figured it might have forensic evidence on it. She was sitting on it in the guzzler, there must have been leakage.

'You can't seriously *want* any of those psychos after this,' I say.

'Kirsten exposed herself on YouTube and nobody's calling her a whore.'

'That's because she's queen, Ross. They're all scared of her.'

'Do you have to scare people to make them respect you?'

That's a good question. All those kings and queens slaughtering people, were they respected? Or just feared? 'I don't think they respect her, exactly, they're just scared of her.'

'I don't want to scare people,' Rossi says in a small voice I haven't heard for years. 'I just want them to like me.'

'Yeah, well, most people don't want to bother with the little guys who just want to be liked unless there's something in it for them. You're better off not wanting to be liked. Then if a person turns out half-decent, it's a bonus.'

'It's going to be all over the school by Monday.'

'All over the world.'

'They called me trash.'

If people say things about you over and over, if all you hear is how you're lazy or stupid, a skank, a whore, trash, you start to believe it.

Peggy, the obese nurse with rheumatoid arthritis, is arguing with a couple of parents. This happens all the time, Mom and Pop refuse to believe they can't buy their way into a private room. Most of the rooms are private anyway but there's one with four beds in it. A couple of newborn twins are in there now. They were diagnosed with cancer before they were even born. Tumours showed up on an ultrasound. I squeeze past Peggy and head for Kadylak's room, telling myself not to freak if someone from the waiting list has filled the bed. I tell myself I'll act normal, get them a freezie then start reading a story. Maybe *Jane Eyre*. I started reading it again last night while Rossi was twitching around. I'm not wild about the second part when Jane's obsessing over old Rochester, but I like the beginning when John Reed beats the crap out of her and Mrs. Reed calls her a liar and naughty and all that. Jane tries hard to please Mrs. Reed, but the old warhorse locks her up in the haunted room anyway. Spooked, Jane starts screaming and Bessie, the maid, lets her out but the battle-axe locks her back in there.

Jane begins to wonder if she really is all those shitty things the Reeds say she is. Which is what I mean when I say if people keep saying rotten things about you, you start to believe them.

I push open the door and it's Kadylak in the bed. She looks up as if she's been waiting for me. She holds out her arms and I hug her and start bawling, which is completely freaky for me. I don't want her to see so I hide my face in the little curve between her neck and shoulder but then my ribcage starts to spasm and I'm making horrible sounds like I'm dying or something, and the tears are burning my eyeballs, which can't be normal. Kadylak just squeezes me harder and we stay like that for ages. She's even skinnier than before, I'm scared I'll crush her. I want to tell her what's happened but I know I can't. I thought I was dealing with it pretty well. I ate Shredded Wheat and had a shower and put on clothes and all that. It was on the subway I felt their hands all over me. And the sharp cold of the bottle. Bonehead's dick against my teeth.

'I missed you,' she says.

'I missed *you*.'

'We should be sisters, then we could live together always.' She has two sisters but they hate her because her cancer stole their parents from them.

'We can be sisters anyway,' I say, still holding her. If she sees my face she'll know something's up. 'I'm so glad you're better.'

'It was a close one,' she says.

'You've got to start eating more.'

'I will,' she says, but I know it's torment eating with sores in your mouth and constant nausea. She stops hugging me and I have to face her, leaving a dark patch where I've soaked her hospital gown.

'Why are you crying?' she asks.

'I'm so happy you're better.'

'I'm not really better. I'm better for now.'

'That's all any of us have, really, if you think about it.'

She grabs Sweetheart the penguin and holds her close. 'What happened to your face?'

'I fell down.'

'Where?'

'In my kitchen. It was the weirdest thing. I just kind of slipped on grease or something.' I've never lied to her before. I feel chains tightening around me.

'It must have hurt.'

'Not really. What do you feel like doing? Do you want to go to the playroom or something?'

'Can we read *Tilly*?'

There's this brutal silence while *Tilly Tilly Tilly* reverberates inside my head, that piece-of-shit book I can't even locate in my memory. I try to believe it's in the bottom of my backpack and that I'll be able to find it in a jiffy. I start feeling around for it. I'm sweating, can't speak.

'Didn't you bring it?' she asks. Her head scarf's falling off. I try to straighten it. 'You thought I died,' she says.

'No, I just forgot, I ... It's been crazy the last few days.'

'Why?'

'I've had a lot of schoolwork,' I lie again. The chains rattle. 'And I've been extremely worried about you.'

'If *you* worry,' she says, '*I* worry. Please don't worry. Mama worries. She's always sick now.'

'Has she come in?'

She shakes her head. 'She's scared I'll get her flu.'

'What about your dad?'

'He comes. He's very tired. He doesn't like Brenda. Why's she so bossy?'

I try to think of a reason other than that Brenda's a miserable sow with a miserable life who gets off making people miserable. 'It's her life purpose,' I say.

'What's a life purpose?'

'A reason to get up in the morning.'

'Why do you need a reason?'

That's a good question. 'I guess because sometimes you feel like it's too much, all the crap you have to deal with.'

'What crap?'

'What a loser you are and all that.'

She thinks about this, fiddling with the tube on her porta-cath. I pull her hand away from it because that's my job, and because I want to hold her hand forever.

'When *I* go to sleep,' she says, 'I'm glad when I wake up.'

I kiss her forehead. 'That's because you're special.'

I scoop ice cream on automatic. Everything looks meaner and uglier, and standing for eight hours proves more challenging after all that kicking and punching. My body aches while customers carp. When they stare at my face I try to stare back but they scare me. They could hurt me. I didn't use to feel this. The movie crowd swarms the food court, bitching about the special effects in some movie. With bulging eyes and guts they bark orders, leaning against my counter, leaving greasy popcorn prints all over the glass. Some Flintstone type, loitering with his wife and kiddies, keeps telling Wilma to shut up. 'Did I ask your opinion?' he keeps saying. 'Shut your trap.' Wilma slumps under the weight of a hostile marriage. Her porcine and needy-looking children shove each other while staring hungrily at the flavours. I imagine the counter collapsing under their bulk, the Flintstones crashing into me, smothering me, shoving their greasy fingers under my clothes.

Wilma goes for the cappuccino. I want to tell her about corn syrup and corn starch and corn oil, how it's put into every prepared food going and that if she wants her kids obese, keep dining at the food court. I want to tell her it's not worth being Fred's semen receptacle. But I don't say anything because Fred might hurt me. In *Jane Eyre* when Helen Burns is dying, she says she's happy because death will end her suffering. She says if she grows older she'll keep making a mess of things and getting into trouble and making people miserable. Dead, she won't have to worry about keeping her drawers tidy or paying attention during lessons. When you think about all the effort that's required to *not* make a mess of things and get into trouble, and make people miserable, and keep your drawers tidy and pay attention during lessons, dying of consumption starts to look like a reasonable alternative. Helen says it's painless, except for the cough.

The Flintstones want different flavours and double scoops. I dig around in the various tubs.

The worst part is knowing those goons have seen my snatch. I told Ross I'd corroborate her story that we got wet in a sprinkler, which is why she was wearing my clothes. I can just see poor old Mrs. Barnfield saying, 'A sprinkler? That must've been fun. You two used to *love* running in sprinklers. How was your date, angel?'

Doyle's hardly speaking to me. He can't feel too swell about his date dumping him to get raped. He asked if Rossi was alright and I said of course she wasn't. He's hiding in the back, doesn't even come out to harass me about the scoops. YangYang, the Chinese girl who has to stand on a footstool, has been accepted to a thousand universities. She's spread their catalogues all over the counter, pages of happy happy students with big futures. She's so busy looking at the catalogues she has no time to wipe things down or rinse the scoops.

I give Mr. Flintstone the wrong change, which is highly unusual for me. He gets uppity and starts bellowing that I owe him eighty-nine cents. 'Sorry,' I mumble, feeling my hands shake, which they never do.

Some kid is circling a table not far from us, gripping two toy cars. I can't see anyone with her, which worries me. I try to smile warmly at her but she looks away and says, 'Fuck you,' to one of her cars. The other car says, 'Fuck you,' back. The girl's head is big compared to the rest of her and I deduce that she's a midget. I'd been prepared to forgive this girl for her foul language, put it down to upbringing and all that. But the fact that she's a midget and is going to get freakier and uglier – and probably meaner – because of all the kicking around she's going to have to endure, makes it hard for me to care about her. Even though she could wander into the parking lot on her stumpy legs with her fucking cars and get run over. Maybe her mother is hoping for such a miracle. I scan the mall for an adult midget but it's the usual suspects. The paraplegic is feeding his parrot frozen yogourt with a stir stick. I really want to care about what happens to this poor, stunted child, but the truth is, she scares me. I can't take my eyes off her, though. My Greek plumber shows up and asks for Cookies 'n' Cream then starts yammering about some Roto-Rooting he has to do. Even he scares me, the dirt under his fingernails, the hair growing out of his nostrils. The midget hauls herself up onto a chair and starts smashing her cars together. Even the paraplegic and the parrot start staring at her. I'm convinced this kid's been abandoned and no one's going to go near her because she's so hideous. I tell myself, if no one comes for her in an hour, I'll call the police. But then two officers suddenly appear. 'Is Doyle Gregg here?'

'I don't know,' I lie.

'He's in the back,' YangYang blurts.

The cops flip the counter and stride around to the back. I try to hear what's going on but it's hard with all the freezer noise and Muzak. The one with the moustache says something about allegations of assault. When I hear Jake and Larry Bone's names I scoot back there pretending to look for napkins. I try to make eye contact with Doyle to give him the opportunity to say, 'She was there, she'll tell you what really happened,' but he doesn't look at me. The cop with the 'stache grumbles, 'Would you mind doing that later, miss?'

'Oh,' I mutter, 'certainly.' As I head to the front I hear Doyle say, 'I want to talk to my lawyer,' like a suspect on TV. His dad's a dentist, he must know a lawyer. The Greek plumber yabbers about how he had to snake somebody's toilet because their son flushed the limbs of his sister's Barbies down it. The nervous woman in the hat creeps up and asks for a smoothie. I prod YangYang. 'Can you make it for her?' I'm about to go back and explain to the two fascists what really happened when out they pop with Doyle in handcuffs. He's taller then both of them. He stares hard at me and I can tell he wants me to zip it.

'He's the manager,' I say. 'You can't take him away.'

'Close early,' the cop with the 'stache orders.

'The keys are back there,' Doyle tells me. 'You know what to do. Don't close till closing time.' He's never shown this kind of confidence in me before and suddenly I'm so scared I want to grab his leg and hang on. 'Tell Mr. Buzny I'm sick,' he says and then they're gone. YangYang doesn't look too impressed. 'Is he dealing drugs?'

'No. They've made a mistake.'

'What happened to your face?'

'I fell down.'

'Is everything alright?' the nervous woman in the hat asks.

'Bitchin',' I say and start making her smoothie. It's when I'm tossing in the strawberries that I notice the midget is gone.

21

They're sitting around eating slop Vaughn's cooked up. I head upstairs.

'Not so fast,' Drew says.

'I'm not hungry.'

'The police phoned. They want you to call them. Detective Sergeant Weech.' She waves a slip of paper. 'His badge number's on there as well.'

I try to look surprised, do some glob-globbing and furrow my brow. 'Why's he calling *me*?'

'I was hoping you could tell me that. He wouldn't discuss it with me. You're sixteen, he doesn't have to.' She leans against the counter with her arms folded in principal mode, which is pretty hilarious considering she's in Damian's old PJs. Vaughn digs around in the slop with his chopsticks. Drew sighs, looks away, then back at me again. 'Are you going to tell me what happened to your face?'

'I fell down.'

'Where?'

'Right here, actually, the floor's pretty greasy, could use a scrub.'

'You're lying to me. Why are you lying to me?'

'I'm not lying.' I watch Treeboy sucking up noodles and try to figure out if he's told her anything.

'Have you been doing drugs?' Drew asks.

'Negative.'

'Did someone hit you?'

'Negative.'

She throws her hands up. Characters in novels throw their hands up but I've never seen it in real life. She does it a couple of times, when she isn't gripping her head like it's about to explode. She sits down again and assumes an air of professional calm. 'I don't understand why you're lying to me. Who are you protecting?'

'Nobody. Maybe there was a robbery at the mall and they're hoping I saw something. Or maybe the midget got kidnapped. There was this midget child hanging around and nobody looking after her. She vanished. Maybe they're holding her ransom. Kidnapping's all the rage these days. Maybe she's in the trunk of a car somewhere.'

Drew starts smoothing out the tablecloth. When she's feeling heated, she smooths. 'I can only help you if you let me. I'm not your mother. You owe me nothing.' I have to admit, it's nice to hear her talking half-normally again, even if she is pissed at me and in Damian's old PJs. 'Detective Sergeant Weech said he would come to the house if you don't call him.'

'I'll call him.'

'When?'

'After I grab a bite. Do we have any pickles?' Maybe if I delay, Weech will head home for Sunday dinner.

'You just said you weren't hungry,' Drew says. 'If you don't call him, I'm going to have to phone Damian.'

'I'll call him.'

'Who?'

'Weech.'

'Want some stir-fry?' Vaughn offers.

'Why not.'

So we sit, the three of us, silent over slop. But old Drew can't help herself. 'Where were you last night?'

'Here.'

'No you weren't. I checked your room and you weren't in it.'

'Oh, you mean later? I slept downstairs.'

'You weren't downstairs.'

'In the basement.'

'Why did you sleep in the basement?'

'Ross was with me. We were at a party and she wanted to sleep over.'

'Since when do you go to parties?'

'Since yesterday.'

Vaughn dishes out more slop but I hold my hand over my plate. 'I'm wasted,' I say, 'could use an early night.'

'Please phone the sergeant,' she says, sounding like she might pass out.

I take the slip of paper. 'No worries.' I hoof it upstairs and run the bath to drown out my call. I get Weech's voice mail. It sounds like he doesn't give a goose's turd if you leave a message or not. I act bewildered in my message. The truth is I don't want to talk to the police until I talk to Doyle. I phone him but there's only his dentist dad on the service who's probably down at the station trying to buy his way out of it like those parents who try to buy private rooms on the cancer floor. I serve milkshakes to cops, they don't like rich people, they call them dicks. I phone Rossi. Mrs. Barnfield answers and says Rossi isn't feeling well.

'What's wrong?' I ask.

'I don't know, dear. I thought it might be food poisoning. What did you girls eat at the party last night?'

'The usual. Tacos and stuff. Pizza.'

'Oh, well, that could be it then. You never know how long those things have been sitting around.'

I can tell she's worried out of her mind, and that Rossi has told her nothing.

'Will you let her know I called?' I ask.

'Will do.'

I feel safer in the bathroom but the mirror is inescapable and, I have to admit, the bruising's nasty. I could pretend I'm sick or something and skip school tomorrow. Except then I'll be home for Weech's call. Purple marks are starting to blossom on my thighs as well, even my breasts. It could be worse. I could be Rossi.

'What's this?' Drew's holding the Ziploc bag containing Doyle's presumably semen-stained T-shirt. Drew doesn't usually barge into my room.

'It's a project for Conkwright. Just leave it alone.'

'What sort of project?'

'A chemistry project. We're freezing enzymes in different mediums.'

She knows nothing about science, did her PhD on some dead poet nobody's ever heard of.

I grab the bag from her. 'It's not supposed to thaw. If it thaws, you'll destroy it.'

She looks a little frightened and for a second I feel shitty about lying to her, but then I think it through – knowing the truth would only make her more paranoid. She wouldn't even go out to bark at the cats.

I jam the T-shirt back into the freezer and scurry to my room. I boot up the computer to check for party gossip about Rossi that might provide evidence. Nobody actually uses the *rape* word. They use every derogatory word known to man to describe the skank's and the dyke's – that would be me – body parts, but our names are never mentioned.

Somebody knocks softly on my door and I know it's Treeboy.

'Yeah?'

'Can I come in?'

'Do I have a choice?'

'Why wouldn't you have a choice?'

'Two against one.'

'Drew's downstairs.'

'Here in spirit.'

'I'll go then.'

'No, it's alright, what's up?'

He sits on the bed and stares at me. 'How badly are you hurt?'

'Not badly.'

'Loggers once beat the crap out of me,' he says. 'I thought they were going to kill me. Later, I thought wow, is that all they can do? I'd been so afraid for so long of what those pricks would do to me. I stopped being afraid after that.'

'Your friend wasn't so lucky.'

'He was afraid and they knew it. You can't show your fear. Ever.'

I pretend I'm shopping on eBay, wait for him to get bored and leave. He's sitting so still it's creepy.

'I took Drew out today,' he says.

'You mean outside?'

He nods. 'We went to the corner to get milk.'

I stare at him to make sure he isn't lying. 'Did she almost bolt or anything?'

'A couple of times. Sudden movements get her going.'

'Did she hold on to you?'

'Of course.'

It hurts that she went out with him, held on to him, and not me. 'That's great,' I say. My alarm clock with the really loud tick ticks away. I shove it under a pile of clothes.

'You going to school tomorrow?' he asks.

'Perhaps.'

'You should.' He stares, I surf. Finally he gets up. 'Good night,' he says.

'Toodles.'

He closes the door gently and all I want is to be with Kadylak, just like Jane was with Helen Burns. I want to crawl into her bed and feel safe.

Nobody and I mean *nobody* talks to me. I sit in the can and read with my feet propped against the door so I'm invisible. Clarissa's on her deathbed in her dank prison with a priest hovering. Old Lovelace refuses to see the error of his ways and leave Clarissa in peace. His former pal, Jack, skewers him in a fit of passion. Meanwhile Clarissa draws her last breath, happy in her delusion that she's on the next plane to the Pearly Gates. Posthumously her parents figure out that they should have forgiven her and booted out her evil brother and sister. You have to wonder what old Samuel wanted us to get out of this ending. A conviction that we should be good even if it kills us? A conviction that we should be bad even if it kills us? Maybe his point is there is no point in conviction. One way or the other it's going to kill you.

I try to nab Doyle after Conkwright's class but it's pretty obvious he doesn't want to be associated with me. Victims of sexual assault don't win popularity contests. People feel sorry for them but that's about it. Plus he's seen my snatch with a beer bottle sticking out of it, which might be a bit of a turnoff. Rossi doesn't show up, which is no surprise, and Tora's made herself scarce, probably having an asthma attack or something. When the going gets tough, Tora starts hacking.

I seek refuge in the library where Mrs. Wartowski is comfortably clueless. She thinks it's time I read *Lady Chatterley's Lover*. I tell her I already read it, went through this intense D. H. Lawrence phase reading about women who needed to come down off their class system and screw labourers. You get the feeling D.H. thought everything was pretty rotten back then. Industrialization pissed him off, and democracy, which wasn't really democracy. He was a Jew-hater, which doesn't win him points, but I guess everybody was kicking around Jews in those days. He took off, travelled, wrote about women getting the big one from gypsies or Mexicans. It's pretty hilarious that this skinny runt with bad lungs was writing about all these virile, swarthy types. Anyway, there he was in the twenties, coughing up blood, despairing about the state of the world and hiding out in Italy. If you think about it, those sickly types like D.H., Orwell, Chekhov *had* to die young or they'd have gone nuts. Because the world wasn't going to slow down for them, the 'progress' they disdained wasn't going to stop. That's another bonus for dying young, you don't have to watch more shit going down.

'How are you making out with *Tilly*?' Mrs. Wartowski asks.

'Great. I'm reading it to a friend of mine. She's really enjoying it. It's got a happy ending, right?'

'Cookson always wrote happy endings.'

Mrs. Wartowski's parents were killed by Polish Jew-haters after the war was over and they came out of hiding. The Jew-haters nabbed them, wired them together, shot her father in the head and tossed them in a river. They didn't shoot her mother because they didn't want to waste the bullet. Mrs. Wartowski's mother drowned wired to her husband's corpse. Mrs. Wartowski told me this after she saw me reading a memoir by an American whose Hungarian father turned out to be a war criminal, one of those types who raped and ripped out gold teeth and wired Jews together and shoved them in the Danube. 'You never know what people are capable of,' Mrs. Wartowski said. The people who killed her parents were neighbours and would have killed her except that she was a newborn and they wanted a baby. They raised her like their own. She only found out the truth after they were dead. So she spent her life loving her parents' murderers. Anyway, what's weird is that Mrs. Wartowski is a really nice person, even when people make fun of her accent and her pumpernickel-and-onion sandwiches. You have to wonder how somebody whose parents got thrown in a river can be so nice and fearless. The guy who wrote the memoir became depressed when he found out his father was a war criminal and started hating everybody, especially his padre. He said everybody looked like a liar to him.

'What happened to your face?' Mrs. Wartowski asks me.

'I fell down.'

She keeps staring at me with the eyeball that doesn't wander, and tapping her pencil against the counter. You have to wonder what it can be like knowing you were inches from being shot or gassed along with the other six million.

'You should be more careful,' she says.

'I'll try.'

'You must always look where you're going.' She touches my cheek, which she's never done before. The gesture is so tender, so caring and all that, it makes me feel sorry for myself. I don't want this. I jet out of there.

Old Huff has us dipping into *Twelfth Night,* which is another one of the bard's dumb-ass comedies about people falling in love before they've even had a conversation. He has me reading Viola, and Kirsten reading Olivia. I have to yammer about her beauty and how my master has the hots for her and all that. This proves torturous due to the fact that she has seen me upside down with a beer bottle up my snatch.

"'I pity you,'" I read.

"'That's a degree to love,'" reads Kirsten.

"'No, not a grize: for 'tis a vulgar proof

"That very oft we pity enemies.'"

Old Huff jumps in. 'Is that true?' he asks. Nobody asks, 'Is *what* true?' because nobody gives a toad's arse. 'Do we very oft pity our enemies?' Huff demands.

'Shit, no,' Taylor in the dog collar says.

'Why not?'

'They're our enemies. Duh.'

'Yes, but are they not flesh and blood, do they not suffer as we do?'

'Shit, no.'

'*I* pity them,' Kirsten says, looking straight at me. 'Because they're ugly and stupid and nobody can stand them.' There's no question that if she could, she would wire me to a corpse and shove me in a river.

'Why,' I ask because I can't read anymore, 'is Viola so hot for the duke?'

'That's an interesting question,' Huff says. 'Why is Viola enamoured of Orsino?'

The class thinks hard. Megan on Prozac says, 'Because he's the duke.'

'Meaning?' Huff asks.

'She's after his power.'

'That is *so* cynical,' Kirsten says. 'She wants him because he's sexy, that's obvious.'

'How is that obvious?' I ask. 'He lies around whining, bossing musicians around. What's so sexy about him?'

'He's the duke,' she says like this explains everything.

'That's what I said,' Megan persists. 'She's after his power.'

Huff licks his fingers and starts turning pages, which means he's about to get us to start reading again. I can't handle this. 'Maybe it's the father thing,' I say. 'Her dad died at sea, she must miss him. Maybe the duke's a father figure.'

'She wouldn't marry him if he was a father figure,' Kirsten says.

'Oh, so you think all those models marrying eighty-year-old billionaires are after their bodies?'

'Okay, so she's hot for his money,' Megan concludes. '*And* power.'

'You are sick,' Kirsten tells her. Kirsten who made sure my friend got raped. While I was sitting around sucking on pretzels.

She doesn't answer the door. I know she's in there, can hear the TV. 'It's me, Ross.' I start pounding.

She flings open the door. 'Cool it,' she says. She looks alright, just tired. No makeup. Baggy clothes for once.

'Why didn't you come to school?' I ask.

'Why do you think?'

'They win if you don't come to school.'

'They win anyway.'

Because I might be short a hymen, I've been thinking about Queen Elizabeth II checking Lady Di's hymen. The old crow got a gyno in there and squinted down the speculum with him. No wonder Di stopped eating.

'So that's it?' I ask. 'You're going to hide out for the rest of your life?'

'They're charging Doyle.'

'Who is?'

'Jake and Larry.'

'For what?'

'The golf club. That's assault with a weapon.'

'Not if he didn't hit them. Did you see him hit them?'

'I wasn't exactly around for most of it.' She stares at the TV.

'How do you know all this?'

'It's on Kirsten's blog.'

Must have been an update since I checked. 'I can't believe you're still reading that. *Stop* reading that.'

She flops face down on the couch. *Super Sweet Sixteen* is on, a reality show in which stinking rich Americans hold outrageously elaborate parties for their buxom daughters, and buy them Hummers and private planes or anything else their pride-and-joys fancy. I turn it off.

'We have to help him,' I say.

'I'm not reporting it. Forget it.'

'Okay, let me get this straight. A guy who rescued you is going to go down for assault with a weapon and you don't care?'

'He didn't rescue me. It was over.'

'No it wasn't. You know it wasn't.'

'I don't want to talk about this.'

'He was defending us, Ross.'

'He was defending *you*. He's got a thing about you.'

'I guess that's why he was so happy to drive me to the party.'

'You've got smarts and you're creative and you just keep shitting on yourself and it's pathetic. He was only going with me because you ditched him.'

'He was going with you because he thinks you're hot.'

'He was on the rebound, Lemon, get a grip. He doesn't even like me.'

'Oh, so I guess that's why he's so keen to go out with you.'

'Fucking somebody has nothing to do with liking them.'

I've never heard her talk like this. 'What's it got to do with then?'

'Power, Lemon. Hello.' She turns the tube back on. Some ancient TV star is talking about a skin cream made from sheep's placenta keeping her looking young.

'Like the plastic surgeon had nothing to do with it,' Rossi grumbles.

'Did you tell your mum?'

'Are you *insane*?'

'She's worried about you.'

'She's always worried about me.'

'It's not too late to go to the police. The semen stays around for a couple of days.'

'Shut up! That is so *disgusting*. Just shut up!'

I sit on the couch beside her, want to hold her like Helen held Jane, keep her safe. 'Please tell me you're still on the pill.'

'Like, how stupid do you think I am, Lemon?'

'People forget to take them.'

'I never forget.' She surfs past car and cosmetic ads. 'What did they do to you today?' she asks.

'Nothing. Just ignored me.'

'So you don't know?'

'What?'

'They're charging *you*. Anyway, they're trying to. A cushion's not exactly a weapon.'

On TV there are before-and-after shots of flabby women in bathing suits who've used a 'firming' gel. I stare hard at their puckered thighs.

'If they charge you,' Rossi says, 'you're going to have a criminal record. Forget university, pal.'

I have a horrible feeling she's pleased. Why? Because I wasn't there for her? I can't ask her this, can't face this.

She picks at a zit on her chin, which she never does because it only makes the zit worse. 'Haven't the cops been after you?'

'Yeah. I haven't talked to them, though. Just voice mail.'

'Well, five guys say you hurt them. I don't know what you were doing out there. Karate or something. Bone says you broke his nose.'

None of this seems real. One of the flabby women in bathing suits says the firming gel changed her life. 'My husband can't keep his hands off me,' she says.

22

I stare in Marty Millionaire's window. Zippy's talking to her ape-man boss, gripping a rag and rubbing furniture. When she finishes she looks up at him and he points at some other furniture which she starts rubbing. Another sex slave. I heard on the radio that there's a sex-slave cult. The female members cook and clean and obey orders when it comes to sex. The 'master' recruits the women from chatrooms, says they have 'a desire to serve.' Zippy starts rubbing the legs of a coffee table near the window and sees me. She jumps up and down like one of those game-show winners, says something to the master and comes charging out. 'Sweetie, pumpkin, what a wonderful surprise!' She kisses and hugs me and this feels familiar. Everything else feels strange.

'Can we go for coffee or something?' I ask.

'Well, it's just me and Lloyd, honey. I can't just take off. I had my lunch already.'

I shouldn't have come.

'What is it, honeybunch? What happened to your face? Did somebody hit you?'

'I fell down.'

'Come and sit for a sec. Lloyd won't mind if I take a few minutes.' She pulls me inside and makes me sit on a bloated couch that smells like animal carcasses. Makes me think of those buffalo being 'hazed' to make room for ranchers' cattle. In the twenty-first century we're still slaughtering buffalo, mothers and babies with umbilical cords attached, gunned down, drowned, all in the name of the burger factory. The older buffalo form circles around the young, trying to protect them from the bullets.

I don't want to live here anymore.

'What is it, sweetness? Did something happen?' She puts her arm around me and I lean into her, rest my head on her shoulder. She kisses my head and strokes my hair. 'What is it, baby?' I can't tell her because I don't even know, exactly. I just want her to make it better. Or offer to kill me. I want us to die together, we should have died together.

'Do you ever try to kill yourself anymore?' I ask.

'Is that what you're worried about? Aren't you the sweetest girl. Of course not, honeybunch, and you know why? I've found Jesus. He loves me and He loves you, baby.'

Where the hell did Jesus spring from? I don't want Jesus between us. I want her like she was, wild-eyed, saying nobody gives a fuck. 'Do you remember when you wanted us to die together?'

'I do, honeybunch, and I'm so sorry. Please forgive me. Jesus forgives me. And He'll forgive you too, sweetheart, if you let Him.'

'I don't want forgiveness.'

'We all want forgiveness, baby.'

I'm so tired.

'I hate to see you sad,' she says. 'Let's think of the good old days. Do you remember puddles? You *loved* puddles. You'd stamp your foot right in the middle, rain boot or no rain boot. *'Plash*, you'd say, *big 'plash!* Then we'd go home and make Rice Krispie squares, d'you remember that?'

'Yes.'

'You were the most beautiful child.'

A Holocaust survivor witnessed a mother pushing her children out a tenth-storey window before jumping herself. She was saving them like Zippy was trying to save me. Now she's found Jesus.

The ape man's gesticulating at her, wants her back rubbing the furniture.

'I better go,' I say, hoping she'll stop me.

'I love you, baby.' She's already moving away from me, rag in hand.

Bradley crawls around with IV lines attached, ignoring the central line in his chest. He shows everybody his shoes, hoping they'll take him outside. I roll around on the floor with him and he tells me where his eyes are. Next he points to his nose. 'Noth,' he says. Then he pats his stomach. 'Tumtum,' he says. Brenda told me to feed him but every time I hand him something he hands it back, not because he doesn't want it but because he thinks he's giving me a present. I bought some grapes for Kadylak and try offering him one. He slobbers all over it before pushing it in my mouth.

'Don't you like grapes?' I ask. I offer him another one, which he pushes in my mouth.

'Okay, now it's your turn,' I say and try to push one in his mouth. He laughs big belly laughs. The grape tumbles to the floor and he scrambles after it before offering it to me again. '*You* eat it,' I say. He pops it in his mouth, squirting juice, which makes him chortle even more. Then suddenly fatigue takes over and he lies still, keeping his big wise eyes on me. I slide over so I'm lying only a couple of feet from him. I roll a Nerf ball toward him. He bats it back. We keep this going for a while and I can tell he's enjoying it. Distraction frees these kids of suffering. Mrs. Bradley shows up and doesn't look too happy about us crawling around on the floor. When he sees her, Bradley gets so excited he starts full-body bouncing. She picks him up and kisses him about a thousand times. Her pain is excruciating, radiates off her. I close the door quietly behind me.

The good news is that Tilly gets a job as a governess. The spoiled rich kids misbehave but she shows them tough love and they decide she's fabulous. Kadylak loves this part, especially the descriptions of the finery in the mansion. The hitch is the lady of the house – who hasn't allowed her husband to knock her boots since the last baby – finds out that the master's been getting some on the side with another lady of a manor. She has a hissy fit, orders the servants to pack up a carriage and off she rolls to Mother's, taking the rotten brats with her. Poor old Tilly's out of a job again and has to go down the mine.

'Why can't she get some other job?' Kadylak asks.

'There aren't any. Towns lived off the mine in those days. It's kind of like where we're headed with Walmart. Pretty soon the only job in town's going to be in the blue smock.'

I keep reading. Miners cough and spew and pass out. It's dark when Tilly goes down the mine, dark when she comes out. Lunch is a crust of bread and hard cheese sprinkled with coal dust.

'How could people do that to people?' Kadylak asks.

'To get rich.'

'I don't believe that. It's just a story.'

I don't tell her that millions of kids still work in mines, and explosives and arms factories, fattening some CEO's bonus. Mrs. Freeman told us that in some countries it's legal to whip, stone or amputate the limbs of children who fail to do their jobs. You'd like to think the execs on the golf course are ignorant of such practices, but then you figure if Mrs. Freeman knows about it, it ain't top secret. Kirsten said she thought it was awesome that movie stars are adopting African babies. Mrs. Freeman said it would be more helpful if the movie stars drew attention to the fact that pharmaceutical companies perform drug trials on Africans. Whenever there's an outbreak of meningitis or some freaky disease, the drug companies get all excited and test drugs they wouldn't test on their dogs on all these desperate Africans. Mothers line up for days to get their kids treated with White Man's medicine. If the kids die or get crippled from the drug, nobody can prove it. Nobody's keeping count of dead Africans.

I straighten Kadylak's head scarf. 'Do you want me to keep reading or should we take a grape break?'

'Grape break,' she says. I wish I could find her a happy novel. The thing is, all this *Tilly* trauma works on her the way the Nerf ball works on Bradley.

Brenda marches through the doors. 'Lemon, can I speak to you for a minute?'

This doesn't sound good. I give Kadylak the grapes and follow the mistress out.

They're the same cops who showed up at Dairy Dream. PC Wigglesworth with the 'stache doesn't look too excited about investigating a girl for assaulting five football players. The catfish tells us to conduct our business elsewhere. I suggest Tim Hortons but they don't go for it, act like they've never eaten a doughnut in their lives. They haul me to the station in a patrol car that stinks of criminals. 'How did you know I was at the hospital?' I ask through the plastic barrier.

'Your mother.'

'She's not my mother.' I hate her for ratting on me.

'What is she?'

'My stepmother once removed.'

The coppers put me in a little room with a chair and a table bolted to the floor. A tiny window on the door slides open and shut from the outside so they can keep an eye on me. Wigglesworth brings in a chair and sits on it but PC Ramkumar stands around taking notes.

'A fella says you broke his nose,' Wigglesworth says, and I get the feeling he's one of those losers who manipulate sex toys via the Net, fingering his mouse in Toronto to make some harlot come in Vegas.

'Yeah, well, he was grabbing at me,' I say.

'How so?'

'I don't know, just grabbing at me.'

'Where? You see, Limone, my problem is I can't see any defensive wounds. Just looks like you smacked your head into the guy.'

I stare at the bolts on the table legs. No way I'm saying anything that might lead them to Rossi.

'Larry Bone says you kicked him in the face on another occasion.'

'You believe a junkie?'

A guy with big glasses slides the door window open and peers in. He slides it shut again and enters.

'This is Detective Sergeant Weech,' Wigglesworth says, giving him the chair. Weech sits, spreading his legs and resting his Molson tumour on his thighs. Wigglesworth summarizes what I've told him. Detective Sergeant Weech doesn't look too impressed.

'Now why would a girl like yourself,' he says, 'with no history of violence, attack a bunch of football players?'

'I was defending myself.'

'From what? Did something else happen? Boys can get pretty wild at parties.'

'I need to pee,' I lie. Ramkumar leads the way. I sit on the toilet lid in a stall. Maybe I'll stay here for a few hours. Women come and go, some hooker talking loudly to herself about how much she hates cops. I unzip my pants. The bruising's spreading like some kind of cancer. Jane Eyre's in my head again, taking all that bull from Rochester. 'I live to serve you, sir,' she tells him. *She'd* make a good sex slave. I don't get why that book's been in print for almost two hundred years. Maybe because there's a whole bunch of women out there who desire to serve the likes of Rochester. Rossi, for example, she'd bend over for a Rochester in a heartbeat. Why's everybody always feeling sorry for the numb-nuts when he's stinking rich and has locked his wife in the attic? He only takes his head out of his ass after he's been blinded, so you have to ask yourself what's a book that's been in print for almost two hundred years telling us? Love a disabled man because a fully functioning one is a self-absorbed asshole? You can only trust him when he's blind? Women can only become equal with the maimed?

Knock knock on the washroom door. I wait for someone to answer. Knock knock again.

'Who's there?' I ask.

'PC Ramkumar.'

'PC Ramkumar who?'

'Are you alright in there, miss?'

'Certainly.'

'Are you coming out?'

'In a minute.'

And why's Rochester always calling her Janet when her name is Jane? And why doesn't she say, 'My name's Jane not Janet'? I lift up my shirt and see finger-shaped bruises on my breasts. Bone's fingers. My legs quit again. I slump back on the toilet. Doesn't smell too bad in here. Cop bathrooms are mighty clean. Little Portuguese ladies must give them a good scrub with toxic substances before they rush home to serve their sahibs. Prisons are clean too. In one of Drew's social-consciousness-raising zines they showed photos of prisons and schools. The prisons were pristine with all the latest facilities while the schools looked like delapidated prisons.

Knock knock again.

'Who's there?'

'Ramkumar.'

'Ramkumar who?'

'It's time to come out, miss.'

'In a minute.'

When you think about it, old D. H. Lawrence was writing about women who had a desire to serve. And Hardy, and the Georges, and those other Brontës before consumption killed them. Our classical literature is all about women who end up serving some schlep.

Knock knock.

'Who's there?'

'Detective Sergeant Weech.'

'Detective Sergeant Weech who?'

'This isn't a game, Limone. Come out or we'll have to come and get you.'

'I'm having bladder problems,' I lie.

Dead quiet for a minute.

'What kind of bladder problems?'

'It's personal.'

'Is this since the party?'

'I'm not sure.' Maybe if they think I'm traumatized they'll leave me alone.

'We can get you some medical help.'

'I'll be alright. Just give me a minute.' I stumble over to the sinks, see some really messed-up girl with two black eyes staring back at me.

Things get worse when Damian shows up. He starts out friendly, *what's up kid* and all that, but when I won't leave the can he starts ranting and I tell him to fuck off because he's not my father. This gets the cops going, who *is* her father then? Who's her mother? They can't believe I'm unaffiliated. Orphan sympathy kicks in. I have to admit it's getting stuffy in the can, and I'm scared my legs aren't working properly. 'Think what this is doing to Drew,' Damian says through the door.

'Think what *you* did to Drew,' I tell him. All these adults running around messing with each other's heads. The door swings open and Weech smiles at me like I'm a lost kitten he's about to grab and flush down the toilet.

'Are you thirsty?' he asks. 'Want a Coke?'

'Sure,' I say, hoping this'll distract him for a few minutes.

'You come out,' he says, 'and we'll set you up with a Coke.'

I hate Coke, it's like drinking cleaning fluid. 'Can I call some-body?' I ask.

'Sure,' Weech says.

'Who are you going to call?' Damian demands. 'Haven't you upset enough people already? What the hell were you thinking?'

I just ignore him, feel legs moving under me that don't feel like my legs. 'Where's the phone?' I ask Ramkumar. He leads me to a desk with a phone and hovers. 'I'd appreciate some privacy,' I tell him. Meanwhile Damian's getting testy with Weech. Accustomed to bossing around illegal immigrants, he lacks people skills.

Weech is telling him I'm sixteen and can do what I want. There's no answer at Rossi's, just her mother's bank-teller squeak on the service. I know Rossi's home, just not picking up. I try Doyle again. His Botoxed mother answers and says he's not home, wants to know who's calling and all that. I just hang up. Ramkumar's checking his BlackBerry. I consider making a run for it but Weech approaches, Coke in hand, with Damian hot at his heels.

'Do you want this man here?' Weech asks me.

'Which man?'

'Your stepfather or whatever he is.'

'Negative,' I say.

'What do you mean "negative"?' Damian demands.

'She means "no,"' Weech translates, and I have to admit, he's alright.

Back in the little room I sip the cleaning fluid. They're all watching me. Must be a slow day.

'Why don't you tell me how it all started?' Weech says.

'What's happened to Doyle?'

'He's been charged.'

'He was defending me.'

'He was swinging a golf club around. Now, if a girl was in trouble and he was trying to defend her, he might have a case. But he didn't say anything about that.'

'Why not?'

'You tell me.'

I fidget with the Coke can, feel the toxic fluid eroding my guts. You're supposed to be able to remove rust with this stuff.

A PC peeks in the window and nods at Wigglesworth who exits. Ramkumar keeps taking notes.

'Limone,' Weech says, 'you've got to answer to these allegations, otherwise I'm going to have to go with their story. Now I have to tell you, the whole thing smells bad. Doyle seems like a good kid, you don't strike me as an attacker, but what am I supposed to think if you don't tell me anything? If you can show me evidence that you were attacked, I suggest you do so because these boys are filing a complaint and you're going to end up with a criminal record.'

'Where's Doyle now?'

'We let him out on his own recognizance.'

'They're all going to testify against him?'

'That's the idea. And they'll do the same for you. Five guys with eighty pounds on you are going to tell the judge you hurt them real bad.'

'What if someone was raped?'

He leans forward, resting his elbows on the table, displaying the busted capillaries on his nose. 'Then that someone should come forward.'

'What if she doesn't want to come forward?'

'Then that's a problem.'

There's this astronomical silence in which the planet turns a couple of times.

'Why wouldn't she come forward?' Weech asks.

'Because girls lose at rape trials.'

'Who told you that?'

'It's not news.'

'Well, I beg to differ. If the girl is innocent, if she wasn't leading anybody on, or drunk out of her wits, or stoned, or high or whatever.'

'Or has a history.'

'What's that?'

'If she's fucked goons before, she has a history. Means she probably asked for it.'

'Your attitude is not helping you, Limone. We're trying to help you here.'

The planet turns a couple of more times. Weech points to the Coke can. 'Want another one?'

'Nein, danke.'

I've served customers like Weech, guys who mow their lawns every twenty seconds and vote Conservative. Guys who, if you were hit by a car, would probably try to help you out.

181

I yank up my shirt and pull up my sports bra. My nipples harden at the exposure. He takes a look, then gently pulls my shirt down. Ramkumar keeps taking notes.

'Who did that to you?' Weech asks.

'The plaintiffs. Doyle scared the shit out of them so they stopped. He didn't hit anybody.'

'Did they rape you?'

'Negative.'

He stares at me and I stare back. A blinking contest. I win.

'Okay,' he says and I know he doesn't believe me. 'We're going to get a female officer in here to take a look at you.'

'What do you mean "take a look"?'

'She's going to measure those bruises. They look defensive to me.' He stands and hikes up his pants, jangling the keys in his pockets.

'You might want to consider getting microchips implanted in your fingers,' I suggest to delay some butch cop coming at me with a ruler. 'So you won't have to worry about keys. It's all the rage in Europe and Asia. They're getting their fingers coded so all they have to do is scan their finger to get into their car or house or something. You can even do ATM with your finger.'

'You don't say,' Weech says. 'Isn't technology great?' He holds the door open for Ramkumar. 'Limone, if you ever happen to talk to that girl who was raped, encourage her to pursue the charges, will ya?'

23

The chair hurts my butt. I start pacing. Periodically some putz slides open the door window and gawps at me. A hostage was on the radio talking about the little room he shared with three other guys in Iraq, all cuffed together. The captors let them out to shit and piss and shower once a month or something. The hostage said the Iraqis weren't mean to him, didn't beat him and always checked to make sure the handcuffs weren't too tight. At Christmas the Iraqis brought them a cake with a decorated palm tree on it and sang 'Happy Birthday' to Jesus for them. They even asked the hostages to sing some carols. They said they hadn't intended to keep the hostages for months and months. All they'd wanted was money to buy more weapons to blow up Americans. The freed hostage wasn't angry at his captors, he said he'd like to see them again, find out if they're alright. He kept referring to 'the war machine,' how all of this terrorist mess is a product of a war machine that costs billions of dollars to run. I thought it was pretty interesting that a guy who'd lived and almost died in Iraq had nothing nasty to say about Muslims. Everybody else is starting to hate them, people who haven't even met any. I figure it's pretty pointless to hate them since there's so many and most of them aren't fanatics. And it's not like they're all in one country we can hate and bomb. It gets pretty tiring hating that many people in that many countries. Anyway, as soon as the oil runs out we won't need to hate them anymore. They'll all be dying of thirst in the desert and we'll be nuking each other for water.

The door window slides open again and a young woman looks in. She enters, camera, clipboard and ruler in hand. She's your regular fat-assed cop. They must make pants in special sizes for these girls.

'Would you mind removing your trousers please?' she asks.

I drop them fast because I want to get it over with. She measures slowly, like she's being tested. She's pudgy-faced, probably fresh out of cop school. She carefully writes down the numbers on her clipboard. I start to shiver, which freaks her out. 'Are you okay?' she asks about a thousand times which only slows the procedure even more.

'I'm fine,' I keep saying but her hands continue to fumble. I don't think she's done this before and I have to admit that the bruises look pretty hideous under the fluorescents. I start to feel sorry for her, this big-thighed girl who's going to have to endure all kinds of macho bullshit to survive on the force. At least they won't want to bang her. It must be hard on the pretty girls.

'I understand there are more bruises on your torso.'

'Can I put my pants back on?'

'Can I just take a quick photo?' She looks embarrassed, fiddling with the camera. Click click.

On go the pants, off goes the shirt. She doesn't gasp or anything but I can see she's having trouble refraining from screaming *ohmygod!* I have this weird sensation that my body doesn't belong to me anymore. It's become a piece of evidence.

It's hard to measure bruises on breasts because they're full of fat and move around. I hold them steady for her. The ruler tickles but I don't laugh. I think about my biological mother, now that I'm down to the wire with nobody else acting even half-normal. You have to wonder if nineteenth-century novelists made their protagonists orphans because parents complicated the story. Much better to start minus all that baggage.

What's really scary about the Jane/Rochester thing is that even after it's proven that he lied to her, she's worried about what he thinks of her. She keeps responding to *his* moods, *his* outbursts, lets him yammer on about how wronged he was by crazy Bertha and her father. Not once does old Jane say, 'You made your own bed, now lie in it. And stop calling me Janet!' Charlotte married some old pastor type in the end and served him well until he got her pregnant and she started puking her guts out. Dehydration from morning sickness killed her.

After more *Playboy* shots the newbie cop says I can get dressed.
'Can I go?'

'Umm ... let me check with Detective Sergeant Weech.'

The hostages in Baghdad figured out how to jam a nail into their cuffs to open them because they'd seen Nick Cage do it in some movie. But one of them was chained to a pipe and they couldn't free him. They knew that if they escaped, the guy left behind would be tortured. So they stayed, took the cuffs off at night to sleep then snapped them back on in the morning. Men of honour. If you cuffed a few politicians together you can be sure they wouldn't be too fussed about leaving one of their comrades behind to have his balls electrocuted. The cuffs would be off and they'd be scrambling over each other.

Weech comes in with a bagel wrapped in plastic. 'You hungry?'

'Negative.'

'When did you last eat?'

'Can't remember.'

'Eat something.' He puts the bagel on the table. I can't imagine getting my mouth around it. Can't imagine doing anything beyond slouching in this tiny room.

'I have to tell you,' Weech says, 'your defensive wounds are consistent with sexual assault. I'm starting to doubt these allegations against you.'

'What about Doyle?'

'What about Doyle?'

'I'm only here because of Doyle.'

'PC Wigglesworth says you work with him at Dairy Dream.'

'Correct.'

'Is he your boyfriend?'

'I never mix business with pleasure.'

'So why are you so worried about him?'

'He's my friend. I want the charges dropped.'

'Too late for that. Once the paperwork gets going there's no stopping it. You should've come in sooner. Shouldn't have made us chase you.'

I stare at a dent in the wall, figure a head made it.

'This whole thing smells bad, Limone. If these guys sexually assaulted you, we can charge them and they get stuck with a record and the stink stays with them. It's up to you.'

'I just want to help Doyle.'

'If you come forward about the rape, and say Doyle was acting in your defence, it'll help him.'

'I wasn't raped.'

'Whatever. Let's call it sexual assault.'

It's the victim thing. If I'm a victim, they win. I stare at a table leg. They must bolt things to the floor because people go nuts in here, smash things, themselves.

'Am I going to be charged?'

Weech leans back in his chair, folds his hands behind his head and gives me a good stare. 'At this point, as far as I'm concerned there is no basis for a charge against you. If they come up with more evidence, we'll take another look at it. In the meantime if you want to charge *them*, that's another story.'

I just want to fade into the walls.

'A girl like yourself stands a good chance against five football players.'

He means an ugly girl in baggy clothes versus a Rossi in a push-up bra.

He leans forward again, squinting. 'Who are you protecting?'

'Myself. I want to go now.'

I find a tree and climb it, disappear. A homeless guy drags his shopping cart to the bench below and sits quietly, looking around like your regular park-bench occupant. His hair's completely matted, his clothes filthy, but he doesn't seem insane or dangerous. He's probably in his thirties, young enough to start over, train for some pod job to keep the machine going. Maybe he doesn't want to. Maybe homelessness means freedom to him. He starts opening coffee creamers and knocking them back like shots. People with life purpose walk by, ignoring him. People who think it's normal to get five hours of sleep a night and have your supervisor on your tail. People who go to movies and eat dinner out and buy package-deal vacations. Normally I feel removed from these people and it doesn't bother me. But now, in pain, with fingerprints all over me, I want to be one of them. It's too hard on the outside.

After the freed hostage spoke, they had some university prof of Middle Eastern studies commenting on the latest terrorist activities. 'They believe they are cleansing their country by blowing up cars,' he said. 'They believe that the decline of their culture began with Western influence. By eradicating Western influence, they believe they can reinstate their faith.' I'd like to know how this is different from Westerners thinking that bombing the shit out of Muslims will convince them that democracy does exist. Amazing how everybody knows what's best for everybody else.

Rossi still won't talk to me. Mrs. Barnfield brews me some instant coffee. I drink the swill because I need an excuse to linger.

'I don't know what's come over her,' she whispers. 'She's not eating, won't go out.'

Mrs. Barnfield looks like death. I've read about that in novels but never actually seen it. Her skin's pasty and hangs off her face. She's got purple bags under her eyes and her lips are the colour of her skin. When she comes home from the bank she's got makeup on so you don't notice. But now she's in her bathrobe, scrubbed for bed.

'Did something happen at the party?' she asks.

'What do you mean?'

'With Rossi. Did she get into any kind of trouble? Kids and alcohol don't always mix.'

'I wasn't with her all that much.'

'Where were you?'

'I was mingling.' I really like Mrs. Barnfield and don't want to tell her that her daughter got raped because it might speed her demise.

'She refuses to go out,' she says.

'Why?'

'Says it's too much work.'

'What is?'

'Getting ready,' she says. 'She has to bathe, shave everywhere and exfoliate. Then she showers because she doesn't like to wash her hair in the bath. After that she has to blow-dry and put on makeup. It's very time-consuming. She says it's not worth doing anymore, she'd rather stay in.'

'She doesn't have to do all that.'

'Don't I know it.' Mrs. Barnfield starts sorting through her junk mail, trying hard to look like she isn't worried out of her mind.

'What about school?' I ask.

'She says she's going to apply to beautician school. You don't need a diploma for that.'

'She'd have to go out, though.'

'You'd think.' She rubs her eyes.

'Could I crash here tonight?' I ask. She stands a little straighter, as though I've lifted a weight off her.

'Of course, if it's okay with your mom.'

My 'mom,' what a joke. I phone Drew. She starts her school-principal number. 'I love you too,' I say and hang up. Mrs. Barnfield and I sit on the couch and watch *Out of Africa*. It gets embarrassing when Bob lies on top of Meryl and tells her not to move. She tells him she wants to but he says, 'Don't.' You have to wonder what kind of sick puppy Sydney Pollack was if he thought good sex is about the guy telling the woman not to move. Which gets me thinking about Rossi, what she did or didn't say when those louts were ramming her. Did she start out acting like she was enjoying it so they'd be nicer to her? Invite her to parties? Drive her around in Daddy's car?

'I wouldn't want to live in Africa,' Mrs. Barnfield says. 'Besides the heat, there's so much unrest there.'

'It's going to get like that here. Once the oil runs out and a potato costs five bucks. The poor will storm the compounds of the rich, get out the garrotte.'

'The what?'

'Garrotte. It's a Spanish method of execution by strangulation. You fit metal collars around necks and tighten them till they choke. Pretty efficient, portable and low cost. People who can't buy a potato can't afford bullets.' Don't know why I'm telling her this when I'm supposed to be cheering her up.

'Oh, it'll never get that bad here,' she says, which is pretty bizarre considering she's being bled by the bank, which is owned by a few billionaire garrotte candidates.

'You're right,' I lie. 'We're way too civilized.'

When things start to go wrong between Meryl and Bob, Mrs. Barnfield spurts tears. She yanks Kleenexes from a box and blows her nose every five seconds.

'It wasn't really like that,' I tell her.

'What wasn't?'

'Karen Blixen and Dennis. I read the book. He was a dick, nothing like Bob. Not as handsome either. He didn't even show up to tell her he was leaving. They hadn't seen each other for months when he crashed the plane. Hollywood put that schmaltz in.'

'What schmaltz?'

'The parting scene, when Meryl's doing longing acting.'

'I think she's a wonderful actress.'

'She's got the accents down.'

I help her make up the couch with sheets and blankets. She's trying really hard to act like a mother and not a damaged individual. I want to tell her it's okay, we're all damaged, but I can't. It's like we have to play these roles.

'Is that everything you need?' she asks. 'Oh, a nightie. I'll lend you one of mine.'

It's white with little skiers on it. I thank her and wait for her to go to bed so I can sneak into Rossi's room. I lie on the couch, listening to the fridge compressor switch on and off about a thousand times, trying to figure out why Rossi won't talk to me. Is she ashamed? Pissed at me for sucking on pretzels? Does she feel so used and ugly she doesn't want to see anyone? Rape probably does that to you, makes you feel dirty for the rest of your life.

189

Every time you have sex after that it feels like rape, but you have to act like you're enjoying it, otherwise the knob thinks you're frigid because you were raped. You feel guilty because you're not enjoying it so you start fucking even more goons, hoping they'll like fucking you even though you were raped and will feel dirty for the rest of your life.

I don't knock this time, just creep in. She's not asleep. 'What do you want?' she asks like I'm an intruder.

'To talk.'

'About what?'

'You can't just stay inside for the rest of your life.'

'Why not?'

'They've charged Doyle,' I say. 'I tried to stop them but it's too late. We should have gone to the cops right away.'

'Fuck off.'

'Don't you care?'

'Was *he* raped? I don't think so. I think Doyle's going to be just fine. His daddy'll hire some hotshot lawyer who'll get him off.'

This may be true. 'He still needs a defence,' I say.

'Spare me, Lemon, okay, just spare me.' She flips on her side, away from me.

'I can't believe you don't care what happens to him.'

'He's a jerk, you told me he's a jerk, so why're you so hot on him all of a sudden?'

'He saved us.'

She faces me again. 'You. He was a bit late for me. I was screaming in case you didn't notice. I'd like to know how nobody heard me.'

'Girls always scream at parties.'

'In pain, in terror?'

'The music was loud, come on, Ross, you were in the gazebo.'

'It has soundproof walls? The truth is nobody gives a shit about me. They're glad I was raped. I'm ugly and fat and stupid. I disgust everybody, they hate me. They figure I deserved it.'

This may also be true.

'Don't we have to get beyond "everybody"?' I say, sitting at her dressing table. 'I mean, there's everybodies everywhere. You have to pick and choose the everybodies you're going to sweat about. If you go to beautician school, everybody there is going to think you're brilliant because you know how to exfoliate and all that. They won't know what happened.'

'I'll know.'

She doesn't even look like Rossi anymore. It's not just that she isn't wearing makeup. Her eyes are different. She's seen hell.

'I'm not too excited about doing it either,' I admit.

'What?'

'Being a piece of evidence for Doyle. Standing in front of those ghouls and saying they did this and that to me. I don't want them looking at me.'

'So don't do it.'

I stare at the Bugs Bunny clock she's had ever since I can remember. His ears make the hands. 'Do you ever want to be a little kid again?' I ask.

'All the time.' She pulls her comforter under her chin.

'I wonder why. I mean, shouldn't we be excited about being free of school and all that?'

'You're only free if you get a decent job and we all know how hard that is.'

'I think going to beautician school is a great idea.'

'I just say that to make Mum feel better.'

'So what are you going to do?'

'Nothing. She wants to buy me a bedroom set.'

'You'll have to go out to do that.'

'I can do it online.'

Her stuffed animals peer down at us from a shelf, which brings to mind *The Velveteen Rabbit* and *The Steadfast Tin Soldier*. Everything works out in those stories. 'Your mum says you're not eating.'

'How would she know?'

'I guess she knows what's in her kitchen.'

'It's not like I don't have pounds to lose.'

'You don't.'

'I'm fat, Lemon. Everybody knows I'm fat.'

'You're female, you're supposed to have fat.'

'Don't talk like my mother. The one good thing about her disease is that she's skinny for the first time in her life. I told her I'll start eating when I'm as skinny as she is.'

'She looks emaciated, Ross.'

'She looks great. Maybe if she'd looked this good five years ago my father wouldn't have dumped her.'

'He didn't dump her. He was a gambling addict.'

'Yeah, right.'

I lie on her fake-fur carpet because I'm tired. She doesn't offer me a pillow.

'Too bad you didn't write that play,' she says.

'Why?'

'Now you're just a total fuck-up like everybody else.'

I don't argue. I drag my ass back to the living room, hoping she'll stop me. I twitch on the couch for a couple of hours before heading out. Old Jane heads out into the night with twenty shillings on her, not even enough to pay the coachman to get her to the next county. He drops her in the middle of nowhere. After he drives off, she realizes she left her parcel with her few belongings on the coach. So she's destitute. Why she didn't ask old Rochester for cash is beyond me, why she had to sneak out instead of saying, 'Look, Edward, you keep calling me Janet, and your little girl, and I think that's perverted. So give me a hundred pounds and I'm outta here.' But no, old Jane isn't happy unless she's suffering. Her first night in the great outdoors she sleeps on some moss under a rock. But then it starts to rain and she sloshes around the village trying to get work, or trade her hankie for a bun or something. Nobody wants anything to do with her because she's not from the village and therefore qualifies as a fallen woman. She trudges through more mud until she finds a beat-up old house with ladies embroidering inside it. She stares in the window then begs at the door but their servant tells her to buzz off. A young pastor shows up and orders the servant to give Jane some soup. Penniless girls had to either become governesses or marry a pastor. Old Charlotte had a couple of pastor proposals before she settled on the deadbeat she ended up serving who got her pregnant.

There's no question it's spooky in the stillness of the night with nobody around and my boots smacking the pavement. I move fast, checking over my shoulder every three seconds. I find a phone booth and call Connie Sheep's Ass. It takes seventeen rings to wake her. 'Hello … ?'

'It's Limone.'

'Who?'

'Your daughter.'

'What time is it?'

'I don't know, I don't wear a watch, it makes me feel like I'm in chains.' I'm babbling because I feel like a jerk waking her and all that. 'I could call you tomorrow if this is inconvenient.'

'No, I'm glad you called. How are you? Is everything okay?'

'Sure.' Her voice sounds familiar for some reason.

'Are you at your stepmother's?'

'No. I'm in a phone booth.'

'Oh.'

'I don't really want to go home.'

'Why not?'

'It's not really my home. I don't have a home. Kind of like Jane Eyre.'

'Who?'

'Jane Eyre. She's a fictional character. Her mother married a man who had no cash so her father disowned her. Jane's mother loved the man, though, and things were going great until they started starving and coughing up blood. They were buried together.'

'Really. I've never read it. I saw the movie, though, years ago. I think Laurence Olivier was in it.'

'What a dick he must've been, swinging both ways, no wonder Vivien was depressed.'

'Pardon?'

Already this feels like a mistake. I bet she never reads. I bet she eats Lean Cuisine in front of the box.

'Anyway, I'll let you go,' I say, 'sorry to disturb you. Ciao.' I hang up. Just a total fuck-up like everybody else. I sit in Tim Hortons with the other rejects with no place to go, thinking about my potential criminal record and how those borderliners are only charging me because they didn't get to destroy me the way they destroyed Rossi. Plus they figure, like her, I won't fight back.

Some podger truck driver is staring at me and I want to rip my clothes off and scream, 'Have a good drool, dickhead!' Let the whole world grab my tits, my ass, my snatch. It's not like it matters.

24

'Shouldn't you be at school?' Peggy asks me. She's walking with a cane, which means her knee's acting up.

'I had a dentist appointment, figured I'd stop by and check on Kadylak.'

'She's been very worried about you. Is everything okay? She said the police were here.'

'Everything's swell. They just want me to witness an accident.'

'I see, well, she's in the classroom, don't disturb her.'

'Can I wheel Bradley out? I mean just outside the hospital?'

'If you're very careful.'

What kills me about Bradley is that he trusts me for no good reason. Right away he's ready to roll. We get his shoes on and collect some crackers for the birds. Sparrows and seagulls know the drill and are pecking at his feet in seconds. He belly-laughs, straining against his seat belt. I let him out to crawl around. A mangy cat shows up and Bradley offers it a half-eaten baby carrot. Sick teenagers slouch in wheelchairs, texting or talking on cells. They don't talk to each other because nobody wants to hang out with cancer patients, especially if you are one. Bradley practices his elemental verbal skills with the teenies but none of them are too interested. I toss him the Nerf ball, which he grabs and flings so I have to go chasing after it. This keeps him guffawing, tossing the ball anywhere but to me. Then all of a sudden he just keels over and lies still in the grass, watching me. I check his temperature and breathing to make sure he's alright. I figure he's just wasted and lie beside him. He stares at me with that wisdom of his. I wait for him to impart some Yoda profundities. He reaches over and touches my nose. 'Noth,' he says. Next he starts digging around in my backpack and pulls out my mother/ daughter scrapbook.

This is a highly personal item and normally I wouldn't let anybody get their glommers on it. 'Don't tear it,' I warn him. He looks intently at the photo of the crying mother of the woman who jumped off an overpass clutching her toddler. Everybody's freaked that a mother could kill her kid but I think it proves she loved him. They were black and poor. She didn't want to leave him behind on Spaceship Earth to get kicked around. Even though she'd managed to get an MBA she couldn't get a job.

Bradley leans in close to the photo, nose to nose with the crying woman.

'Her daughter died,' I explain.

The jumper stopped taking antidepressants when she was nursing. She paid her rent on time and told everybody she was fine. She spent all day with her son, took him to the park and the library, was teaching him English and French. Her landlord said, 'She took really good care of that kid. Everything was about that kid.' So she killed him. I understand this.

Bradley scrutinizes another photo of a crying mother who tried to kidnap her seventeen-month-old twins from their adoptive parents. She says she was forced to give them up because of postpartum depression. She says, 'How will they ever understand why they were kept from their mother when their mother wanted them so desperately? How will that ever be explained to them?' Bradley can't keep his hands off the photo of the twins. I guess he figures they're his buddies, short people like himself. Their mother said she could never *ever* tell them she gave up on them, and she never will. Unlike Connie Sheep's Ass who just remembered I exist.

I started reading *Anna Karenina* again – talk about a woman pining for some guy. I like the atmosphere, though, all those samovars, sleighs and furs. Reading dead Russians always makes you glad you've got central heating. Anyway, it's pretty obvious judging from what old Vronksy does to Kitty that the putz has zip moral fibre. But he looks good in a uniform and all that.

Bradley's onto my Progeny of Prostitutes page. They like to think Mommy loved them, only handed them over because she couldn't turn tricks with her bundles of joy crawling around. Some of the prostitutes' babies, if they aren't damaged by drugs or alcohol, get adopted. Others live with relatives who treat them like they treated their mommies so the girls grow up into prostitutes. They don't know who their fathers are, although usually it's pimps because most of the johns use condoms. Pimps rape their girls to show who's boss and don't have time for condoms. On the radio they were freaking about child prostitution again. What kind of man wants to do that to a child, the non-compos host asked. Seems like most of them. A child prostitute who'd graduated to hooker said she'd been hired by men from 'all walks of life.' She said that while they were doing perverted things to her, she told herself it meant they weren't doing it to their daughters or nieces. She convinced herself that she was saving some little girl somewhere. She ended up a crackhead.

Bradley rolls on his back and squints at the sky.

'Do you see any animals up there?' I ask him. His eyelids droop. I lie beside him and point at a formation. 'Elephant,' I say.

'Elfalant,' he says.

'There's a bunch of elephants in India searching for their elephant sister,' I tell him. 'They don't know that she fell into an irrigation ditch and drowned. So fourteen of them have been marauding villages, looking for her.' I roll on my side so I can watch Bradley fall asleep. I keep talking even though he doesn't understand a word I'm saying. Talking distracts these kids from pain. 'There's hardly any forest left so the elephants end up searching for grub where there's people. The villagers get hysterical, and chase them with firecrackers and pitchforks. Sharpshooters kill the ones they can't scare off. One rogue male was so feared they called him Osama bin Laden.'

Bradley's asleep. At peace. I adjust the stroller to the reclining position and lay him in it.

My favourite mother/daughter story is about the fifteen-year-old girl who escaped from her burning house with her little brother. On the street, crowded with fire trucks and gawpers, she couldn't see her mother. She started screaming 'Mummy!' and ran back into the burning house to rescue her mother. What she didn't know was that her mother had already jumped out her bedroom window and was being treated by paramedics. The girl died from smoke inhalation, searching for her mother. In the photo the girl's wearing braces and those felt antlers kids wear at Christmas.

Kadylak's staring at a corner of the room.

'What is it?' I ask.

'It's the man in the black coat.'

She's seen him before. It could be the drugs making her hallucinate or the fact that she hasn't eaten for days.

'Tell him to back off,' I say. 'Tell him to go spook around someplace else. Is there anything you want to eat? What about noodle soup? Do you want me to nuke one of those for you? Or what about some custard?'

'Are the police going to arrest you?'

'Nope. It was one big snafu. They thought I was some other girl. I brought *Tilly*.'

'Is she still in the mine?'

'She is, but the master's there with her.'

'Why?'

'He went down to make sure all his serfs were earning their stale bread.'

'Where's Simon?'

'Milking cows or something.' I don't tell her Simon's in his barn, stuffing the very same lady of the manor the master was diddling.

'Can you read?'

There's trouble down the mine. Old Clive, the master, gets trapped under a falling beam and can't move his legs. Tilly holds his hand and tells him not to worry, sir, they'll find us. Clive says he's less frightened with her there. She demonstrates her desire to serve by feeding him her stale bread.

'Are there rats in the mine?' Kadylak asks.

'Probably.'

'In my country, when men get trapped in mines, they eat rats.'

'Well, I don't think Ms. Cookson's going to want her heroine eating rodents.'

We read on and, bless my soul, Tilly and Clive are rescued. But tragedy has struck. Old Clive will never walk again.

'How will he work?' Kadylak asks.

'He doesn't work. He's an aristocrat.'

'What's that?'

'Someone who inherits all kinds of land and cash made off the sweat of poor people.'

'I like Clive.'

'He's alright.'

'It will be hard for him to be in a wheelchair.'

'Maybe he'll get a couple of slaves to carry him around. They had all kinds of slaves back then. That's how the aristocrats got even richer. All those black people on plantations.' I pass her a juice box.

'When they were picking cotton,' I continue, 'they had to stay bent over. Imagine spending all day hunched over, tearing sticky cotton off bushes and getting whipped every time you tried to straighten up.'

Kadylak's looking at me, sucking on her straw. It's good she's keeping liquids down.

'What did the other girl do?' she asks.

'What other girl?'

'That the police wanted. What did she do?'

'Oh. I'm not sure. Shoplifting or something.' It's getting easier to lie to her.

'What's shoplifting?'

'Stealing.'

'You wouldn't do that.'

'Hell, no.' Speaking of shoplifting brings to mind the spinning tops. I dig around in my backpack and spin them on her table. She gasps as if I've performed a magic trick. The tops teeter and stumble. 'You try,' I tell her. It feels like a miracle, being here with her, spinning the tops. It feels like a dream.

Drew's watching some documentary on Susan B. Anthony they keep recycling on the History Channel. They make like we've come a long way, baby, since Sue cast her vote. Like there's no glass ceiling anymore, and boys and girls get equal pay.

'Have you seen this?' Drew asks me.

'Yep.'

'She was an extraordinary woman.'

The sombre photo of Sue comes onscreen. The narrator insists that, before Sue adopted the black dress and red cloak, she was actually a very perky person with lots of suitors. I guess that makes her a real woman, the fact that she wore pretty dresses and had lots of suitors before she became a crusader for women's rights. The narrator says giving up pretty clothes and suitors must have been a sacrifice for her. *Au contraire, mon garçon.* Sue probably figured out the dudes were dullards, probably wore black to scare them off.

I look in the fridge, which is loaded with healthy food I didn't buy. Ergo Treeboy must have been shopping. I resent being robbed of the opportunity to feign normalcy at the Valu-Mart. I find a yogourt and aim for the stairs but Drew heads me off. 'Are you going to tell me what the police wanted?'

'Some girl was shoplifting. They thought maybe I saw her.'

'Did you?'

'What?'

'See her?'

'Nope.'

'How did they know you were there?'

'Where?'

'At the store. Or was she shoplifting ice cream?'

'They saw me on the surveillance camera.'

Drew grabs her head again. 'Why are you lying to me?'

'Why are you so concerned all of a sudden? It's not like you're my mother.'

This gives her pause. She stops grabbing her head and squints as if I'm very far away and she can hardly see me.

'I'm going to bed,' I say.

'Why didn't you go to school today? Don't turn your back on me, young woman.'

'Go fuck yourself,' I tell her and, I have to admit, it feels pretty liberating saying it. I guess I've been wanting to say it for years but have been afraid she'd boot me out or something. Now I don't care. I say it again, spacing the words this time. 'Go ... fuck ... yourself.'

She just turns away, goes back to Susan B. I was hoping she'd try to garrotte me or something.

The worst part is nothing's changed. Except that I dream about glass splintering inside me.

I saw David Weiss outside Dollarama. I went up to him because I wanted to say I was sorry and all that. He pretended not to recognize me.

All these horrible things happen and the world keeps turning its back on you. Mrs. Freeman was talking about the Armenian genocide, how the Turks keep pretending it didn't happen. They didn't have cellphones in 1915 so the only evidence is what people choose to remember and if you're a Turk you don't want to remember that you raped and killed mothers with babies. You want to think your great-great-granddaddy looked swell in a uniform with a sabre on his belt.

I dig around in the yogourt for the jam at the bottom. I'm supposed to be working on that essay for Swails but I can't get interested. He always gives me shitty marks.

There's knocking on my door and I know it's Treeboy.

'What?' I demand.

'Requesting entry.'

'Don't let me stop you.'

He sits at my desk and stares at me for about an hour. I start singing 'The Hokey Pokey.' 'You put your right hand in, you put your right hand out. You put your right hand in and you shake it all about. You do the Hokey Pokey and you turn yourself around. And that's what it's all a-bout.'

The Tree Frog doesn't budge. Maybe he thinks I can't see him on the bark. I roll on my side so my back's to him. 'Don't mind me,' I say, 'just need to grab some shut-eye.'

'I'm finding it hard to believe they didn't hurt you.'

'Try harder, sonny.'

The fact is I could shower a million times and it wouldn't get their prints off me. I'm marked for life.

25

I always thought the Aztecs were smart agriculturalists and all that but Drew's *National Geographic* says they were constantly sacrificing people to some god or other, then eating the leftovers. They had no livestock, just corn and beans, so eating each other not only kept the population down but provided protein. They were always starting wars so they could convert the POWs into chow. They lined them up by the hundreds before cutting out their hearts. The ribcage was too tough to penetrate so the holy men would slice open the victim's belly, reach up under the bones and grab the beating heart. They'd yank it out and show it to the sacrificee before shoving it down the mouth of some statue. When they ran out of POWs, they started rounding up the locals. Nobody rebelled because they figured that's what you had to do to keep the sun coming up. No sun meant no crops, which meant they'd die anyway. The sun god, Huitzilopochtli, was a big eater. When old Cortés showed up with his ships and armour, Moctezuma figured *he* was a god and offered him some bleeding hearts. Cortés, being a canny European, used his god status to mindfuck the Aztecs who were already pretty obsessed with the collapse of the universe and all that. The way Moctezuma saw it, Cortés wasn't just any god but the Feathered Serpent god, Quetzalcoatl, who wanted to be the *only* god. Which meant they had to stop feeding hearts to the other gods to keep the Feathered Serpent god – Cortés – happy. He kept acting displeased, which totally freaked out the Aztecs. They got more and more stressed about which gods to feed and even more freaked about the world ending. They started beating up on each other, which made it easy for Cortés to divide and conquer. Which brings to mind our current situation. We're all freaked about pollution and war and all that, but instead of doing something intelligent about it we make more pollution and war. We're going the way of the Aztecs and we don't need a Spaniard to get us there.

I hear knocking.

'You have to go to school,' Drew says through the door.

'Who says?'

'You have to go to school, or tell me what's going on.'

There's no way I'm letting her feel sorry for me.

'I'll go to school if you drive me.' I know she won't leave the house.

'Since when do you need a drive to school?'

'Since today.' I hear nothing, just a pregnant pause. You always read about those in novels.

'Fine,' she says. 'I'll drive you. Let's go or you'll be late.'

'There's no way you're driving that car.'

She's thrown her raincoat over Damian's PJs. She pumps the gas. *Vroom vroom.* It stalls. I start singing 'The Hokey Pokey' again.

'Please stop that,' she says, jamming the ignition. I stare at our old camping gear hanging on the garage wall. I enjoyed those trips, scampering around the woods, pretending I was an Indian collecting herbs and barks for medicines. Only I wasn't going to give any to the white people, Damian and Drew. I'd let them die of scurvy, couldn't wait to see their gums rot and their teeth fall out. I have a picture of the last living Beothuk girl. White folk made her a servant and the master raped her and all that.

The engine starts up again and Drew backs out of the garage. Rush hour's in full swing. Stressed-out drivers rush to dead-end jobs. I turn on the radio and learn that in the last ten years the top 1 percent of rich Americans have amassed more wealth than the bottom 99 altogether.

'Hope you've got your licence on you,' I say.

She keeps her eyes on the road, looking grimmer than I've ever seen her.

'Watch out for joggers,' I caution. 'One got mashed the other day, was out burning carbs, then *slam*. Her hubby and kiddies were home waiting for her. They'd just ordered pizza.'

'Why do you retain these horrible, horrible stories? What does it do for you?'

'Makes my story less horrible.'

'Your story isn't horrible at all. You're spoiled rotten.' She slams on the brakes, avoiding a squirrel. She hit one once and watched it quiver forever, stood in the street getting hysterical. I stayed in the car pretending I didn't know her.

'How long is Vaughn staying?' I ask.

'I don't know.'

'Doesn't he have anywhere to go?'

'Don't you like him?'

'He's alright.' I'm thinking there's some sick Oedipal thing going on between them. They're not even related. 'I just think it's weird he's around all of a sudden.'

'Why is that weird?'

'Because he's never been around before.' I heard them murmuring to each other this morning. They sounded like lovers. 'He said you went to the store with him.'

'Do you have a problem with that?'

'Doesn't he have his own mother?'

'She works for Dupont.'

'What about his father?'

'He works for Dupont.'

'So he can't stay with them because they work for Dupont?'

'What about *your* mother, Lemon? You won't even talk to the poor woman.'

'Which one?'

'You know very well which one.'

'Oh, you mean the one who dropped me in the Walmart toilet?' Why's she mentioning my bio mother all of a sudden? Does she want me out? So her and Treeboy can frolic happily ever after?

'She most certainly did not drop you in a Walmart toilet. She gave you up out of necessity. You know nothing about her, or even the circumstances, and yet you've already condemned her.'

'She condemned *me*.'

She pulls up outside the schoolyard and digs around in the glove compartment for her shades – probably because she doesn't want to be recognized. She looks scared out of her mind, her lips twitch and her shoulders vibrate around her ears. She hasn't been here since she was knifed. 'Nice place, eh?' I ask. 'Aren't you glad you brought me here?'

'What am I supposed to do, Lemon? I'm doing the best I can here. *You* tell me what I'm supposed to do.' I can't see her eyes behind the glasses.

'You're the grown-up,' I say.

She grabs the wheel the way she's been grabbing her head lately. 'Do you hear yourself? That snide, self-important tone? It's rude, it's disrespectful and I've had it, really I've had it.' She keeps shaking her head, staring at the misfits in the yard. Suddenly old Blecher flings herself against the driver's-side window. Drew yelps.

'It's only me,' Blecher shouts through the glass because Drew isn't rolling down the window. 'Sorry, I didn't mean to startle you. It's so good to see you. How are you?' Drew stares at her hands on the wheel.

'I was thinking about you the other day,' Blecher shouts, 'and I thought, Drew just has to work through it. It's like a splinter, it just has to work itself out.'

I push open my door and dissolve into the mob where I hear the predictable chorus of sick words: *cunt, slit, gash, twat, yo bitch, where's your lesbo friend?* I keep my head down, think of animals – they don't bother you if you avoid eye contact.

On the steps I look back and Drew's still there, immobilized by Blecher, and for a second I feel sorry for her but then I remember that she doesn't need me anymore, that I'm spoiled rotten, snide, self-important. She has Treeboy now.

Megan, the former mute who is now empowered by Prozac, says it's disgraceful that Toby Belch and his buddies lock up Malvolio. 'Why are they so hostile?' she demands.

'That's an interesting question,' Huff says. 'Why are Sir Toby and his cohorts so hostile toward Malvolio?'

'Because he's a dick,' Taylor in the dog collar offers.

'Define *dick*,' Megan says.

Some dick left a note on my locker saying I'll get worse treatment than Rossi if I testify. Slade the blow-job freak has been wearing my ripped underpants on his head. Some psychologist on the radio said humans are angry primates out of control.

'He's a fag,' Bonehead says.

'Totally,' Taylor adds, 'he's like, wearing fucking stockings.'

'Since when does how someone dresses make them homosexual?' Megan demands.

'That's a good question,' Huff says, leaning on the back of his chair. 'Since when does attire define the man, or woman for that matter? Limone, what are your thoughts?'

'You is what you wears,' I say.

'What does that make Malvolio then, cross-gartered in yellow stockings?'

'A faggot,' an angry primate concludes.

'Nobody has the right to lock someone in hideous darkness,' Megan declares. She's had her hair cut short. It used to hang over her face and she chewed on it. 'Think Guantánamo,' she persists, '*children* were being held at Guantánamo.'

'Gwan-what?' the primate says.

'That's what's wrong with the world,' Megan concludes. 'Men thinking they can just go ahead and lock people up.'

'Or kill them,' I offer.

I tell Mrs. Wartowski I think Vronsky's a jerk and I don't see how Anna could leave her little boy to shack up with him.

'Only because her husband won't let her take the boy with her,' she argues.

'That's no excuse. You don't desert your kid. It's *your* responsibility.' Then I remember that Mrs. Wartowski's biological parents were wired together and thrown in the Danube by her adoptive parents.

'One day you'll fall in love,' Mrs. Wartowski says, 'and then you'll understand.' She gazes at me, all dreamy and delusional.

I grab a science rag and sit with my back to the wall. There's nobody around but Chester Gropp, the pimple farm, popping bubble wrap. I read about all the plastic in the oceans. Some ship lost a container over the side and dropped ten thousand plastic ducks into the Pacific. The albatross thought they were food and started eating and regurgitating them to feed their babies. The albatross couldn't figure out why their babies were dying. All kinds of sea creatures eat the plastic bobbing on the ocean and don't know that it's killing them.

I read about cancer and stem-cell research. You can slash, poison and burn but if one cancerous stem cell remains, the cancer's coming back. I figure in twenty years current cancer treatment will look barbaric, like leeches and bleeding.

Chester stops popping bubble wrap to pick his nose and wipe his fingers on his jeans.

It turns out a cheap, simple drug that has been used for years to treat metabolic disorders also happens to kill almost all cancers. But it's not patented, which means drug companies aren't interested in carrying out clinical trials using the drug because there's no money in it. I read that scientists are messing around with human/cow and human/rabbit hybrids. I read that they've created genetically modified chickens to lay anti-cancer eggs.

Mrs. Wartowski scrambles toward me. 'The principal wants to see you.'

'Frankly, we are all shocked and disappointed with your behaviour,' Brimmers says. She's wearing purple eyeshadow, looks like she's been in a fight.

'Mr. Lund in particular feels that you betrayed his trust. He believed in your talent.'

'What exactly are we talking about here?' I say.

'I think you know very well. You are a disgrace to your mother.'

'Which one?'

All this pretense that they give a rat's fart makes me want to throw things.

'I think it's time to seek professional help. Mrs. Blecher has done everything she can for you.'

'Did she say that?'

'Not in those exact words.' She rests her hands on her sex-goddess hips.

'What *were* her exact words?' For some reason I don't want Blecher quitting on me. All of a sudden I want to be in her cubbyhole watching her eat cheese triangles.

'I can't remember exactly what she said.'

'Then don't quote her.'

'There is a psychologist associated with the school. I think it's time you saw him.'

Him? I don't want to see any hims.

'Have you bumped uglies with Inspector Power yet?' I demand because I just want one true thing said.

'Excuse me?'

'Or is he married? Don't cops marry when they're twelve or something, then get hoochie on the side? Child prostitutes? School principals?'

'If you were not Drew's daughter ... '

'You'd suspend me. Now that's a scary thought. You don't even know what's going on in this school. You've got your head so far up your ass, you can't even *see* the suffering. Kids are *dying* in this school.' I shove the African violet off her desk, can't even get it together to throw it. She stares down at it, her glossed lips glob-globbing. I jet out of there.

Doyle's still not talking to me except to give orders. He wants the joint cleaned because Mr. Buzny told him the health inspector is planning a visit. 'That's a line,' I replied. 'No way does the health inspector give a heads-up.' Doyle just shrugged and went on giving orders. YangYang's busy trying to decide which university to grace with her presence so I get down on my hands and knees to clean the fridges. I don't mind it because I can see I'm having an effect. The water in the pail gets dirty, I change it, it gets dirty again. Maybe I should become a cleaning woman. They make twenty bucks an hour, cash, and you get to snoop in people's medicine cabinets, steal their drugs. The hitch is you have to clean their toilets.

YangYang's uncustomarily chatty. Usually she doesn't have much to say to poor minority white trash like myself but she's giddy about her future prospects, Masters and PhDs and all that. 'I worry I'm an Internet addict,' she admits. 'In Shanghai, a man played online games for six years. He's stuck in a sitting position. His back is fused at a ninety-degree angle. Doctors say there's nothing they can do.'

I ask her to move so I can clean where she's standing.

'And a boy played World of Warcraft for thirty-six hours in a row, then jumped off his high-rise. His suicide note said he was off to meet the game's characters.'

'I don't think Internet addiction is unique to China,' I say.

'It's a serious problem. They're shutting down Net cafés and have national addiction helplines.'

Nobody sees it as a disease over here. You're expected to live in a virtual world, to lose yourself in technology and shut the fuck up.

YangYang clasps her hands under her chin. 'I have to cut back.'

I'm thinking about those female elephants in the South African reserve. Humans are drugging them with elephant-size contraceptive pills because there are too many elephants in the park. They consume three hundred kilograms of grass, leaves and twigs a day and they're messy eaters: 60 percent gets wasted. It's pissing off other species, especially the black rhinos. The female elephant usually breeds every four years and doesn't mate while nursing. On the pill she comes into heat every four months but doesn't get pregnant, so the bulls keep banging her. The bulls can be four times her weight and the stress of the frequent copulation equals abuse. Female elephants are being raped to death. The conservation 'experts' say the only alternative is to start culling elephants again. Cull humans, would be my recommendation. If civil war can't do it, get some suicide bombers in there.

Waldo the security guard shows up for his swirl softee. 'This guy,' he tells me, 'got in *The Guinness Book of Records* by making the biggest rubber band ball ever. It took him a year. He had to wear safety goggles at the end.'

'There's a life purpose for you,' I say.

'What I want to know is, what was he doing for cash all that time? I mean, he must have been living in his mother's basement or something. Working people don't get to be in *The Guinness Book of Records*, they're too busy working.' I can see he thinks he's being witty. He leans over the counter. 'Have you seen that homeless guy around?'

'Which one?' I wouldn't tell him even if I had because all Waldo does is chase the poor buggers out.

'The one with the plastic bags.'

'They all have plastic bags.'

'The one with the toque. He's always wearing it.'

'The Hugh Hefner look-alike was digging around in the trash.' I think it's swell Hugh got married to another twenty-year-old. He's only ninety or something.

'You let me know if he bothers you,' Waldo says, puffing his pecs.

'Roger that.'

Waldo licks his softee. 'Some guy tried to shove a cell down his girlfriend's throat. His excuse was she got drunk and was trying to swallow the cell before he could grab it and find out who she'd been calling.' Waldo stiffens like a hound spotting a squirrel. The homeless guy in the toque is exiting the can. 'Hey, buddy,'

Waldo says, bounding after him. 'I'm going to have to ask you to leave.'

'What for?' the homeless man asks. 'I'm not doing nothin'.'

'Well, I heard different. A lady tells me you spit on her.'

'I didn't spit on anybody.'

'Well, I've got a lady here says you spit on her.'

'What lady?' He looks around.

'She's not here at this present moment but her description fits you, buddy, and we can't have people spitting on customers. So you know what we have to do now, we have to get you out.' The homeless man doesn't resist, just clutches his plastic bags.

The nervous woman in the hat shuffles over to order her smoothie. I have to make it because YangYang's on break even though she hasn't lifted a finger since she got here. 'How are you?' the nervous woman asks.

'Tootin'. Would that be strawberry or blueberry?'

'Strawberry, please.' She watches me like she always does, making sure I don't shortchange her on berries.

'What happened to your face?' she asks.

'I fell down. Are you the one who said the homeless guy spit on you?'

'What? No, of course not.'

'If he spat on somebody, they were probably asking for it. It's not like he can plug 'em or anything. *I* might start spitting on people. You'd have to work up a good glob, though, if it's going to travel. You can't be too spontaneous.'

'Limone,' she says, which startles me because I didn't think she knew my name. 'I'm Constance. I'm your mother.'

I stare at her parched face for what feels like a couple of hours.

'I'm sorry to have to tell you this way,' she says, 'but it's been difficult contacting you.'

I recognize her voice now.

'I'm hoping we can be friends,' she says. 'I know this is all very strange and sudden. But I thought we might start a dialogue.'

'You've been watching me for months.'

'Yes.'

'Checking me out, making sure I'm not some kind of freak.'

'Not exactly. More just trying to find the right moment.'

'And this is the right moment?'

'To be honest, I'm not sure there is one. All these years I've wondered if you would try to find me.'

'Why would I try to find you? Who the *fuck* are you?'

Doyle appears in time for the bad word, gives me one of his über-boss glares. 'Is there a problem here?'

'Not at all,' the woman in the hat says. 'Limone is making me a smoothie.'

'Is that what she's doing?'

I resume mashing berries, thinking about my useless life and that the only thing that gets me through is Kadylak, holding her, reading to her, building houses with doors. I don't want anything from this nervous woman in the hat. I want her to go away. I want my dreams of Mutti back. The blender wails. I work the register, take her cash. Her fingers are bony, witchy, but the nails are ridged and flat like mine. I've always hated my nails, always wanted the smooth round nails of hand models. This woman left me with her nails. I slap her change on the counter. 'Have a nice day.'

26

M rs. Barnfield spears a chicken croquette and waves it in front of Rossi who's on the couch watching a hospital show. The model types in scrubs huddle around a body, trying to jolt its heart into action.

'Please eat something, angel,' Mrs. Barnfield says. 'I made them specially for you, they're your favourite.'

Rossi pays no attention to her. I can't understand why she's tormenting the only person who loves her. Mrs. Barnfield's even laid the table with placemats and napkins and little swirls of butter. I jab at the croquettes in front of me.

'How 'bout a little salad, sweetheart? I bought low-fat Ranch dressing.'

'I'm not hungry.'

It's over for the corpse. The model types in scrubs sigh and shake their heads.

'These croquettes certainly are delicious,' I say. I can't remember the last time one of my mothers cooked me a meal. Mrs. Barnfield strokes Rossi's hair, which hasn't been brushed in days.

'I'll just go sit with Lemon,' Mrs. Barnfield says, 'and you come join us if you feel like it.' She swallows some gruel out of a can. She looks worried out of her mind, her eyes flitting back and forth between Ross and me. I get the feeling she's hoping I'll make conversation.

'One of my customers,' I say, 'is a total Nazi freak. He likes talking about the bunker, and Hitler having strokes and ranting about vegetarianism and all that. Apparently old Adolf had this German shepherd called Blondi he was always talking to. Eva Braun hated the dog, was always kicking it when lover-boy wasn't looking. The hound would start whining and Adolf would get all concerned, trying to figure out what was wrong with the mutt. He poisoned Blondi before he poisoned himself and Eva.'

'Isn't that interesting,' Mrs. Barnfield says, watching Rossi staring at the model types stitching up gunshot wounds.

I eat more mini carrots. 'These carrots are delicious,' I say in Rossi's direction. 'There's nothing like butter swirls on steamed carrots.'

An ad for a fabric softener comes on. A damsel in a negligee rolls around in sheets like she's getting off on it.

'I'm not sure I buy that vegetarian stuff,' I say. 'I heard that old Adolf had some chef from Vienna cook him Wiener schnitzel.' I smear a butter swirl on one of the Pillsbury dinner rolls Mrs. Barnfield's just baked. 'I've never been able to figure out how anybody could eat baby cows. They chain their feet together so the calves can't walk. It keeps the meat tender.'

On the wire wave communicator a happy family is chowing down at Red Lobster. The Ken-doll dad ruffles his shrimp-eating daughter's hair.

'Why is your friend so interested in Nazis?' Mrs. Barnfield asks.

'He's not my friend, actually, just some weirdo. He told me Mrs. Goebbels killed her children in the bunker. I always thought Mr. Goebbels did it, but apparently the frau drugged them unconscious then shoved cyanide capsules down their throats. Old Joseph wasn't even in the room, couldn't handle it, was off diddling some starlet.'

A couple of the model types start swapping spit in a stairwell.

'If you think about it,' I say, 'Mrs. Goebbels was saving them. What with old Adolf dead and the Russkies barking at the door, she knew she'd be separated from her kids and her husband would be executed. She figured a world without National Socialism wouldn't be exactly friendly to her Aryan spawn. It wasn't like the Commies would be too thrilled to hear the Nazi anthems she was always getting her kiddies to croon for Uncle Adolf. Offing them was an act of love. She figured she'd meet them in heaven.'

'Did she take a capsule too then?'

'Nah. She made hubby shoot her before he shot himself. She played a game of solitaire first though. I don't think she was that wild about old Joseph, probably because he was always off banging demoiselles.'

Mrs. Barnfield swallows more gruel. 'I don't know what kind of mother could poison her own children.'

'A courageous one. Or crazy, depending on how you look at it.'

The girly in scrubs who was swapping spit in the stairwell is being stalked by a former patient who wants her to give him a rectal or something. He charges around Emerg in a New York Yankees cap.

'A lot of bunker Nazis blew their brains out,' I say. 'At the end. There they'd been snug as bugs while civilians were being bombed. Old Adolf didn't give a buzzard's ass about the German people getting blasted, no way was he going to surrender.'

Mrs. Barnfield pushes some lettuce around on her plate, pretending she's going to eat it, and I get the feeling this isn't the kind of conversation she was hoping for but I can't think of another topic. '"Ze broad mass of a nation,"' I say, doing my Hitler impression, '"vill more easily fall victim to a big lie zan to a small one." Adolf's exact words.'

Mrs. Barnfield fiddles with the tassels on her placemat. A gaggle of orderlies swarm the stalker in the Yankees cap. The girly gasps in a corner while the brawny lad she was swapping spit with comforts her.

'A lot of those Nazis lived into their nineties,' I say, 'which makes you wonder about conscience, how you live longer if you don't have one.'

'Could you shut up for *one* minute?' Rossi says, actually facing me for the first time in days. Her eyes look uninhabited.

'She speaks,' I say.

'Who asked you to talk about that shit? Nobody wants to know about that shit. You think my mother needs to hear that?'

'I don't mind,' Mrs. Barnfield says.

'You *do* mind, Mother, you're just too polite to say anything. Lemon's a fucking psycho. Any sick topic out there, she reads up on it. Don't even get her started on animal testing.'

I look down at the melted butter hardening around my carrots.

'You're sick, Lemon, you should get help and stop hanging around my mother, she's got enough problems.'

'It's nice to have company,' Mrs. Barnfield says.

'You call her company? She wrote a sick play. She made people audition for it by fake-fucking doggy-style on her couch.'

Mrs. Barnfield looks at me the way she'd have looked at Frau Goebbels.

'Did it ever occur to you,' Rossi spits at me, 'that what happened to me might have something to do with what *you* did?'

'What happened to you, angel?' Mrs. Barnfield asks.

'You fucked everything up,' Rossi hisses, getting off the couch and heading unsteadily toward me. 'They went at me because of what *you* did, your sick, fucking non-existent play.' She already looks thinner, weaker. I know she's planning to starve herself so she'll die before her mother. 'Now get out and leave us alone.' She yanks on the back of my chair. 'You're not welcome here.'

'You can't blame me for what happened,' I say, knowing she can.

'*What* happened?' Mrs. Barnfield pleads. 'Please, girls, tell me what's going on.' She grasps at Rossi's arm.

'Why won't you tell her?' I ask.

'None of your business.'

'What's none of her business, please, tell me, angel?'

Rossi jerks the door open and stands with her hand on her bony hip, waiting for me to exit. Everything in the apartment that I have known since kindergarten, the figurines, the china plates, the kitten paintings, have turned hostile. All those days sitting here drinking Kool-Aid, feeling safe. I am no longer welcome.

'Where's Bradley?'

Brenda stares at the monitor. 'He's been transferred.'

'Why?'

'Is that your concern, Limone?'

'Where are they taking him?'

'What parents decide to do with patients is none of your business.'

'He can't travel, he's too frail.' I picture him being bounced around in planes, trains and automobiles, with no one to play Nerf ball with.

'He'll be fine,' Brenda says to the monitor and I can't believe she thinks I'm stupid enough to believe her. This has happened before, when parents with cash don't like what the doctors are telling them. They outsource their kid to the States or India or somewhere and pay doctors to tell them what they want to hear. I'm used to kids coming and going when I'm not on watch, but it's worse with Bradley. I stand outside Kadylak's room waiting for my blood to start moving again, clutching the grapes I bought him, seeing his wise eyes looking at me. He'll be so lonely. He won't understand why I'm not there.

Kadylak refuses the grapes but gets pretty excited when old Clive, the master, hires Tilly to be his housekeeper. Kadylak hasn't figured out that Clive wants to stuff the young lass, even though he's in a wheelchair. On the news they showed some sick creep in a wheelchair who gave his three-year-old daughter gonorrhea. Explain that to a teenager. You're sterile because your father raped you when you were three. You've forgotten the incident but fortunately he posted it on YouTube.

There I go with those Sick Topics again.

'Why are the other servants so mean to Tilly?' Kadylak asks.

'Because she's got the top job. They don't want to take orders from some coal miner.'

'But she's nice.'

'Since when does being nice make you popular?'

I can't shake Bradley, can't believe I won't be able to pick him up again, jostle him, make him belly laugh.

Kadylak grabs hold of Sweetheart the penguin and strokes her wings. 'I think they should be nice to her because she isn't bossy.'

'I agree. Unfortunately, that's not how the world ticks.'

She kisses Sweetheart's head and tucks her under her covers. She's lost so much weight the veins stick out on her temples and neck. 'A lady my mother cleans for is always telling my mother what she did wrong. No matter how hard Mama works, Mrs. Bandakar finds something wrong.'

'Which proves my point because your mother's nice.'

Kadylak looks at me for a long time. The blue of her eyes looks darker, deeper, full of shadows. 'My parents wish they never came to Canada.'

'They told you that?'

She shakes her head. I try to straighten her scarf.

'I don't remember my grandmother,' she says. 'Mama tells me about her because she doesn't want me to forget her. I pretend to remember.' She rolls on her side. I untangle her lines and adjust the bed to the horizontal. I kiss her cheek, feeling chemo heat against my lips.

'Can you spin the tops again?' she asks.

I slide the table close to the bed and spin the tops until she goes unconscious. Her breathing sounds a bit raspy but I don't want to call anybody because they'll wake her and shove instruments at her. I lie on the sofa bed. There's no way another kid is disappearing on my watch.

Brenda's nudging me. 'You can't sleep here.'

'I wasn't sleeping.'

'You were most definitely sleeping. I've just about had it with your antics.' Her breath stinks of tuna.

'I'm sorry, I didn't mean to fall asleep.'

'Go home now, please.'

'What if she wakes up?'

'You are not family, Limone. The sofa bed is for family.'

'Her family has to work all the time.'

'We all know that she is attached to you, and for that reason we have been tolerant of your behaviour. But we have our limits. You are not being professional.'

'I'm not a professional.'

'Even volunteers should not get emotionally involved with the patients.' She holds the door open for me. I think of kicking it shut, fighting the old catfish, but she'd just call security and ban me from the ward. I walk out of there feeling the air being sucked out of me.

The subway's full of zombies. Some Korean guy in dark glasses stands by the doors with his arms crossed and his index fingers pointed like guns. I change trains, glad to be free of him, but sure enough he shows up in my car, still by the doors with his arms crossed and his fingers pointed like guns. A leering lubber in a track suit parks across from me. Sphincter-loosening anxiety is becoming chronic with me in public places. Some woman was raped on a cruise by a security guard. Her cabin door didn't have a peephole so she opened it, thinking it was her friend. The security guard says it was consensual sex. The FBI aren't pressing charges because they say it's a 'she said, he said' case, meaning no evidence. The rape victim was on the radio crying about it. She said the fact that nobody believes her feels like being violated all over again.

Sick Topics.

I get off the train and walk, inhaling car exhaust, and check out recycling bins to find out how the normal people are getting by. Lots of wine bottles and pizza boxes, Bagel Bites, sugared cereals, mini Danishes, frozen lasagna, fries, pop cans, chip packets. When in doubt they reach for junk and booze. I step in dog shit and spend an hour trying to get it off my boot with a twig. How did they do it in the seventeenth and eighteenth centuries? Or did they just buck up and get used to having shit on their shoes? They had to get used to shit on their houses because they dumped it out the windows. During the rain the drainage ditches were bunged up with shit, slop and dead babies. Things are supposed to be better now because we've got plumbing and no bugs in our beds, and light bulbs instead of tallow candles made from sheep's hooves. We feel superior, showered and shaved in our shit-free Nikes, sucking back CO_2s.

The worst part about the nervous woman in the hat is that she's torpedoed Mutti. Even though I suspected my mother was trailer trash, I'm not willing to let go of Mutti. She's been living with me for years; I can almost touch her, smell the potato latkes on her. I mix her up with Anne Frank's mother who, even after she was separated from her daughters in the camp, managed to smuggle food scraps to them. The nervous woman in the hat sat watching me for months, folding her napkins into little squares, making dents in her Styrofoam cups with her thumbnail. Once I saw her break a Styrofoam cup into little pieces. I've done this. Without even realizing it, suddenly there's a pile of Styrofoam bits in front of me. It's just a question of time before I start wearing hats. Already my hands are starting to look witchy, don't feel like my hands. I don't want them on me.

Some creep's following me. When I cross to the other side of the street, so does he. I cross back. So does he. I hightail it down a side street and look for a house with an open-door policy, or a kind pedestrian. There's nothing, just the racket of my boots and breathing. Turning a corner, I smash into a shopping cart and hear a yowl as plastic bags fly in all directions. I fall hard on a patch of grass and just lie there with my face in the dirt.

'What did you do that for?' a homeless man wearing a hat with flaps demands. 'Can't you at least say you're sorry?' he demands.

'I'm sorry.'

'Why don't you look where you're going?'

'I was running.'

'Evidently.' He speaks clearly, like he's educated.

I help him stuff the bags in the cart. They smell of piss and mildew. I look around. No sign of my pursuer. The homeless guy starts spraying Lysol into a can of Coke.

'Can't drink it straight?' I ask him.

'You try it.'

'Why don't you go to a shelter?'

'They want you in by nine.'

'Is that so bad?'

'When's Mommy want *you* home?'

'I don't have a mommy.'

'Aren't you lucky.'

'Where's yours?'

'Pushing up daisies.'

'So I guess you don't miss her.'

'She made grand martinis.'

All of a sudden Treeboy trots up, breathless. 'Lemon ...' he begins.

'What are you doing here?' I demand.

'Looking for you.'

'Was it you chasing me?'

'Trying to catch up.'

'Why don't you leave her alone?' the homeless guy says. 'Can't you see she wants to be left *alone*?'

'He's right,' I say, cramming in the last of his bags. He shoves his cart down the street to get away from us riff-raff.

'Please come home,' Vaughn says.

'It's not your home, where do you get this idea it's your home?'

'I didn't say it was my home.'

'You said "home." You didn't say "come back to Drew's," you said "home." What the fuck are you doing there anyway? Don't you have your own home? Your own mother? It's sick the way you're hanging around. It's fucking perverted.' I start walking, telling myself I'm lucky it was only Treeboy tailing me, lost without his forest. Although I wouldn't have minded dying a hideous, sexually deviant death. Because then Rossi would have heard about it.

'Why do you think it's perverted?' he asks. I don't even look at him, just hear him panting behind me. My lungs are fully recovered, pink and steaming.

'It's obvious that you two have a bit of a thing going,' I say.

'What thing?'

'Oh please.'

'We're friends.'

'Right.'

'She needs help right now.'

'She needs to get laid. She's not happy unless she's got some dickhead taking her water-skiing or something.'

'Really? Hunh. So you think I should take her water-skiing?'

The homeless man looks over his shoulder then accelerates, trying to widen the gap between us.

'Drew's house is that way,' Treeboy says, grabbing my arm, which gives me an excuse to go at him. I jab him under the jaw, swat the side of his head. When he tries to shield himself with his arms, I kick his shins and jab my boot into the top of his foot. He yelps. I have to admit, it feels great, inflicting damage. I leave him in pain. 'Get a job,' I tell him.

I smear butter on my mini baguette. Don't know how much longer I can loiter before they figure out I'm sleeping here. Shouldn't drink any more coffee. Can feel myself ticking, thinking about those short people 1,800 years ago in Thailand who had huge cerebral cortexes, which meant they were way smarter than we are. They didn't start wars or destroy ecosystems and were only four feet tall. A volcano wiped them out. Why them? Why wipe out peaceful people with huge cortexes?

A small-cortexed codger wearing a fedora over his toque keeps glancing up from a tabloid to check me out. The headline on the tabloid says, 'Who's Had a Full-Body Makeover?'

I read in *National Geographic* about Africans killing Africans. Hutus ranting on loudspeakers about what cockroaches Tutsis were. Which is how every genocide gets going, I guess. The more aggressive side mouths off about what scum, filth, lying, cheating, degenerates the weaker side is, and how these loathsome, despicable vermin are to blame for all the shit that goes down, and that if we go out and machete them, our problems will be over. We're about due for a genocide in North America, although it's hard to say who's going to slaughter whom. The boys showing up for school killings are all breeds. It doesn't take a genius to figure out that committing mass murder would lose its attraction if it wasn't the fastest road to fame. The shooters just look like regular dweebs hoping someone will be nice to them. You have to wonder if, before the rampage, somebody *had* been nice to them, invited them out for a cup of joe or something, the massacres might not have happened. Pretty sad how they have to talk themselves into it, dress up like action heroes and post their psycho rantings. Although I guess once you taste contempt, it's pretty easy to make the jump to murder. It's something in our angry-primate wiring. All it takes is a little circuit change. And desperation. I guess we just aren't desperate enough yet in old Amérique du Nord for a full-scale genocide. Once the oil runs out maybe the religious right will round us up and get some systematic killing going, convert the non-believers into biofuel to keep their guzzlers running.

I'll forget about Bradley eventually. You get better at knowing you'll get over stuff as you get older. All those people standing around during genocides, they know they'll get over it if they just look the other way while their neighbours are being exterminated. Just like I'll get over the fact that I sat around sucking on pretzels while Rossi got raped.

A three-hundred-pound lady in an oversized tank top and leggings squeezes into a chair a couple of tables over. She's clutching a croissant and a book. I try to read the title because I always check out what people are reading. It's usually *Chicken Soup for the Soul* books or *How to Become a Positive Thinker* or something. She puts the book down to butter her croissant. It's *Pride and Prejudice*. She's reading about Lizzie pining for old Darcy, wondering what the hell happened to *her* Mr. Darcy and how she got so freakin' fat.

At least Kadylak's getting better, off the ventilator and all that.

I'm definitely hyper because my witchy hands have shredded my paper cup into bits. I didn't even roll up the rim to win. I dig around for the bits of rim, find one with the tip of the big yellow arrow and roll it up. *Play again*, it says.

Usually when I sit in trees I listen to bird and squirrel sounds, rustling leaves and all that. But it's night and they're sleeping and all I hear is cars and humans. I'm hoping Drew's noticed I'm missing and is regretting all the shitty things she's ever said to me. More likely Vaughn's consoling her, cooking up slop and finding her G-spot.

I feel around in my backpack for my mother/daughter scrapbook and tuck in the story about the mother wrongly convicted of killing her baby due to some inept pathologist. Her older kid was taken away by the Children's Aid Society. Eventually his foster parents wanted to adopt him. His real mother had to concede that, since she wasn't allowed to have him, he'd have a better future with the adoptive parents. Otherwise he'd be passed around in foster care, which would lead him straight to a jail cell. So even though it nearly killed her to give him up, his real mother did. She wasn't allowed to see him until he was eighteen. But they could write to each other and send pictures and all that. Well, he couldn't forget her, and was writing to her all the time about how much he missed her, and remembering little things they did together and asking her if she could remember them. It tore her up every time she read one of his letters because she remembered every little thing, but she didn't know if she should encourage him to miss her or if she should try to help him forget her. Now she can see him again, hold him again, tell him she remembers everything. I hope it works out; probably won't, though. He'll be taking drugs to fill the gaping holes inside him. She'll freak about what's happened to her boy and start zoning out on antidepressants, fondling his old letters.

Staying out all night is harder than it looks in movies. Time drags. Plus I'm getting cold. I hang around outside Zippy's for about an hour. There's no light in her windows. Not sure if it's worth the hassle. I could never trust her to keep a secret, she'll probably flip out and phone Damian. He'll haul my ass to the police station, or Drew's, which would be even worse.

Moments like this it's best to think about somebody worse off than yourself. That African girl who got her hands cut off, for example. Boy soldiers figure people without hands can't mark ballots. One of them held a gun to her head while the other two held her arms down. The girl crawled to a village and eventually some agency hooked her up with Canadians who wanted to help her. She lives here now and goes to school with kids who can't figure out the hand thing, like how that could happen. The girl says she has moments when she forgives the boy soldiers, which I can't figure out. She assumes her family has been killed, but has somehow managed to get a B average and is planning a career in office administration. How do you type with no hands? Meanwhile us Americanos are taking antidepressants because kissing ass to keep our twelve-hour-day jobs gets depressing. Not to mention knowing we could be replaced by an even better ass-kisser who'll work fourteen-hour days. Can't see them hiring an African with no hands though. Maybe for about five minutes for the photo op.

I buzz Zippy's, a man answers. It's the ape man from Marty Millionaire. I scram.

She picks up on the first ring.

'I need somewhere to sleep,' I tell her.

'Where are you? I'll send a cab.'

Her house is narrow and antiseptic with abstract art on the walls.

'Can I make you some tea or coffee? Would you like some juice?'

'I'm hungry, actually,' I say, staring at the art to avoid staring at her.

'What can I get you? Bread and cheese? Some fruit? I could scramble some eggs.'

'Bread and cheese is fine.' Her place is open concept, meaning there's no place to hide. While she messes around in the kitchen, I scan for family photos. There are none, probably because they'd clutter the designer look. The furniture is metallic and leather, angular. A child could never live here. A child would skewer herself on the furniture.

Constance puts the food on the cleared dining room table. At Drew's these days, tables are never cleared. They breed paper and dirty cups.

She sits across from me. Without the hat I can see her hair-line, which, of course, is exactly like mine. She has bed-head, her mouse-coloured hair stands out in tufts. So much for my mouse hair turning an actual colour someday.

'Do you work?' I ask.

'Not anymore. I'm on permanent disability.'

'Why?'

'Fibromyalgia.'

'What's that?'

'A muscle disease. It's not fatal but very disabling.'

'You don't look disabled.'

'I have chronic pain, and tire very easily.' She keeps tugging on the chain around her neck.

'Is it genetic?'

'I don't think so.'

'What did you do before?'

'I worked for the Ministry of Foreign Affairs.'

'A government job. Must have been nice. Big cheques, big benefits.'

She lays out napkins. 'It had its moments.'

'So I guess us taxpayers are subsidizing your disability.'

She slices a tomato. It bleeds all over the plate.

'So why didn't you abort?' I ask.

'I thought I'd be able to manage.'

'What happened?'

She sips her tea, nervously, of course, wrapping her witchy fingers around the cup. 'I kept you for months. You cried incessantly. I thought I was losing my mind. I suspect it was post-partum depression, although they didn't call it that then. I probably should have sought counselling. But I had my thesis to defend.' She tugs at the chain around her neck again. 'It just wasn't working.'

'Isn't it great chucking stuff when it just *isn't working*? Like why bother to try and fix it. Get rid of it. Computers, babies ... '

'You have every right to be angry.'

I shove bread and cheese in my mouth and chew for about an hour, waiting for her to continue.

'You're probably wondering why I've contacted you after all these years,' she says, ripping a slice of bread into little bits. 'I just felt ... it was time.'

'For what?'

'To make peace with my past. You can't run forever.'

What a crock. 'You were lonely and happened to notice you'd totally fucked up your life. You're hoping I'll make it better for you.'

'I don't think that's fair.'

'Did you give me a name?'

'Of course. Cecily.'

'You've got to be kidding me.'

'What's wrong with Cecily?'

'Did you stash me in a handbag?'

'I don't think you should make light of this. It wasn't easy for me.'

'Me neither.'

Stalemate. She nibbles on one of her bits of bread.

'Cecily Charity,' she adds.

Cecily Charity Ramsbottom. Now there's a reason not to live. I wolf down tomato slices, waiting for her to weep and plead for forgiveness. She starts shredding one of the napkins.

'Why don't you have any photos of anybody?' I ask.

'How do you mean?'

'Your parents or anybody.'

'Oh. I've never been close to my parents and my sister is ... my sister is mentally ill.'

'She's locked up?'

'They don't lock them up anymore. I'm not sure where she is.'

'Homeless.'

'That's a possibility.'

I start buttering more bread, might as well stuff myself before she discovers I'm not the long-lost daughter of her dreams and

229

boots me out. 'So,' I say, 'you go spying on the daughter you ditched, but you don't give a buzzard's ass about your sister who's probably licking cat food out of a can somewhere. Is it genetic?'

'What?'

'Her condition.'

'I don't know.'

'You don't know much.' I talk with my mouth full, spraying bits of bread on the glass-topped table. 'What about my father?'

'What about him?'

'Who is he?'

She looks at me as though I'm speaking Chinese. 'You know who your father is.'

'I do?'

'Don't you?'

'Is this a trick question?'

'No, it's just ... I thought you knew. I thought he'd told you. He said he would.'

'Gee, I guess he didn't.'

'I see. Well, I really don't know if it's my place to tell you.'

'Tell me or I'll fucking rip your face off.'

She looks at me the way she probably looked at me when I was incessantly crying.

'Tell me,' I repeat.

'Damian is your father. Your adoptive mother doesn't know. He didn't want to hurt her.'

Suddenly I'm down the mine with Tilly, choking on coal dust, covered in soot.

'I met him while he was renovating our offices,' she explains. 'He didn't tell me he was married.'

He's never worn a ring, says he isn't the ring type.

'We were careless,' Constance says, going at her napkin again. 'And anyway, our affair took place in ... in awkward circumstances.'

'Behind dumpsters,' I suggest, 'in storage rooms, on top of the drywall. He's been at it for years.'

'Yes, well, I certainly had the impression he'd had some experience.'

'Which is what attracted you to him. A little walk on the wild side after all that shit-eating and paper shuffling.'

'He seemed like a good man. I think he is a good man. I mean, he arranged the adoption, was very understanding. I really thought it was for the best.'

'Did you ever meet Zippy?'

'Who?'

'His wife. My mama.'

'No.'

'Why not?'

'We thought it would complicate things. Damian wanted to keep it simple.'

'So you handed your baby over to a complete stranger?'

'That's not unusual with adoption.'

'She was fucking psychotic,' I say. 'A total nutcase. She tried to kill me.'

'He told me she fell in love with you on sight.'

'And you didn't ask questions. How'd the thesis go?'

'Very well. I worked night and day on it for months.'

'Kept you up like an incessantly crying baby.'

She goes back to tugging on her chain, pulling it from side to side, sawing at her neck.

'I have to sleep now,' I say. 'Is there a spare room?'

I follow her up narrow stairs past more aborted art. I lie rigid on a narrow bed. I don't even like this woman.

Who needs a past anyway? Look at that Amazonian tribe with no long-term memory. Out of sight is out of mind with these folks. They don't sweat about years gone by. All they need is a few pots and pans, a machete, a knife, a couple of palm-leaf bags, and wooden bows and arrows. They're total hunter-gatherers. Missionaries and government agencies have been trying to teach them farming and religion for decades. The tribe doesn't give a monkey's turd. They arrived in the Amazon between ten and forty thousand years ago but the only history that means anything to them is what someone living has seen or heard. When asked about Creation they say, 'It's always been this way.' They have no fixed words for colours, no words for left and right, and their only numbers are one and two. Their language is driving linguists nuts because one word can mean many different things depending on how they say it. When the missionaries try to interest them in Jesus, the tribe's people say, 'Have you met this man?' A guy who died two thousand years ago doesn't draw crowds. Only immediate experience counts. They don't live in the past or plan for the future. They don't search for long-lost relatives. They don't get stressed and fat and cancerous and diabetic. They don't take pharmaceuticals.

I listen to Constance moving around, tidying up after me. If she really cared she'd be at my door apologizing, begging me to understand. I think if she begged me to understand, I might be able to. If I could see the neediness in her that I've been living with for years. All I've ever wanted was someone to really care about me. I mean *really care*. Die for me. Animals die protecting their young. Mutti was ready to die for Marianne. Anne Frank's mother starved herself to feed her daughters. Anne Boleyn had her head chopped off to protect Elizabeth. Mrs. Barnfield would die for Rossi, *is* dying for Rossi.

I start snooping in drawers. Nothing but sheets and sweaters and little scented sachets, a heating pad. The books on the shelves are drivel, all about diet, exercise, living with chronic pain, how to make your money work for you, and a couple of award-winning novels people buy but never read.

I lie back down, try to sleep, but I'm caffeinated.

I miss my hamster, Alice. When I couldn't sleep I'd build her wonderlands with toilet rolls and egg cartons. I cut windows in cardboard boxes so she could waddle in and out of them. She was so curious, so eager to keep moving. Which is what humans are before shit keeps happening. What was shitty about Alice's life? Why was she shutting down when I took such good care of her? She started limping and couldn't trust her legs. She stopped coming out and slept more, ate less. At first I could tempt her with grapes, slices of pear or apple. When she was too weak to eat even that, I tried giving her juice through an eye dropper but she wouldn't swallow and the juice soaked her fur. She was dying and there was squat I could do about it. Zippy said there was no way we were taking a ten-dollar hamster to the vet to pay seventy bucks to have some whitecoat tell us there was nothing he could do. I saw her point. Alice was letting go, finally escaping her cage. Her courage and dignity astounded me. She lay on her side in the cedar chips, staring nowhere. I made sure she was warm, put some extra bedding around her and waited while blood leaked out of her butt. I couldn't eat, just watched for her breathing to stop. It seemed unfair that death took longer than birth, that it only took minutes to be born and days to die. Zippy tried to make me go to school, but I didn't want Alice dying when I wasn't watching. She did, though. When I woke, her eyes were closed and she was getting cold. I didn't tell Zippy because I knew she'd get hysterical about a dead rodent contaminating the air or something. I lay still, as still as Alice. When Zippy figured out what was going on she charged at Alice with rubber gloves. 'Don't touch her!' I screamed.

'We can't leave her here.'

'I'll take care of it.' I wrapped her in lilac tissue paper and placed her in a Celestial Seasonings tea box. I buried her behind the building, placed a couple of rocks over her so the raccoons wouldn't dig her up. They dug her up anyway. I wrapped her mauled body in more paper and dug her deeper, put bigger rocks over her. I visited the grave daily until Damian dragged me off to the new frau.

So that slug is my father. That oily, balding, brainless lech is part of my DNA. I knew all along, despite my dreams of dads in Father's Day ads, that mine had to be a deadbeat. I stare at a full-length mirror. Constance has a lot of mirrors. What's she looking at, the angle of her hats?

I lean in closer. There's something about the nose. People used to say we looked alike. I thought they were being polite. Nope. I've got the slug's nose.

So rather than let Zippy in on his rolls in the sawdust, he lived a lie. Made me live a lie.

There's something about the shoulders, the way they slump. The neck's too long and the arms too short. We're deformed and I only just noticed it.

I take off my clothes. I don't have a mirror at Drew's because I can't stand looking at myself. But now I want to see him, her, the bruises. Purple turning yellow around the edges. I've got her witchy hands and feet but they're *his* meaty thighs. And his ass. He's got this little round ass that looks weird on a guy. It's my ass. I get closer to study the eyes and the mouth. Hard to say. Maybe they're from past generations. I met Damian's mother once. We visited her in Florida. She was always mopping up after me, chasing me with a sponge. I couldn't stop spilling around her. 'What's wrong with this child?' she demanded. Maybe it's the old trout's mouth.

I locate the bathroom, all coordinated. Peach and cream walls, towels, mat, shower curtain, bath salts. I stand under the shower for a couple of hours, trapped in a body that is not my own. I use all her towels and leave them in piles on the peach and cream floor. I squirt peach lotion all over the body that is not my own. I dig around in her makeup case, find a lipstick and scrawl on the mirror: YOU'RE GOING TO DIE ALONE.

28

At first light I am the last human on Earth. I see traces of humanity, signs posted on telephone poles: Oh My Junk Removal, Nanny Wanted, Sod Laid, Bikini Booty Camp, K9 Walker, Salsa for Tots, Fuzzy Love Pet Sitting. All posted with hope rendered meaningless now that I am the last human on Earth. If only they'd known. Although they did know, didn't they? Unlike the dinos, we were given a heads-up.

These boots were made for walkin'. Clomp clomp clomp go the witchy feet, squelch squelch squelch go the meaty thighs, bounce bounce bounce goes the round ass. The slug nose sniffs the human detritus, the slumped shoulders shudder under the weight of Sick Topics.

I grab one of the tomato's cherub lawn ornaments and smash it into his driver-side window. Glass shatters, jewels sparkle on the asphalt. Beep beep beep goes the alarm. I sing loudly, 'Oh, what a beautiful mor-ning. Oh, what a beautiful day. I've got a wonder-ful feel-ling, everything's go-ing my way.'

Padre appears, scruffy in a striped bathrobe. The tomato hovers in something slinky, claws on mouth.

'What the ... ?' he begins. Neighbours peer through blinds.

'Oh, what a beautiful mor-ning. Oh, what a beautiful day ... '

'Would you stop that?' he says, scrambling back into the house for the car remote. The two of them squabble. 'I left the fucking thing on the sideboard,' he shouts. 'What'd you do with it? Your crap's all over the place, purses, gloves, scarves. It's a fuck-ing boutique in here.'

'I've got a wonderful feel-ling, everything's go-ing my way.'

A suited neighbour skiddles past, hurrying to kiss ass at the corpse. 'Everything alright here?'

'Tootin',' I say. 'I'm his daughter. There's no place like home.'

The honking stops and Padre stands aghast, hands jabbing the air before he rushes to assess the damage to his beloved guzzler. 'Happy now?' he asks.

'Not really.' I ram my boot into his fender.

'Stop that, just stop it, alright? You've got my attention, is that what this is about? Do you need bail money? Those bastards wouldn't tell me a thing. What's going on? Come inside, for God's sake.'

'I don't want to go inside.' Nobody's watching anymore, they're back at the morning hustle.

The slug's examining his fender.

'How do you like dem apples?' I ask.

'Jesus, Limone, what's got into you?'

'Why didn't you tell me?'

'What?'

'What do you think?'

'I have no idea. This is ... this is delinquent behaviour.'

'Unlike fucking on drywall. He's still at it, you know,' I shout at the tomato skulking in the doorway. 'Been tested for HIV lately?' She slams the door.

He slouches against his guzzler, exposing the widening bald patch at the top of his head, and for a second I feel sorry for him, the sad old bon vivant running out of tail.

'I presume your mother contacted you,' he says.

'Which one?'

'I thought it might be best coming from her, mother to daughter.'

'Wrong again, son.'

'She's a good woman.'

'She said you're a good man. Isn't that convenient? While we're at it, you might tell me about any good bastard siblings you know about. I'm kind of hoping for a family reunion. Something big, depending on how many there are, of course. I'm thinking of booking the Four Seasons ballroom.'

He rubs his brow. Poor lad, I'm such a trial.

'So what's the deal?' I persist. 'Any sibs?'

'No. I'm always very careful. It was different with Connie. She was ... an unusually passionate woman.'

'Ga-ross,' I cry. At least parentless I didn't have to picture Ma and Pa in the missionary position.

'She's had a hard life,' he says.

'Yeah, the civil service really takes it out of you.'

He spits on the cuff of his bathrobe and rubs his precious fender. 'What do you want from me? Is it money? What are the police saying?'

'Why didn't you tell me?'

'What?'

'Here we go round the mulberry bush.'

'If you mean why didn't I tell you I was your father, let me be frank. You are a difficult girl, Limone. I didn't want to make you more difficult.'

'How would that make me more difficult?'

'Look at you, you're just ... you're an embarrassment, really. You seem incapable of finding any kind of direction. You alienate anyone who tries to help you. Look what you've done to Drew.'

'What *I've* done to Drew?'

'Don't start with that. She was a grown woman, capable of making her own decisions.'

'But I wasn't grown, remember? I was a wee lass.'

'Yes, yes, we know, who always felt sorry for herself. Well, that doesn't fly anymore, kiddo. According to the police you're old enough to be responsible for your actions. So go for it, Limone, just leave me out of it.' He turns his back on me, climbing the steps to his hideous house. I grab a handful of the tomato's decorative pebbles and hurl them at him. They miss by a mile. He is behind the door and out of my life in seconds.

I try the old think-about-someone-worse-off-than-yourself trick. Those Chinese girls in one of Drew's human-rights rags. After the Jap invasion, 'comfort stations' were set up for Jap soldiers so they could rape Chinese girls. Getting raped fifty times a day meant they couldn't walk anymore. A father bribed the Japs with chickens to get his twelve-year-old daughter out. Back in the village she was raped by more Jap soldiers. She had a miscarriage and was left infertile. Sick Topics.

No sign of the catfish. I scamper to Kadylak's room. Her stuff's still there. Maybe somebody's taken her for tests. I can't wait in here, could get caught. I scoot back to the elevators.

The Second Cup is jammed as usual. I line up with the relations of sick children. An old biddy takes six hours to choose a cookie. Her cross-eyed daughter tries to hurry her along. 'Come on, Maw, there's people waitin'.' An obese woman behind me huffs and puffs. Her yellow-skinned companion, probably in need of dialysis, probably on the verge of death, says, 'My worst fear when I retire is that I'm going to be busy busy busy being unproductive.'

I hunch in a corner, surrounded. The cross-eyed daughter fits her mother into a chair. 'It just goes to show,' she says, 'money and ej-a-cation don't make you happy and all that stuff.'

I see the catfish and cower. She always orders soy vanilla something or other. While she's deliberating over munchies, I charge back up to the floor. Kadylak's still absent and I'm starting to freak. I pace, periodically checking the corridor. Peggy sees me but doesn't seem to know I'm persona non grata. 'Have you seen Kadylak?' I ask.

'She was with her dad.'

'She was?' Right away I feel a thousand times better knowing he's here. Maybe he'll hold my hand again. Maybe we'll talk more, the three of us. *They* don't think I'm difficult.

But then I see him coming out of the elevator with her unconscious in his arms.

'Help me, she not *breathing*!' he shouts. 'She not *breathing*!'

They're rushed to ICU where a tube will be shoved down her again, more lines attached to her, more blood sucked from her. Surrounded by technology, she'll be far away from me.

I get *Tilly* out and put it on her bed. I straighten the covers and place Sweetheart and Mischa on her pillow. No one will come in here now. I lie down on the sofa bed.

I hear the click of the door and duck for cover behind the bed. The catfish spies me anyway. 'I can't believe you're here again,' she blasts. 'This is pathological. The police were looking for you. Am I going to have to call security?'

'How's Kadylak?'

'That is no concern of yours.'

'What time is it?'

'Time to leave, Limone. Right now. This minute. Go.'

I walk the halls. Clomp clomp clomp go the feet, squelch, squelch, squelch go the thighs, bounce, bounce, bounce goes the ass.

I find him hunched over a pay phone. I watch his back, the heaving ribs. He is choking in his language, trying to explain something he cannot understand. He bangs his forehead into the phone box, talking more loudly. His frustration at being unable to explain what he cannot understand causes him to shout and then, abruptly, slam the receiver into its cradle. He clutches the phone box as though he has been shot. I grab him from behind, hold him steady, press my forehead between his shoulder blades. He takes my hand and holds it over his eyes. His tears heat my palm then tickle my wrist. Against my other hand his heart punishes his ribs. We are the last humans on Earth.

'Are you using the phone?' demands a short man in short pants and wearing a golfer's cap. 'If you don't mind, I need to use the phone.'

I take my palm away from Mr. Paluska's eyes, slide it down his arm and grip his hand. He moves slowly, as though tranked, moaning softly. We shuffle along the wall, making room for the people with life purpose.

'I have to get my wife,' he mutters.

'Where's your van?'

He's forgotten what parking level it's on, has confused the letters and numbers. He keeps covering his eyes and gasping as though he can't breathe.

'What colour is it?' I ask.

'White. No rear windows.'

'Licence plate?'

He stares at an exit sign.

'Can you remember any of it?'

He looks back at me. 'What happen to your face?'

'I fell down. Can you remember any of your plate numbers?'

'KWR 395.'

'Okay. You wait here.' I prop him against a humming machine room. 'Promise me you'll wait here.' He nods and the slug's meaty thighs move fast. I scale stairs, dash across parking spaces. My eyes, with laser precision, scour licence numbers. My armpits soak my T-shirt and I worry that I smell bad. Then it's there, a dirty white van. I run back to him. He has slid to the floor, is staring up at a caged fluorescent. 'I found it,' I shout, expecting him to jump to his feet. 'I found the van, we should get your wife.'

He grabs my hand and pulls me down beside him. He puts his arm around me and talks softly into my ear. 'She told me ... "The man in the black coat is back." She told me, "It's okay, Papa, I go with him."' He starts gasping again. 'She told me, "It's okay, Papa." She told me she *so* tired.' I pull his head to my chest and stroke his hair.

'*So* tired,' he says.

He wraps his arms around my waist and holds tight. It's just us, at the end of the world. I brace myself against his sobs. He pulls me onto his lap and grips me harder. Straddling him, I feel the pain in his chest, the warmth of his breath, the heat of his groin. He rocks me gently and I want to stay here forever. The last humans on Earth.

But then other humans rush from level B to level C. Car doors slam, engines start up and drive out. Engines drive in and shut down. Car doors slam. Bodies rush from level B to level A.

'I have to get my wife.'

'Okay.'

I get off him but he won't let go of my hand as we climb like the wounded to level D.

'She told me it's … okay,' he says, opening the passenger door for me. 'She *so* tired.' I don't release his hand. I slide it under my T-shirt and hold it against my breast. He looks at me, trying to understand. I feel my nipple hardening.

'Don't leave me,' I say, understanding finally that Kadylak is gone and that he is all I have and that I want him to fuck me to death.

He climbs in after me and guides me between the seats to the rear. He lays me down among the paint cans and rags. He pulls up my shirt and caresses my breasts, sees the bruises. 'What's this?'

'An accident. When I fell down.'

'Do you hurt?'

'No.' I pull his head back down to my breasts and he gently sucks on my nipples. I pull off his shirt and run my tongue over him. He tastes of salt and paint solvent. He moves up to my lips and I want to share his breath, his life. The last people on Earth. His hand is down my pants and I can hear slippery sounds as he moves his fingers in and out. I unzip his jeans and reach for him, massaging his testicles. It is his sperm that made Kadylak. In seconds I'm up and over him, guiding his penis into me, denying the pain, wanting only that he ejaculate into me, stop this need, fill this void. But he won't fit and I'm afraid I'm too small, too virginal but he rolls me onto my back and begins to push and it feels as though I'm being ripped apart but I see Kadylak in his eyes. Then he comes, causing my head to bump paint cans but I don't care, I want him inside with the blood, his blood. Kadylak's blood. He lies over me and we breathe as one.

'You not come,' he says.

'That's alright.'

He slides his mouth down my body and sees the blood. 'No,' he says.

'It's alright,' I say.

'First time?'

'It's alright.'

'My God,' he says, pulling away from me.

'It's okay,' I say. 'I wanted it.'

'This is not right,' he says and I know it isn't. We are not the last humans on Earth.

He pulls up his jeans. He is leaving me. 'I am so sorry,' he says.

'Don't be sorry, *please* don't be sorry.' I think of clinging to him but it never works. I've seen Zippy cling to Damian, Drew cling to Damian. Scarlett cling to Rhett. It never works.

He climbs into the driver's seat and starts the engine.

29

I don't need to see her dead. They wash and shroud them, tie their hands and feet like chickens, wrap them in plastic before sending them to the morgue.

I wrote down my number for him. He'll never call. I am no longer an ally, just another person to fear. I watched him drive away, wanted to run after him. Just another heroine pining for some guy.

Zippy doesn't see me at first because she's busy opening and closing doors on an entertainment unit she's pitching to a big-haired couple. They don't seem too interested, keep glancing around for something with more wow factor. Zippy follows their gaze, which leads her to me. This time she doesn't jump up and down like a game-show winner. She holds up a finger and mouths, 'I'll just be a minute,' but I know she'll be licking the big-haired couple's boots till they gag. I flop on a grotesque easy chair and keep an eye out for the ape. Pop music blares from the unit, that song by that guy who needs a haircut, louder and louder, about how am I supposed to *live* without you? And I start trying to figure out how I'm supposed to live without Kadylak. I plug my ears and start singing, 'O-klahoma, where the wind comes sweepin' down the plains. Where the wavin' wheat can sure smell sweet, when the wind comes right behind the rain.' The big-haired couple look at me like I'm off my nut and head for the door with Zippy in tow. She seems pretty desperate, flapping her hands around. Maybe the ape only pays her on commission.

Somebody prods my shoulder. It's the ape, of course. 'What do you think you're doing, young lady?'

'I'm waiting for Zippy.'

'I don't know if you've noticed but she's busy right now. Why don't you come back when she's done her shift?'

'I need to talk to her now.' I try not to stare at his unibrow. There's no question he's hairy all over. I wait for him to start pounding his chest.

'Well, I hate to break it to you,' he says, 'but working people don't get to socialize when they're working.'

'I just need to talk to her for a second.'

Zippy scuttles our way, all a-flutter. 'I'll take care of it, Lloyd.'

'You better,' he warns.

She grabs my arm and pulls me into a corner. 'I'm still on probation, Limone. You can't keep popping in like this.'

'Can I stay at your place?'

'What? Why? Did she throw you out?'

'No, I just need a change. Please, I won't be any bother.'

'Shouldn't you be in school?'

'I'm a bit feverish.' This always works. She's fever-phobic.

She feels my forehead. 'You do feel a bit warm.'

'Zippy!' the ape bellows.

'I'm just getting her my keys,' she says, scrambling behind the cash and digging around in her handbag.

'What're you giving her keys for?' he demands, no doubt worried he's going to have to shag her with me around.

I start singing, 'O-klahoma, every night my honeylamb and I sit alone and talk, and watch a hawk makin' lazy circles in the sky ...'

'Can it,' the ape says.

She bustles back and hands me the keys.

'Don't tell Damian about this,' I say, knowing she will. 'If you tell Damian, I'll never speak to you again.'

'Don't talk like that, honeybunch, of course I won't tell him.'

I exit belting it like the singer who needs a haircut, 'And when we say hay-a-yippy-i-o-ay, we're only sayin', you're doing fine Oklaho-ma, OK!'

Her building is subsidized, meaning all kinds of rejects live there. The place stinks of fried food and rotten carpet. In the elevator a hundred-year-old man breathes poisonous breath in my direction. It takes him six hours to figure out which button to press. I offer to help but he must be deaf. I feel for the guy, being ancient and all that, but I'm pissed at him for being alive when Kadylak is dead.

I don't know what the Paluskas will do with her body; it's a few thousand bucks no matter how you disappear it. What happens to her corpse if they can't pay up? Don't want to think about it. I dig around in Zippy's fridge for some processed food, find those crumpets with holes in them. When I was little I used to fill the holes with butter. Zippy leaves her butter out so it gets nice and goopy. Drew keeps hers in the fridge, or anyway used to, before the peanut butter diet.

I lie down to eat because I don't want more of his semen dribbling out of me. I put pillows under my ass and pull my knees into my chest to help his sperm swim up my tubes. Our baby will look like him and Kadylak. Our baby will show no trace of the Witch or the Slug. Our baby will grow healthy and strong and never have cancer. I'll take her with me wherever I go. We'll never be parted. I'll teach her how to read and make soap. We'll travel around the world discovering exotic ingredients for our special bars, which we'll sell in the markets. We'll learn about different places and cultures by living in them. I'll be the most important person in her life and she'll be the most important in mine.

The phone rings and I know it's the Slug and he's probably sent the cops after me. It rings twenty-six times. I wipe buttery fingers on her bedspread that's got the ape's excretions all over it.

Zippy's shaking me. 'You should go home now, Limone, or she'll be worried about you and I'll get into trouble. You know they think I'm a bad influence.'

'Did you tell him?'

'Of course not.' I know she's lying, she always goes crying to Damian. No doubt he instructed her to turn me in, probably said he'd washed his hands of me. He always washes his hands of people when they get out of line. I consider telling her that he lied to her all those years – before he washed his hands of her – that he bumped uglies with an unusually passionate bureaucrat and out I popped. But she doesn't deserve more torment.

'Who are those people?' I ask, noticing blobby types in the living room ripping open chip packets.

'We're having a prayer meeting. You can't stay here.'

'Why not? I won't bother you. I'll be totally quiet.'

'I don't want you singing or anything, Limone.'

'Cross my heart.'

She sits on the bed and pats my hand. 'Jesus would watch over you, baby, if you'd only let Him.'

'Maybe if I listen in on the prayer meeting, I'll feel Him and let Him watch over me. I'm still a little feverish so I think I should stay in bed.' Sperm can survive forty-eight hours. I don't want to disturb it.

'Promise me you won't sing, honeybunch, it's so embarrassing when you sing.'

'Cross my heart. Can you bring me some juice and chips?'

I can't make out what they're saying. It's almost spooky. They hold their hands above each other's heads, I guess to heal each other or something. Every twenty minutes one of them keels over in a fit of Jesus fever. They all huddle around the forgiven until he or she can stand up, then they start praying again until the next sinner keels over. Must sound pretty strange in the apartment below. All that believing works up a sweat, it's starting to smell like a locker room in here.

I eat chips, drink juice, keeping my pelvis elevated. I have a life purpose.

'What did you think?' she asks after the last blobby type departs.

'Awesome.'

'Could you feel Him?'

'Definitely.'

'He'll forgive you, baby, if you forgive yourself.'

She brews chicken soup from a package and grills some cheese sandwiches. This used to be my favourite meal.

'Maybe you can come to the next one,' she says.

'What?'

'Prayer meeting.'

'I'll have to check my calendar.'

'You have to *demonstrate* your devotion, Limone. He can't be deceived. And He knows there is not one human on Earth who has never sinned. His wish is that we all come to repentance and stop rebelling against the truth.'

'What about Mars? Is there not one Martian on Mars who has never sinned?'

'You can make as much fun as you want.'

'Seriously, does He oversee the whole universe or just Earth?' I shove more grilled cheese in my mouth.

'If you let him,' Zippy says, 'He will help you to be obedient by giving you the power to become a true witness and follower.'

I stick my fingers into the pickle jar and wriggle out a cornichon.

'There is no other name among men,' she says, 'whereby we can be saved.'

'Are you eating?' I ask.

'Jesus will free you if you let Him,' she says. 'He'll help you overcome every wicked habit that you can't conquer on your own. Promise you'll come?'

'Where?'

'To the next prayer meeting.'

'I'll try. Drew's in pretty rough shape these days. I don't like to leave her alone too long.'

'I thought you said you needed a change.'

'Right, well, I just meant for a night or two.'

'You felt Jesus calling you, baby, that's why you needed a change.'

'Maybe that was it.' I suck up more noodles.

'I was so lonely before I let Jesus in,' she confides. 'You're so lonely, honeybunch, I can see that.'

'I'd kind of like to just be with *you* for a bit, no offence to Jesus.'

'He's watching us, baby. He's all around us.'

It's worse than when she was on drugs. On drugs it was just the two of us. Who wants Jesus hanging around?

We watch a movie about grand theft auto. Nick Cage skulks around in faded denim. He's tired of being a car thief and wants to live the quiet life in Monterey. But his associates say, 'Just one more time, boss, it's the Big One, it'll set us up for life.' So old Nick has to chase the dollar and neck with Angelina who's also in faded denim. I keep getting distracted by his rug. Is America ever going to be ready for a bald Nick Cage?

The commercials are bursting with perfect people and children and I start thinking about Kadylak again, the fact that I can't touch her, smell her, hold her. That she's gone. My only friend. A lung-stiffening panic sets in and I start sweating and hyperventilating and I know this can't be good for conception. I try to think about the baby, that she'll have Kadylak's eyes and she'll look at me the way she did and I'll be able to hold her whenever I feel like it.

'What's wrong, honeybunch?'

'Nothing.'

'It's Jesus, isn't it? Don't fight Him, baby.'

'It's not Jesus, for fuck's sake, would you shut up about Jesus?'

She pulls away like I've slapped her. I've hurt her, I didn't mean to hurt her.

Nick Cage drives a stolen Ferrari at high speed over a bridge.

'It's just I want it to be you and me again,' I say. 'Like the old days. Why can't it just be you and me?'

'That's very selfish, Limone.'

A chopper shot reveals that the bridge is blocked by traffic and that Nick is going to have to stop speeding and get nabbed by the LAPD.

'I am grateful for what He has done for me, Limone. And you should be too.'

'He hasn't done shit for me. My best friend died today. He *killed* my best friend. So you can take Jesus and shove Him up your ass.'

Nick guns his engine and drives up over the cars in front of him. Cops scurry out of their cruisers, shaking their heads in disbelief. Zippy closes her eyes and starts talking to Jesus.

She lets me sleep beside her on the bed. We used to do this. She's always talked gibberish in her sleep, sounding anxious and afraid. I used to pat her shoulder till she settled down. I don't tonight. Let Jesus do it.

I'm woken by voices in the living room. At first I think she's talking to her Saviour again but then I hear the ape. He's got her bent over the sofa so he can do her up the backside.

'Stop that!' I shout.

'What the fuck ... ?'

'What kind of sick pervert are you!' I scream because I need to scream at somebody. I start kicking him the way I kicked Bonehead and company. The ape, with his plumbing dangling, starts swinging at me. I grab an umbrella and aim it at his eyeball while he's yanking up his pants. 'That is one ugly set of jewels,' I tell him. 'Now get out before she calls the cops.'

'She's not calling anybody.'

'Pick up the phone, Zippy,' I order. '*Now*. Pick it up now.' She does and holds the receiver as if it might catch fire.

The ape tries to snatch the umbrella but I keep swinging it the way Doyle swung the golf club. The ape retreats but of course has to say, 'Don't bother showing up at the store tomorrow,' before he slams the door. Zippy puts the phone down and squats on her pouffe.

'Where's Jesus when you need him?' I say.

'You hurt people and you don't care,' she says. 'You're destructive. That's what they've always said about you.'

'I care about *you*.'

'No you don't. You just lost me my job.'

There's no point in saying she's a whole lot better off without the ape plugging her orifices. 'I'm sorry,' I say.

'No you're not.'

I don't argue. She starts rocking on the pouffe, humming some hymn.

'I want you to leave in the morning,' she says in a voice that doesn't sound like hers, more like the Almighty's. This is not good. I was planning to lie around eating crumpets with my ass held high.

'I'm still feeling a bit feverish,' I say.

'*Please* leave in the morning. You *must* leave in the morning.' She runs her hands over the scar tissue on her wrists from all that self-mutilating. She won't look at me.

'If that's what you want,' I say.

She closes her eyes and talks to Jesus.

30

I don't stomp but walk carefully with my secret inside me, staying far from school and the mall where I might be detected. I talk to her in my head, tell her about all the fun we're going to have, all the places we're going to see. I sit in a park and watch the children, awed by their freedom and wonder. I watch the old people, gnarled and broken. What happened to their freedom and wonder?

I sip steamed milk, slumped on an overstuffed chair at a Starbucks. The milk warms my womb as the wired around me fiddle with their techno-gadgets. A woman wearing a ponytail so tight it looks like it'll rip her face off speaks heatedly into her cell. 'I'm confronting you as a mature man. Am I wrong in presuming that you would like to be treated as a mature man?' Outside the window a little shaggy dog is watching her with its tongue hanging out. 'I thought you could handle this,' the woman says. 'Clearly I was mistaken. It's obvious you're putting that up as a block.' The dog yaps and paws the glass. 'That's baloney. That is *absolute* baloney. You are *so* not the man I thought you were.' Who is? I want to ask. Who *is* who we thought they were? Didn't we make it all up?

I linger in the baby store, press my face into fuzzy sleepers. Two hugely pregnant women can't get over the news that some teens glued broken glass on slides and monkey bars. 'They could have seriously injured somebody,' the squatter one says.

'What's the world coming to, I ask you,' the other responds. I could tell her, but she wouldn't listen. She'll buy albatross-killing plastic baubles for baby and speed off in her guzzler, not

251

believing that Junior could grow into a teenager who glues glass on slides and monkey bars.

I only have eight bucks on me, not enough for cute little slippers decorated with animal faces. I decide to choose a pair anyway. Kittens or puppies? What about bunnies? The saleswoman hovers. 'Can I help you with anything?'

'I'm just looking, thanks.'

'How old is the baby?' She has pencilled lips and tweezed eyebrows.

'It's not born yet.'

'Do you know if it's a boy or a girl?'

I want her off my case but act dull-eyed because I want to stay here where it's warm and fuzzy and pink and blue. Full of potential.

'Because we have some really cute unisex slippers in green,' she says. 'Do you like turtles?' She holds up turtle slippers. I smile like a good cretin. 'And these are skid-proof,' she says. 'You'd be amazed at how many baby slippers aren't skid-proof.'

Saved by the bell. She gets on the phone to plot with hubby. He'll take Kyle to hockey, she'll take Emma to gymnastics. Dinner plans cause friction, nobody has time to stop at the store, to cook. 'Fine, we'll have pizza again,' she snipes. I sense the chat drying up. I stuff the pink bunny slippers in my jacket and exit before she hangs up.

I walk softly, cradling the slippers. I take them out of the plastic and rub their fluff against my face. I sniff them, trying to smell Kadylak. I think of Mischa and Sweetheart the penguin on the bed waiting for her.

White vans without rear windows pass me by. I scan the licence plates. KWR 395. Don't know what I'd do if he were in front of me. Couldn't stand it if he looked away.

I withdraw my last twenty bucks and sit in the library, staring at baby books while desperate folks reeking of the street nab the seats around me. Can't stand the photos in the books, everybody happy happy happy, plus all the rules about looking after baby – doesn't baby make the rules? I pitch the baby books and read Emily Dickinson:

> *I stepped from plank to plank*
> *So slow and cautiously*
> *The stars about my head I felt*
> *About my feet the sea.*
>
> *I knew not but the next*
> *Would be my final inch –*
> *This gave me that precarious gait*
> *Some call experience.*

She became a recluse, never left her house, died at fifty-six. Childless. The way Drew's headed.

'Have you seen my umbrella?' a hyper Jamaican woman demands.

'No.'

'I left it right here.' She points where I'm sitting.

'I didn't see it,' I say.

'I left it right here. Did you see it?' The cuffs of her jacket are frayed, buttons are missing. I look behind and under my chair, go back to Emily.

> *The earth reversed her Hemispheres –*
> *I touched the Universe –*
> *And back it slid – and I alone –*
> *A Speck upon a Ball –*
> *Went out upon Circumference –*

'Have you seen my umbrella?' the Jamaican woman demands of another bottom-feeder. 'I left it *right here*.' She points at me again and I know she thinks I've swiped it. 'It was striped.'

'I can't see it anywhere,' I say. 'Sorry.'

'I left it *right here*. Striped.'

The movie theatre should offer peace. I buy popcorn and sit at the back, try to get interested in a romantic comedy about some blond and a stud with get-rich schemes. He thinks she won't want him unless he's rich. She thinks he doesn't like her because he never asks her out. She's educated, he's streetwise. How many times have we seen this movie? I try to catch some shut-eye before they discover they truly love each other and get naked. But movies are so loud these days and there's the inevitable spit-swapping going on a few seats over. I move up, keeping an eye out for geezers with hands down their pants. I hook my knees over the seat in front of me to tilt my ass up. The streetwise stud is stalking the blond in the rain. She meets up with a male co-worker who our hero takes to be a rival. He festers with jealousy in the rain while the blond and the co-worker grab a latte. I close my eyes and try to make a plan. I could steal from Drew. I know her PIN. If I can sneak in without her, or Treeboy, noticing. Around three in the morning. Take out the daily max till it twigs that her card's missing. Find some cheap digs and buy myself some time. Sleep. Research the soap thing, maybe track down that human-rights lawyer, offer myself as an apprentice. Move to the country. Let baby grow. I'm so tired. Should get some prenatal vities. The books say the early stages are crucial, need that folic acid.

An usher hustles me out. 'This is not a shelter,' he says. His stitched harelip gets me thinking about those Chinese baby girls in orphanages deemed unadoptable because of harelips. Grotty rooms full of growing girls with broken mouths. They're sent away at sixteen, no doubt into slavery. Or the sex trade. Sick Topics.

More time to kill before nightfall and the burglary. And no money. I count it. Enough for a juice, stay away from coffee, not good for baby. Time crawls when you're homeless. But I'm calm, at peace, looking forward for once. I see her learning to walk, chubby with golden curls, grabbing hold of whatever's in reach, stumbling, crying. I pick her up and kiss the salt off her cheeks.

I tickle her and she starts to laugh, big belly laughs like Bradley. I know he's dead. It doesn't take them long to die. Like Kadylak, he just let go. They don't hang on like the grownups. They who have so much to lose let go too easily.

I sip an OJ very slowly, avoiding eye contact with the servers who must be figuring out I'm a street kid. I try not to watch the clock, try to think positively, think of a good role model with a life purpose. Florence Nightingale. Everybody thinks she just hopped over to Crimea to bandage soldiers, but the fact is she was one of the first people to tell doctors to wash their hands, gowns and surgical instruments. They ignored her, of course, kept mutilating one person after another with their dirty knives. Patients were dying from infections but this didn't faze the doctors. Bloody smocks and blades were badges of honour with these duffers. Florence changed nursing care, made it respectable. She fought for the poor not only in England but in India where old Victoria was named empress. Millions of Indians were starving while old Victoria was gumming crumpets, pining for dead Albert. Florence was always in poor health, and got no support from her family who disapproved of her humanitarian efforts. They wanted her to marry a gent with cash and settle down. She died alone and blind.

Maybe I'll call her Florence.

It's 1:37 a.m. I stare at a paper, more adults in a flap over cyber-bullying. I look for ads for baby stuff, strollers, Exersaucers, high chairs. Although we won't need all that crap. We'll live like peasants. Grains and beans. Slung on my back she will feel safe. I will feel safe.

I use the back door, don't turn on lights, grope and creep, bumping and squeaking. It smells different with him here. All that slop cooking. I feel my way to the front hall, stumble over the table where she leaves her purse. I stop and listen. Just fridge noise. I dig around for her wallet, take out some bills but can't see which

255

is her bank card. I sneak to the basement, close the bathroom door and switch on the light, shove the cash and card in my back pocket. Wouldn't mind taking a shower but it's bound to wake Treeboy who'll show up and stare, offering profound insights like *you can't let them see your fear*. They don't need to see it, dickhead, they can smell it.

I wash my hands and face, squirt toothpaste on my finger for my teeth. I'm in no rush to go out there again where striped umbrellas vanish. At least not until dawn. I can snooze here, on the bath mat, dream of baby Florence, watch her running through fields of buttercups. I take out her slippers and hold them against my face, promising to take her to forests and meadows, to show her wild animals and sparkling fish in rocky streams.

I pull down my pants to piss and see blood.

All is quiet, the last person on Earth. I alone a Speck upon a Ball.

It's different from the busted hymen blood. I watch it swirl in the toilet bowl. I wad toilet paper and hold it between my legs. It has to stop. It *will* stop. I lie on my back with my feet on the toilet seat and beg Jesus. 'Please, Jesus, don't take her, I'll stop rebelling against the truth, please don't take her.'

Dying babies, the preemies in the neo-natal unit plugged with tubes and electrodes, forced into an existence they tried to avoid, squirming on their backs like fallen featherless baby birds, destined for a life crippled by brain damage. Kadylak's falling from me, limbs awash in blood. 'Please let me have her, Jesus. I know I have sinned. She's all I have, *please* ... '

The blood conquers gravity, volcanic gushes of useless uterine lining soaking the toilet paper and dribbling down Damian's ass. I do not deserve to live, conceived in plaster dust by the Witch and the Slug. Loveless, soulless, destructive, an embarrassment. Grotesque. I will not live trapped inside this body that is not my own.

I scrabble back upstairs, dripping blood, grab her Xanax, which she never takes. I chew a few and feel around for her keys, gulp tap water en route to the garage. It stalls, of course. I try again with purpose. The engine awakens and idles soothingly. I take her notepad and pen out of the glove compartment. I write down everything Bonehead and company did to me, every humiliating detail including dick in mouth and beer bottle. I write it down so Doyle will have a defence. I don't mention Rossi. I date and sign it and leave it on the dash. I open the windows and turn on the jazz station but they're off the air. It's just the usual all-night pop drivel. I switch it off and sing, 'Fly me to the moon and let me play among the stars.'

I've taken her anxiety drugs before, they take forever to kick in. My dead baby floats in the toilet bowl, bloodied chunks of flesh, curls, tiny severed hands. She's gone. Never was. As the blood oozes from me so does salt water. My lungs are filling with ocean. I push the seat back and feel the tears dripping into my ears.

'I hate you, Jesus,' I croak while I'm drowning. Try to hum, keep my mind off the blackness. Stay calm. Float. I'll be with her, won't I? She's waiting for me with her arms outstretched, isn't she? I'll bury my face in the soft curve between her neck and shoulder. We'll build Lego houses with doors in case somebody nice comes to visit.

Starting to breathe the carbon monoxide finally. Slow going with a low-emissions vehicle. Still no drugs kicking in. Not like in the movies. I try the radio again. Céline Dion yowling. I switch it off. Slide my fingers into the tiny slippers. The preemies are constantly in crisis, constantly being resuscitated. Let them die, why can't they die? The parents stand on the periphery, believing the doctors are helping, not torturing, not disabling their beloved baby. Why life at any cost? Why can't we *die*? Who says we have to put up with this shit day in and day out, these lies, these betrayals? My eyes and throat are burning. I'm so thirsty. So tired. She was *so* tired. Where's the man in black? Come get me, you fucker. I'm so thirsty. *So* tired. Fly me to the moon.

31

Massive headache. Can't move. Mask gripping my face. Where is she? Can't kick, scream. Scared shitless. Fluorescents obscure, curtains swish. Mouth tastes of ashes. They've squirted charcoal down my nose, the fuckers. Tired, so tired. Where is she? Find me, come find me, the fuckers have hooked me up, can feel it, IV, oxygen monitor pinching my finger. A whitecoat is jabbing at my wrist, sucking more blood. Can't lift my head, scream. So tired, sick, choking on vomit. Can hear the ECG monitor beep beep beep. Fucking heart pumping. *So* tired. Let me die, Jesus, *please* let me die.

'Lemon, can you hear me?'
Don't rise to the surface. Sink where they can't find you.
'Lemon, please nod, love, if you can hear me.'
What's she want? Get out go go go go.

Yak yak yakking at my feet. Shut the fuck up, you meddlers. Can't move my arms. Where is she? She was here with Mischa and Sweetheart. I saw her.
'Lemon? Please nod, love, if you can hear me.'
My botched suicide got her out. She sits there like a gargoyle. Get out of my face, go go go go.

A broken heart can kill. The adrenals go berserk, blasting an overdose of stress hormones. *Please* let me die. She was here. I could smell her, touch her. Why won't she take me with her? Every time I surface she's gone. Must stay down, down.

The meddlers won't leave me alone. Have to escape. Must act grateful to be alive, won't do it again, doctor. It was a cry for help, you understand. Just write me a scrip and I'll take my antidepressants like a good little girl.

'Lemon, can you hear me?' the gargoyle asks. 'Please nod if you can hear me.'

I nod because I need an ally.

'Lemon, listen to me, you can't act crazy or they won't let you out. You were pulling at the tubes, that's why they tied you up.' She leans over the bed rail, her eyes deranged, and whispers, 'I'm serious, they're like the cops, they can throw away the key. I read your note. Nobody else has. You can pretend you never wrote it. I'll burn it if you want me to. I haven't told these morons anything.'

She's right. I have to act normal before I can sleep in front of a train. They're not far from her house, always toot-tooting, uselessly, endlessly coming and going.

A woman moans on the other side of the curtain.

'I tried to kill myself once,' Drew says. 'I hated my rescuer. She was our cleaning lady, a little Italian who hardly spoke English. I wanted her dead. You probably want me dead.'

Just get out of my face. Go go go go.

Close my eyes. Sink. Where is she?

A resident who looks like a boxer pulls off my mask. 'How are you feeling?'

'Excellent.'

'I guess you'd like us to remove the restraints.'

'Hell no, I enjoy them.'

'You're doing great,' the boxer says. 'You've got a good ticker. We're going to have you assessed. Obviously the concern is that you might try this again.'

'Obviously.'

'Do you think you might try it again?'

'Absolutely not. Not worth the hangover.'

'That's the spirit. Well, Dr. Fireman should be here shortly then we'll talk more.'

'Can't wait.'

The boxer trots off. The gargoyle strokes my forehead.

'Did he say Dr. Fireman?' I ask.

'He did.'

'Where's Dr. Policeman?'

'Guess he's busy.'

'I have to get out of here.'

'Then act normal, and don't be a wiseass.'

'I'm thirsty.'

'They're allowing you ice chips.' She hands me a Styrofoam cup.

'What was *your* method?' I ask.

'Same as yours. Except gasoline had lead in it in those days, packed more of a punch. They thought I had neurological damage, wouldn't let me out. Hospitals weren't quadruple-booked back then.'

'Why did you do it?'

'It's pretty maudlin and not very original.'

'A broken heart.'

'Bingo. Dawson Frost destroyed my life.'

'Dawson Frost?'

'His wife wrote an obituary for him a while back and there he was, fat and smug. She said he was a gentleman and a gentle man.'

'You beg to differ?'

'He was an unctuous sociopath.'

'Was he fat when he broke your heart?'

'No, but certainly smug. I seem to go for those.' She looks a mess, still in Damian's PJs.

'How did you get here?'

'Ambulance.' She holds my still-restrained hand, meaning I can't pull away. 'I'm not leaving without you.'

Dr. Fireman is one of those balding types who shaves his pate to disguise the fact that he's balding. Behind his rectangular glasses are the agitated eyes of the overworked. He sniffs repeatedly, which suggests a cold or a cocaine habit. He removes the restraints and asks my 'mother' to leave to preserve patient confidentiality. He wants her gone so I will reveal hidden truths.

'How are you feeling?' he asks.

'Better.' I rub my wrists like the recently cuffed.

'Very good.' He starts making notes. 'Let's start with family history. Any psychological illness in your family?'

'I have no family. I'm adopted.' Don't tell him about the crazy aunt.

'So that woman is your adoptive mother?'

'My stepmother, actually. My adoptive mother passed on.'

'I'm sorry. When was that?'

'Years ago.'

'Do you miss her?'

'Not really.'

Sniff, sniff. 'Are you in high school?'

'Yes.'

'What is your previous medical history?'

'Don't have any.'

'Psychiatric history?'

'Ditto.'

'Do you use drugs?' Sniff, sniff.

'No.'

'Not at all? At parties and so on?'

'Not at all.'

'Alcohol?'

'Not much.'

'What does "not much" mean?'

'Almost never.'

'Have you attempted suicide before?'

'Absolutely not.'

'Okaaay.' He scribbles more. 'Limone, is there any psychological trauma you can tell me about, or a history of depression?'

'Nothing springs to mind.'

'Okaaay.' Each time he says 'okaaay' he pauses briefly, narrowing his eyes, as though in deep concentration. 'Can you tell me what precipitated this event?'

'It's pretty maudlin and not very original.'

'Can you tell me about it?'

'I was in love.'

'Ah.' Sniff, sniff.

'Dawson Frost ... ' I look away, pausing for effect, 'broke my heart.'

'Okaaay.' His eyes narrow. 'I gather Dawson did not return your feelings?'

'Everything was going swell at first. I really thought he loved me. He even invited me to the prom.'

'What changed, do you think?'

'Her. That ho Wendy. I saw them together. She was supposed to be my BFF.'

'BFF?'

'Best Friend Forever. I wanted to die.'

Recognition ignites behind the rectangular glasses. Okaaay, just another teenage girl spurned, attempting suicide after a breakup. Herr Freud would say her daddy spanked her and she got off on it. 'Can you tell me something about your bruises?'

'That was Dawson. We had some pretty athletic sex.'

'Okaaay.' His eyes narrow. 'Was it consensual?'

'Totally. I left some marks on him as well.' This is stretching it but the fireman doesn't flinch, just jots it down, no doubt convinced Herr Freud was right.

'Had you planned your suicide attempt or was it spontaneous?'

'Spontaneous.'

Sniff, sniff. 'Did you really wish to die or were you hoping to be discovered?'

'I didn't really think about it.' Noncommittal is probably the way to go. 'My moon was in Mercury but now it's in Jupiter.'

'Okaaay. How do you feel *now* about being alive?'

'Great. It was a mistake. He's not worth it.'

'Will you be seeing him again?'

'No way, he took off, that's what started it. He didn't tell me he was leaving. He just up and left with that skank.'

'Okaaay. How do you feel about Dawson and Wendy now?'

'Good riddance. They deserve each other. He was no good from the start, I was just fooling myself because the sex was so hot.'

Sniff, sniff. 'What made you realize he was no good?'

'I guess just lying here thinking about it. I mean, no guy is worth dying over.'

'So you no longer wish to die?'

'No way. My stepmother's really made me realize how lucky I am.'

'How so?'

'I'm young. I have a whole future ahead of me. Plus my moon's in Jupiter so I'm feeling a whole lot better. I saw a want ad for baristas at Starbucks and I'm think I'm going to go for it. I really want to be part of a team.'

'Very good.' Sniff, sniff, more scribbling. 'Okaaay. Limone, I have a proposal for you. Would you consider signing a treatment contract which states that if you go home you vow not to try this again? And that if you do feel the urge to try again you will contact the psychiatric crisis team immediately?'

'Absolutely.'

'We would still want to see you for follow-up. In a couple of days then weekly.'

'No problem, Doc. Today is the first day of the rest of my life.'

'Very good.'

Behind the curtain the woman moans.

'Okaaay,' Fireman says. 'How would you feel about going home with your stepmother?'

'Could I have a word with her in private first? I don't want to impose.'

'Of course.' He ushers her in and disappears behind the curtain.

'I told him it was over a guy,' I whisper. 'Dawson Frost. So don't blow my cover. I told him he left town.'

'Did you tell them anything about me? The agoraphobia?'

'No. So act normal. We both have to *act normal.*'

She nods solemnly, my conspirator in the asylum. She has always despised the medical establishment, *drug pushers,* she calls them. 'Fireman told me to remove any dangerous materials from the environment,' she says. 'Hide the car keys, pills, toxic chemicals, sharp instruments. Do I really have to do that?'

'Nah, I'm over it. Cry for help and all that. Are you going to be able to get in a cab with me?'

'Yes. I think I'm getting better. I've been going to the corner store by myself.' She says this with pride, the kid who's pulled off her first solo spin on the bicycle. She seems courageous to me suddenly. More courageous than I have ever been.

'Call the fireman.'

The bloodless city thrums. Looks the same, although I'm not. Grim types rushing, clutching purses, briefcases, techno-gadgets, united in their determination to find purpose in the pointless. Drew grips my arm, trying to hold me or herself together. Traffic clogs, drivers honk like it matters.

She's going to want to talk to me later. I don't want this.

'Are you okay in there?'

She thinks I'm slitting my wrists. 'I'm fine. No worries.' The faucet drips, resonating off the tiles.

Treeboy made us some slop. He's rearranged the kitchen, added weird-looking utensils and a wok. Still doesn't say much. Maybe he comes alive in the sack.

Knock knock. Pretend to be asleep. Comes in anyway crackling a paper bag.

'Someone left this for you,' she says.

I open my eyes. 'Who?'

'I don't know, they just left it, didn't ring the bell. And I found these in the car.' She pulls out the bunny slippers and holds them inches from my face. Something corrosive spills inside me. I can't look at the slippers.

'Did you think you were pregnant?' she asks.

'They're for a baby at the hospital.'

'Oh. Okay, well, they called, and they don't want you back for a while. Maybe I can mail them for you. Do you have the baby's full name?'

'They don't want me back ever?'

'They're concerned about your effect on the kids. Brenda, is it Brenda? She said you get too involved. She told me about your friend dying.'

'Just leave the slippers. I'd like to be alone now, thank you.'

She lingers, waiting for hidden truths. 'Whatever I can do for you, Lemon, I will.'

'I just need to be alone now, thank you.'

She gently closes the door of the sick room. I shove the slippers in the trash.

Can't believe I'm back here. All that effort wasted. Don't even remember the me who lived in this room. I stare at the paper bag, my name printed in block letters. A booby trap from my adoring fans? My ripped underwear plus an assortment of used condoms? A hate package from Rossi or the Witch? I crawl over to it, sniff and shake it to see if it explodes. It's a book and something soft. I look inside and see Sweetheart the penguin. The book is *Tilly*. I fling it against the wall. No note. Some of Kadylak's drawings. Brightly coloured birds with stick legs always under a smiling sun. Drawings I watched her pen intently with felt marker, wondering why the sun was always smiling. She who could not go outside for fear of burning her chemo-blasted skin always drew smiling suns. I believed she would survive because of those suns. Those smiling suns would protect her. I start shredding them before I realize they're all I have of her. My lungs stiffen again as

I search for the tape, can't find it in the wreckage that was my life. I stomp around pulling out drawers, shoving crap aside on what was my desk, unable to piece together the birds.

'Are you alright in there?'

Why won't she leave me alone?

My tears are blotting the felt marker. The stick legs bleed. 'Fine. No worries.'

He left without ringing the bell because he didn't want to see me. He is ashamed. And thinks I'm a slut, just another easy North American girl.

I hold Sweetheart against my face, try to smell Kadylak but she's gone. Hug Sweetheart to my chest, hear myself moaning like the woman on the other side of the curtain.

Cold. Should have brought a jacket, didn't want to look for it and risk waking my captors.

I listen for toot-tooting, or a distant rumble. There's probably less action at night. I might have to wait. They're behind a housing development. The streets are all crescents and dead ends. Keep walking north, follow the drinking gourd. Dogs bark behind fences. All the houses look the same. Pay attention to the street signs: Cedar, Pine, Poplar, Beech. Not a tree in sight, just houses that look the same. I'm tired, *so* tired, clutching Sweetheart, trespassing, trampling flowers. If I rest my head on her penguin belly, I won't feel so scared. Enter a laneway of two-car garages. Walk down it till I get to the wire-mesh fence. It's tall, barbed wire strung across the top. Try to climb up but my boots are too big. Shake them off, stuff Sweetheart in my belt, push my toes through the mesh, haul myself up, but Damian's ass keeps dragging me down. And the wire scorches the Witch's fingers. Fall back on the Slug's ass. Can't even *do this*. Smash my head against the fence. The Witch's mousy hair catches in the mesh, rips out. Bash the Slug's nose.

'You're going to hurt yourself.' Treeboy has me in a shoulder lock.

'Get your own fucking life, will you?' I shout. 'Get your own *fucking life*!'

'You're part of my life.'

'Since when?'

'Since we share a mother.'

'She's not our mother.'

'Best mother I've ever had.'

'Is that why you're fucking her?'

'Who said I was fucking her?'

'Oh please.' Dogs bark again. 'Just go, would you please *go*?' I jab at his shoes with the Witch's feet. 'Just because your friend fell out of a tree doesn't mean you have to save me. I'm not your friend. Fuck off, go go go!'

'You keep this up, Mr. and Mrs. Jones will call the cops.'

I slump against him, tired, *so* tired. He lifts me in his arms like Rhett lifted Scarlett.

32

One of them is always on watch, always listening, always tense. I don't want to do this to them but they won't let me go. They don't ask questions. Days are formless, endless. I wake up and remember she's dead.

They've started forcing me to go for walks. I know it's hard for her, that she's only going out to get me out. Although she seems to be getting better daily. He walks on my right, she on my left. I consider making a break for it to see if they'll chase me, but where would I go? They like to sit and sip designer coffees on patios while June buzzes around us. I'd forgotten what it's like to sit with people. Nobody bothers you, lubbers don't stare.

When I asked if she knew about Damian, she said she'd had her suspicions but he'd denied it. 'You don't look like him,' she said, which opened a breathing hole. Sometimes I can look in the mirror and not see the Slug.

We burned the letter but I called Detective Sergeant Weech to tell him I would testify. He said the charges had been dropped. Rossi was right, Doyle's dentist dad struck a deal. I phoned to tell her but she wouldn't talk to me. Mrs. Barnfield sounded haunted.

Weech wanted to know if I'd considered laying sexual assault charges. 'Limone, if you don't take them to court they'll just do it to some other girl.' They'll just do it to some other girl anyway.

We sleep like Bedouins in the living room because I don't want to be in that room that was mine and they don't want me to be alone. They aren't rutting. Vaughn told her what I said and she laughed. Hadn't seen her laugh since before the knifing.

'He's too earthy for me, Lemon, you know I go for those seemingly confident plastic jerks.'

I'm not alone in the dark because she's been having insomnia. Sometimes we talk about Extraordinary Women. Sometimes we read to each other. She's rediscovered William Blake:

> Man was made for Joy and Woe;
> And when this we rightly know
> Through the world we safely go.

Sometimes we plot cat murders knowing we'll never do it, that in the end they are just animals crapping and digging as we will once the water runs out. I have nightmares about the world ending, taps running dry, crops shrivelling, the earth cracking. I wake up knowing it's only a matter of time.

'Do you have any summer shoes?' she asks the sales clerk. 'Canvas sneakers, do they make those anymore?'

'For you?'

'All of us.'

His name tag says Bosko. His accent is like Mr. Paluska's. His hair is like Mr. Paluska's. Grief shifts its bulk again, throwing me off balance. I squat on a stool. People dying all over the world, fighting for life, and here am I.

'We all need *summer* shoes,' Drew emphasizes, 'light on the feet.' She has been obsessing over this, remembering when she was a child, how freeing the canvas shoes felt after the confinement of winter boots.

Bosko speeds off in search of sneakers. Tweedledee and Tweedledum hover, groping the shoes on display. 'They're all so built up,' Drew says. 'How are you supposed to feel the world under your feet?'

'You're not,' Vaughn says.

'I have Keds for the ladies,' Bosko says, 'and high-tops for the gentleman.'

'Oh, I *love* those,' she says, shedding years as she grabs the polka-dotted pink pair. 'Lemon, do you want stripes or dots? We shouldn't get the same, should we? We'll just get them confused.'

Vaughn slowly, deliberately laces the yellow high-tops. He never rushes, never panics. I wish I could do this.

Drew is up, bouncing on the balls of her feet, she who sleeps three hours a night. 'These feel *amazing*. Come on, Lemon, try them.'

Bosko is at my feet, helping to remove my army boots, retrieved from the tracks by Vaughn. I worry that my feet stink. I want to touch Bosko's hair and ask him if he knows the Paluskas, ask him what they did with her body.

He slips the turquoise-striped sneakers on my feet. Tweedledee and Tweedledum wait for my rebirth. Vaughn rocks slowly back and forth on his high-tops while Drew pirouettes. I try to stand, to join in the celebration because they mean well, these two. Vaughn puts out his hand as he often does to steady me or remind me he's there. His palms never sweat but are never cold.

I waver, unanchored, shorter without my boots. How will I kick in faces with canvas shoes?

'Aren't they fantastic?' asks eight-year-old Drew. 'Wiggle your toes. Can you wiggle your toes?'

I wiggle my toes. The shoes feel spongy, light. I bounce on the soles of my feet. 'I can fly in these.'

'Yes,' she says. 'And that's what you will do, fly.'

They want ice cream, of course. I still can't look at the stuff, drink water while they slurp and dribble. 'Don't drip on your shoes,' I warn. His feet look enormous in the yellow boats. I suggested the green but he said yellow reminded him of bees. We sit on a bench, me in the middle as always. She turns her face toward the sun; she who spent months indoors is rediscovering Mother Earth. She crosses one leg over the other and swings her foot. 'It's hard to be miserable in June,' she says, licking her Cherry Garcia.

It *is* hard to be miserable with blossoms abounding. I turn my face toward the sun and tell myself she's up there, free of pain, building houses with doors in case someone nice comes to visit.

They're cooking lasagna. Something's up, there's a charge in the air. She spoons the sauce and the ricotta, he lays the noodles, they both sprinkle cheeses. 'Don't drip on your shoes,' I warn.

'Can you set the table, Lemon?'

I put out the linen napkins so we don't kill trees. Vaughn's backpack is out. I don't like this, don't know how much of Drew's recovery is because of him, don't want her cracking up again, can't fix her on my own. Can't fix myself.

'Serve up the grub,' Drew says. As usual, Vaughn overloads our plates.

'Are you leaving?' I ask. He finishes serving then gives me the tree-frog stare.

'Yes,' he says.

'Why?'

'Because I'm not doing anything here.'

'Where are you going?'

'Sherwood Forest.'

'You're going to be Robin Hood?'

'I'm going to save some trees.'

'I can't believe you're still doing that.'

'Why not?'

'They're going to die anyway. Everything's going to die.'

'We don't know exactly when, though, do we? Might as well do what we can while we can, don't you think?'

'It's pointless.'

'Who says there has to be a point?'

'That's a point,' Drew says. 'Who says there has to be a point?'

I dig around in the pasta. I don't need him anyway, don't need anybody. All they do is let you down, over and over and over again. Or die.

'The thing is,' Drew says with tomato sauce on her chin, 'he wants you to go with him.'

I stare at them, trying to figure out what's real and what isn't.

'You need to get away from here, Lemon,' she says. 'You need to see something different.'

'I can't leave you,' I blurt, stunning even myself. Since when do I care?

'I'll be fine,' she says. 'I'm going to work in the garden this summer, tend my veggies, and go back to school in the fall. I have to get back to work, earn some cash. I'm looking for a smaller school.'

She's moving on, they're both moving on while I just want to sit on benches between them. I didn't even know I wanted this. You never know what you want until you can't have it anymore.

'I'm not a tree sitter,' I say.

'Who says you have to be a tree sitter?'

'Isn't that what you'll be doing?'

'Nope. There's plenty of work on terra firma. You can get people to sign petitions, can't you?'

'I'm buying you an open ticket,' she says. 'So you can always come back.'

'You might not want to come back,' he says. 'You might meet an English lord and find romance.'

'Vaughn's got rich relatives over there with spare rooms.'

'They go to the south of France in the summer. Leave me the dogs.' He keeps eating like we're discussing a spin to Buffalo. 'Makes a good base camp.'

'I'll give you some cash,' she says. 'But Vaughn's the king of thrift. He can live off twenty bucks a week. He's been a world traveller since he was twelve.'

I pull up weeds as instructed. At least I hope they're weeds. 'How did you recover from your friend dying?'

'Who says I've recovered?' He's digging another bed for Drew.

'You seem to have accepted it and all that,' I say. 'You're supposed to accept it and move on.'

'Who says?'

'I don't know. Everybody. The stages of grief.'

'It's in stages?'

'You start with denial and anger and all that, then move to acceptance.'

'Well, I can't deny he's dead, have to accept that.'

'Are you still angry?'

'Of course.' He jabs at more turf. 'But I don't think he'd want me sitting around with my thumb up my ass.'

'Would he want you to sit in trees?'

'Doubt it. Even said *he* was getting too old for it. It was supposed to be his last sit.'

Out she bustles in her straw gardening hat offering popsicles. She has an interview tomorrow. She's going alone in her car. We wanted to go with her but we're getting on a plane.

She's determined to come into the terminal with us even though Vaughn has been a world traveller since he was twelve. She parks and we check our baggage then sip burnt coffee while the airport drones around us. She has fussed over me for twenty-four hours, made certain that my backpack contains everything a girl on her first transatlantic voyage could possibly require. I wait for her to ask me to promise to write.

'I'm worried about you,' I say.

'Don't worry about me.'

'Worry about *me*,' Vaughn says.

'We never worry about you,' Drew says.

Beside us a sagging woman announces that she has lost eighty pounds and asks her scrawny companion's advice regarding what hats to wear now that her face is thinner. 'I like that sixties look,' she says. 'You know those little peaked hats? Those are cute. Would I look good in one of them?'

Vaughn holds both our hands. 'Time to go or you'll be late for your interview.'

'Yes.' She stands, unfamiliar in her still loosely fitting principal clothes. Gone are the pink polka dots and the straw gardening hat. 'Take care of each other,' she says, hugging him and then me. She feels thin but alive, an animal strengthened by her injury. I don't let her go because I'm afraid she'll disappear, or die on me. 'You'll be fine,' she whispers in my ear. She pulls away without asking me to promise to write. She digs in her purse for her car keys and I can tell this is hard for her, that pushing us away is another act of courage.

'You're allowed to cry,' he tells her.

'Oh, stop it,' she says. 'I'm gone.' And she is, sharply in her pumps, soon to be swallowed by the crowds and sliding doors. It is only when she is out of sight that I realize she is my mother.

Cordelia Strube is an accomplished playwright and the author of seven novels. Her first novel, *Alex and Zee*, was shortlisted for the W. H. Smith/*Books in Canada* First Novel Award, and *Teaching Pigs to Sing* was a finalist for the Governor General's Award and a recipient of a Toronto Arts Protégé Award. Her novels *Blind Night*, *The Barking Dog* and *Planet Reese* were shortlisted for the Relit Award. Her play *Mortal* won the CBC Literary Competition and was nominated for the Prix Italia. She lives with her family in Toronto, where she teaches at Ryerson University.

Edited and designed by Alana Wilcox
Cover art and design by Jason Logan and Una Janicijevic
Author photo by Peter Bregg

Coach House Books
401 Huron Street on bpNichol Lane
Toronto, ON M5S 2G5

416 979 2217
800 367 6360

mail@chbooks.com
www.chbooks.com